Marguerite Kaye writes hot historical romances from her home in cold and usually rainy Scotland, featuring Regency rakes, Highlanders and sheikhs. She has published over forty books and novellas. When she's not writing she enjoys walking, cycling—but only on the level—gardening—but only what she can eat—and cooking. She also likes to knit and occasionally drink martinis—though not at the same time! Find out more on her website: margueritekaye.com.

Also by Marguerite Kaye

Invitation to a Cornish Christmas

Matches Made in Scandal miniseries

From Governess to Countess
From Courtesan to Convenient Wife
His Rags-to-Riches Contessa
A Scandalous Winter Wedding

Penniless Brides of Convenience miniseries

The Earl's Countess of Convenience
A Wife Worth Investing In
The Truth Behind Their Practical Marriage

And look out for the next book
coming soon

Discover more at millsandboon.co.uk.

THE TRUTH BEHIND THEIR PRACTICAL MARRIAGE

Marguerite Kaye

MILLS & BOON

First Published in Great Britain 2019
by Mills & Boon, an imprint of HarperCollins*Publishers*
1 London Bridge Street, London, SE1 9GF

ISBN: 978-0-263-26941-3

MIX
Paper from
responsible sources
FSC
www.fsc.org
FSC‑ C007454

This book is produced from independently certified FSC™ paper
to ensure responsible forest management.
For more information visit www.harpercollins.co.uk/green.

Printed and bound in Spain
by CPI, Barcelona

Prologue

*October 1832—Castle Duairc,
County Kildare, Ireland*

A flurry of rain rattled the windowpane, and a gust of wind found a gap in the casement, making the curtains billow. Shivering, Estelle curled up under the sheets, knowing that sleep would never come. How could it, when in a few short hours she'd finally discover the true reason for her husband's tortured and self-destructive behaviour.

Another strong gust of wind blew the window open. Jumping out of bed, she wrestled to close it over. A storm was brewing in more ways than one. A shaft of moonlight pierced the thick cloud casting a shadow on the lake, illuminating the ruined tower on the island. It looked stark, brooding, ominous, as befitting a place harbouring dark secrets.

Secrets which had already blighted their marriage. They had lived—no, barely existed—in the shadow of those secrets for far too long. Was it too late to salvage something from the wreckage? Tomorrow, the past would be dug up and the truth unearthed. Whatever that turned out to mean, she was determined not to let it destroy them completely.

Chapter One

∽∾∽∾∽

May 1832—Florence, Grand Duchy of Tuscany

She first became aware of him in the Piazza della Signoria. It was a Monday morning and she was enjoying her ritual morning coffee. He was perched on the stone balustrade of the Neptune fountain set in the middle of the *piazza*, trailing his hands languidly in the water, his back to the looming Palazzo Vecchio. His gaze roamed over the same milling throngs that she had been idly observing, a mixture of tourists and Florentines enjoying the morning sunshine.

There were any number of well-dressed and presentable young men among the crowd. What was it about him that particularly caught her attention? Perhaps it was the fact that he was so obviously not Italian. But then, so were a good many of the passers-by. Was it his looks? But he was not handsome, not in the flamboyant, peacock manner of the local dandies who didn't so much walk as strut. He had light-brown hair, close-cut, with strong rather than striking features. His skin looked weathered rather than tanned, and his nascent beard could have simply been the result of neglecting to shave for two or three days. Unkempt, that was the word that sprung to mind, for his hair, though short, had a rumpled look, as if it were a stranger to a comb, and his clothes, though clearly the product of expensive tailoring, looked as if they had been donned straight from a valise without the intervention of either a valet or a hot iron. Yet she couldn't take her eyes off him.

How long she had been staring before their gazes clashed and held, she had no idea. Her insides jolted. It was not recognition, for they most certainly had not met before, but an *urging*, as if it was imperative that they should meet. He didn't stare openly in those attenuated moments. She had the impression of being subject to a cool assessment, then surprise was registered in the slight raising of his brow, before he turned away as if shielding himself from view, resenting the intrusion on his thoughts.

In the aftermath, her cheeks heated. Had she been ogling him, the very thing that she loathed being subjected to herself? She had become accustomed, now that she had finally come out into the world, to being assessed, to being leered at and even occasionally accosted. Her flamboyant looks gave men the impression that she welcomed close attention. She did not, but she'd come to expect it, and had become practised too, at rebuffing it. Yet this man had done none of those things. She was being fanciful, she decided, for the *piazza* had been crowded and he was at least twenty yards away. But the fleeting encounter haunted her for the rest of the day.

She saw him again the next morning, in the same square. Not that she deliberately sought him out, certainly not, it was simply that she went to the same café every morning, at the same time. In the ten days she'd been in the city, it had become her habit to sip one of the small, syrupy cups of Italian coffee there, on the pretext of planning her day. In reality, it was simply another way of whiling away the time—something the Florentines did with élan and at which she had been surprised to discover she too was rather adept.

She wasn't looking for him, but he was there, and her stomach fluttered when she spotted him, not quite as she'd remembered him but—goodness, if anything even more intriguing! He really wasn't handsome, and yet that added to his attraction and, as far as she was concerned, made him stand out from the crowd.

He wasn't sitting at the fountain this time, but inspecting the Medici lions in the Loggia dei Lanzi. He was very tall and solid-looking, built more like a man who earned his living from hard labour than a man of leisure. She liked his dishevelled appearance, it spoke of a man who had more important things on his mind, who had neither any need nor interest in setting out to impress. She cupped her chin in her hand, allowing herself to study him while his attention was focused on the statues. He wasn't wearing a hat or gloves. Unconventional. That too appealed to her. What was he doing here in Florence? Was he alone? He certainly didn't have the air of a man with an entourage. Or a valet to iron his rumpled clothes!

She smiled wryly to herself, perfectly well aware that she was bending his circumstances to her will. But where was the harm, after all, in indulging her imagination? Wasn't it one of the reasons that women ventured abroad, to seek romance safe from society's gaze? Most decidedly *not* one of her objectives, but she understood well enough the disconnection from reality that travel offered, that allowed a person to behave completely out of character, to flout the conventions which usually bound them. Florence, in the heat of the southern sun, was a city in which passions of all kinds flourished. Until now, she had been a mere disinterested observer, but this man fired both her imagination and her senses. She allowed herself to picture their eyes meeting again as they had yesterday, only this time he would cross the square, sit down beside her and smile shyly. She would smile in return to demonstrate his attentions were not entirely unwelcome.

He looked up, and once again their eyes did meet but, appalled that her scandalous train of thought might be transparent, she dropped her gaze immediately, concentrating on her coffee and the sweet flaky pastry which constituted her breakfast. When she next raised her eyes he was gone, and though she quickly surveyed the *piazza* she could see no sign of him, as if he really was a figment of her imagination, and had vanished into thin air.

* * *

On Wednesday morning, he was seated two places away from her usual table in the café. He nodded, quirked a smile at her, then returned his attention to his notebook. His eyes were blue-green, with a permanent fan of lines at the edges. There were permanent lines on his brow too, and a furrow that deepened above his nose as he studied his notebook, his mouth turned down at the edges with concentration. Every now and then he looked up from his scribbling to stare off into the distance, to smile to himself, then continue writing. And every now and then, when she had been consciously looking in the other direction or concentrating on her pastry, she had the distinct impression that he was studying her, as covertly as she was studying him.

What was in his notebook that he found so fascinating? It was not a journal, she decided, for his absorption seemed far too genuine. Diarists and journalists, she had noticed, made much of their occupation, making a show of setting out their writing and sketching implements, gazing down at the page in search of the perfect word or well-turned phrase, ensuring that those around them understood that they were *serious* travellers engaged in a *serious* endeavour, creating a tableau for onlookers to observe the creative process as deliberately as if they were on stage. But this man—no, he didn't give a damn who was watching him.

This time, she forced herself to leave before he did. He looked up as she pushed her chair back, then hurriedly looked away.

It was Thursday, in the Uffizi galleries that they finally met. She was not particularly drawn to the collection, which was so vast that she felt quite overwhelmed by the sheer opulent beauty of the paintings and the tapestries, but she loved the sense of history that seemed to seep from the walls, even if she knew little about it. As ever, she wanted to see behind the public façade, to open all the locked and hidden doors, to discover the beating heart and all the lost corners too, of what had, extraordinarily, once been an elaborate set of offices. She loved the architecture, the simplicity of the exterior belying the extravagance within. And in particular she loved the view through the high arch at the end of the long narrow courtyard of the River Arno and the buildings jostling on the opposite bank. This was her favourite picture, framed by the gallery itself.

She didn't see him at first, being absorbed in a little drama that was being played out between a mother and her two children, who had as little interest in the art as she did, and were begging to be left to their own devices to play in the courtyard by the Arno. Their flustered mother was clearly tempted, and equally clearly reluctant to accede to their demands. Eventually, the woman threw her hands up in surrender, signalling that the family dose of culture would have to wait for another day, marching the jubilant pair towards the exit.

She turned, smiling to herself, and walked straight into him. 'I beg your pardon,' she said in English, not at first realising that it was *him*, immediately correcting herself. *'Mi spiace.'*

'No, I'm sorry, it was my fault.'

Surprise, recognition, embarrassment and a kick of raw excitement made her skin flush. 'You're Irish!' she blurted out, for his accent was unmistakable.

'And your own mellifluous tones betray the fact that so indeed are you. Aidan Malahide, at your service.'

'Estelle Brannagh.'

He sketched a bow. 'It is a pleasure, Mrs Brannagh.'

'Miss,' she corrected him, blushing as she curtsied.

'Miss Brannagh.'

Was she imagining his gratification at her single state? They smiled awkwardly at each other. He shuffled his feet, as if he was about to move on, but he made no move. Was this it then, the beginning and end of their briefest of acquaintances? In England, without anyone to make formal introductions, it would be. But they were not in England.

'What do you make of the...?'

'Are you enjoying...?'

'Please,' she said, indicating that he should continue.

'I was merely wondering whether you were enjoying the paintings.'

'I was—it is—there is so much to take in,' Estelle floundered, unwilling to lie, but not wishing to be branded a Philistine. 'It can be a little overwhelming. I was going to ask you the same question.'

'I'll be honest. I think the building more interesting than the content. The proportions and the perspective of the architecture—that, I could study all day.'

'I'm so glad you said that, for it allows me to be honest too. This,' Estelle said, indicating her favourite view, 'I think it quite beautiful. As to the paintings—sadly, I find myself quite unable to go into raptures over them, let alone transcribe those raptures into my journal.'

'As every other visitor to Florence does!' To her delight and relief, he laughed. 'There now, I knew from the moment I set eyes on you, taking your coffee in the *piazza* on Monday, that you were different. Most ladies taking coffee on their own have a book or a journal, but you seemed quite content in your own company. Not,' he added hastily, 'that I've been spying on you, it's merely that I noticed you.'

'It's my hair.' Self-consciously she put a hand to the nape of her neck. 'Redheads are not very common here on the Continent.'

He studied her for a moment, one brow raised. 'You must know perfectly well that you are a beauty, and an uncommon one at that.'

'Not so very uncommon at all, actually. I have two sisters, both also redheads and very similar in looks.'

'Ah now, I've put your back up and I didn't

mean to. It's why I didn't speak to you, though I wanted to. I reckoned you must be sick of being accosted, and—well, as I said, you'd an air about you, of being perfectly content in your own company. Which I'll leave you to now.' He sketched another bow. 'It was a pleasure, Miss Brannagh.'

It took her until he had turned his back and taken two steps to summon up the courage to call him back. 'Mr Malahide, don't go just yet.' But as he turned, her nerve was already crumbling. 'You probably prefer to be alone—I noticed that you too seemed very content in your own company, but if you would like—oh, this is too awkward.'

'It is indeed,' he said with a wry smile. 'You know nothing about me, and under normal circumstances, my being very much aware of that fact, I wouldn't dream of inviting you to take coffee with me.'

'Or perhaps an ice?'

'Or indeed, an ice. *Would* it be presumptive of me to issue such an invitation?'

'An ice, in a café in full public view,' Estelle said, 'hardly an unseemly suggestion. Admiring art is very tiring work. Your invitation isn't in the least presumptive, Mr Malahide, it is very welcome, and I am happy to accept it.'

* * *

They sat in a café in another of Florence's many *piazze*. Mr Malahide drank coffee. Estelle ate a gelato flavoured with lemon.

'What brought you to Florence?' he asked her.

'The pedantic answer is a ship. I sailed from Nice to Leghorn.' She contemplated a spoonful of ice, allowing it to melt on her tongue before continuing. 'In terms of my thinking, notwithstanding my views on art, all the guide books insist that no trip to the Continent is complete without a visit to Florence—so here I am.'

'You're travelling around Europe on your own!'

'Is that so surprising?'

'Yes,' Mr Malahide said frankly. 'You must be an extremely intrepid young woman, with a remarkably complacent family back in Ireland.'

'Oh, as to that, my parents died ten years ago, and I'd label them rather more indifferent than complacent. But that is not to say that I've no one to worry about my welfare,' Estelle added hurriedly, castigating herself for her indiscretion, even if it was the truth. 'My Aunt Kate, who took us girls in when we were orphaned, would do plenty of worrying, were it not for Eloise—that is my eldest sister. She has done a great deal to grease the wheels of my wandering, so to speak, and to ensure that none of them worry needlessly about me either. I have a portfolio of names and addresses, letters of introduction, lists of people in every city I can turn to if I need help of any sort.'

'Your sister must be extremely well connected.'

'And practical. Her husband is—was—in a senior position in the government. Thanks to him, I've had my currency changed, accommodation recommended, and my papers accepted at every border without question. I promised to ensure that someone on my list knows that I have arrived, and someone knows where I am headed next so that my sister can keep track of me. So, you see, I'm not really very intrepid at all.'

'I beg to differ. Intrepid, and modest with it,' he insisted, eyeing her with flattering respect. 'How long have you been travelling?'

'I left England back in June. Since then I've been to France, Spain, Portugal and now Italy.'

'Good Lord, that's quite a tour. Will you be publishing your journals when you return home?'

'Shall I? *Tales of a Single Lady Traveller*,' Estelle opined, slanting him a mischievous smile.

'It's the whole point of travelling, isn't it, to share one's experience with the world, to prove that travel is *elevating*.'

Mr Malahide eyed her sceptically. 'I could be wrong, we have only just met, but you don't strike me as either a diarist or an educationist.'

'You are sadly right. To be honest, I have not once felt in the least bit *elevated* by any of the paintings or the tapestries or even the statues in the Uffizi, though I assure you, it is not for want of trying. They say, don't they, that the more one stares at a painting, the more one appreciates it. Well, I have stood in front of countless Old Masters trying to *absorb* their greatness. I am beginning to think,' she concluded sorrowfully, 'that I am a heathen. Or perhaps my female mind is too feeble for the task.'

She was pleased to note that he was not in the least bit taken in. 'And I am beginning to think that your female mind, far from being feeble, takes great pleasure in making fun of conventional wisdom. I'd also hazard a guess that what you really like is to observe real people, rather than portraits on a wall. An Englishwoman alone would sit in that café only long enough to finish her coffee,' Mr Malahide added, seeing her surprise. 'You take your time, content to simply watch the world go by.'

'Ah, but that may be because I am simply empty-headed.'

'I already know that is far from the case.'

'But indeed, Mr Malahide, my ignorance of culture knows no bounds. My education was—well, let's say sporadic, at best. My parents, like many others, it seems to me, considered education wasted on girls, and therefore money spent on governesses squandered, so we three sisters had scant experience of either.'

'Three sisters?'

'I have mentioned Eloise. I also have a twin. Phoebe is a chef—chef patron, actually, for she owns her own restaurant in London. Le Pas à Pas, it's called—have you heard of it?'

'I'm afraid not. I haven't had cause to visit London in some time. Is it a popular restaurant?'

'The most lauded in the whole city,' Estelle said proudly. 'It only opened in April, but already she has plans to open another.'

'I know little of such things—I'm afraid I view food as fuel—but isn't it quite unusual to have a female chef patron?'

'Extremely. In fact Phoebe may even be unique.'

'So the pioneering spirit runs in the family?'

'If it does, then my sisters have the full quota between them. I'm no pioneer, Mr Malahide, I'm simply a purposeless wanderer, who has taken up far more than her share of the conversation.'

'Sure,' he replied in a much-thickened accent, 'are we Irish not famed for having the gift of the gab?'

'Nevertheless.' Estelle pushed her empty dish to one side. 'That's quite enough about me. Tell me, what brings *you* to Florence?'

'I've come to study mathematics. I know,' he said, holding his hands up and laughing at her bemused expression, 'a confession guaranteed to stop any conversation in its tracks. I'm also well past student age, but that's what I've been doing none the less, for the better part of the last year. And now I can see you're revising your opinion of me entirely, from someone you're happy to while away a convivial hour or so with, to a crusty academic who prefers equations to words.'

'Or a puzzle you've tempted me into solving, more like,' she retorted. 'You're as likely a crusty academic as I am a—a...'

'Blue-stockinged diarist?'

'Precisely! Good grief, I hardly know what

to make of you now. Do you intend to become a teacher? Or a college fellow—if that is the correct term?'

'Neither. I study for the sheer pleasure of acquiring knowledge, having granted myself a year's sabbatical. Though that's up at the end of August.'

'And what is it, may I ask, that you took a sabbatical from?'

'Real life?' His smile faltered. 'I turned thirty last August, just before I left Ireland, and it seemed to me that I needed to—to get away for a while. So that's what I did.'

Get away from what? Estelle wondered, but before she could ask, he pre-empted her. 'I'm lucky, I've an excellent estate manager, but it would be unfair to expect him to hold the fort indefinitely, so I'll need to return home soon. What about you, is there any end in sight to your sojourn?

There should be. After almost a year, she had a right to expect to have resolved her dilemma, or come up with alternative plans for how she intended to spend the rest of her life. Estelle pushed this increasingly persistent worry to one side. 'I have nothing in my sights, save luncheon.'

She meant it flippantly, simply as a means of changing the subject, but Mr Malahide checked his watch, looking dismayed. 'I don't know where the time has gone. We've been sitting here for more than an hour.'

'Really?' Estelle exclaimed, 'I had no idea. I—I've enjoyed our conversation, Mr Malahide.'

'I have too, Miss Brannagh, very much. I've talked little but mathematics for nigh on nine months, and barely a word of it in my own language.'

'You must have an excellent command of Italian.'

'I studied here when I was younger and picked it up then. Your own linguistic skills must be impressive, given that you've managed to negotiate France, Spain and now Italy.'

'Impressive is not the word I'd have chosen. I learned from textbooks, not from a tutor. I've been the unwitting source of hilarity in several inns and restaurants. Eggs, I have found, are one of the trickiest words to pronounce in any tongue. In France I ordered *oafs*, in Spain *hoovos*, and here in Italy, *oova*.'

He laughed. 'Then what talent do you possess, for I refuse to believe as impressive a young woman as yourself is not blessed with some gift?'

'I am fond of music,' Estelle said, rolling her eyes inwardly at this understatement. 'I have a good ear and a facility for playing almost any instrument.'

'Now I am truly impressed, for though I enjoy music very much, I'm tone deaf and have a singing voice reminiscent of a distressed Wicklow lamb. Did you know there is a strong connection between music and mathematics?'

'I did not.'

'Shall I bore you with it over lunch? That is, if I've not intruded too much on your time already?'

Estelle had received many invitations to dine. Having naively accepted several in the early days of her travels, she had quickly realised that an invitation issued by a single man to a single woman tended to imply a hunger for something other than food, rather than a genuine desire to get to know someone. Thus, it was her policy to refuse all but those issued by names on Eloise's list. It was perfectly acceptable for a woman to eat alone, she had discovered, and she had enjoyed doing so. Which made it all the more curious that she accepted this invitation with alacrity.

'That's not an offer a person hears every day,' she said, pushing back her chair. 'I'd be delighted to join you for lunch.'

Chapter Two

Resisting the urge to take her to one of Florence's more prestigious *ristorante*, Aidan decided to risk sharing his favourite humble *osteria*. 'The food is simple,' he said, 'but it's much more typical of the region. The kind of dishes that would be served at home, the receipts handed down from mother to daughter.'

'I thought you viewed food as fuel, Mr Malahide?'

He shrugged sheepishly. 'I'm Irish, a bit of blarney comes naturally. The truth is, I like food well enough, provided it's honest and authentic.'

'That is precisely the kind of food my sister Phoebe loves,' Miss Brannagh replied, to his surprise, 'despite the fact that she trained in Paris, in the kitchen of the great Pascal Solignac's restaurant, La Grande Taverne de Londres.'

'Judging by the somewhat contemptuous tone in your voice, you are not a fan.'

They were walking along the banks of the Arno, the more scenic if less direct route to the *osteria*, and Miss Brannagh stopped to gaze up river to the view of the Ponte Vecchio. 'I am not a fan of Monsieur Solignac the chef *or* the man,' she said, her mouth curled into a sneer. 'More importantly, I am very pleased to say, neither is Phoebe, nowadays. Excellent ingredients, traditional receipts, that is what she serves at Le Pas à Pas. The kind of food that people enjoy eating, not the kind that is served up to be admired.'

'Is that what Monsieur Solignac does?'

'I've never eaten his food, nor ever will. That man is a—' Miss Brannagh caught herself short, biting her lip. 'He treated my sister abominably,' she finished, her eyes sparking fire, 'but Phoebe—Phoebe has risen like a phoenix from the ashes. To see her presiding over her stove, in her own restaurant as I did just before I set out on my travels, made me immensely proud of her.' She blinked, turning her gaze back to the river. 'Excuse me.'

'Don't apologise. You clearly love your sister very dearly.'

'I love both my sisters very much, we are very close, though of late, seeing them both blossom in their own ways, it's made me wonder if we've been *too* close.'

'Is that why you decided to travel the world, to escape them?'

Miss Brannagh laughed. 'I'm not running from something or someone, I'm looking for something. Inspiration, you could call it. Both of my sisters are happily settled in their different ways. I envy them that—you know, the *certainty* they have, that they are making something of their lives. I'd like to do the same, but what I want I don't seem to be able to find, and so far, I've not been able to think of an alternative.'

'Would it be impertinent of me to ask what it is you're looking for?'

'Not impertinent but irrelevant, since I've had to accept that I am unlikely to find it.' She shook her head impatiently. 'I sound like a malcontent, when I am very much aware that I'm extremely fortunate to be able to do nothing at all, if I choose. You know I can't imagine how we came to be talking about me again.'

'Because you're far more interesting than me?'

'I cannot agree with you there. I know everything there is to know about me, and almost nothing about you, save that you are a mathematician—and I've never met a mathematician before. What is it about the subject that you find so fascinating?'

'The fact that there is a rational answer to every problem,' Aidan replied promptly. 'No ambiguity, no doubt, no guesswork. Find the key, and the problem is solved.'

'If only life were like that!'

'My thoughts exactly.' The dark shadow of the one question he knew now that he'd never resolve dampened his spirits for a second, but Aidan closed his mind to it. Looking down into the expectant face of the lovely Miss Brannagh, it was an easy thing to do. He felt he ought to pinch himself, just to make sure he wasn't dreaming, but if he was, he didn't want to wake up. Though for a man who might be dreaming, he'd never felt so alive. It wasn't only her looks, though she was quite beautiful, with her heart-shaped face and big hazel eyes, lips that really were the colour of cherries, and that hair—true Titian red. Beautiful—yes, she most certainly was that, but it was her earthiness—dreadful word—which made heads turn as she walked past. Her figure was voluptuous. Her smile was generous. She possessed a certain vibrancy, like the warmth of the setting sun. She positively glowed with life. And she seemed determined to live it too. She could not be more different from…

'You much prefer order, then, Mr Malahide? Mr Malahide?'

'Order?' He nodded furiously. 'Indeed I do. And certainty, and logic. Predictable outcomes. Recognisable patterns—that's where mathematics and music cross paths. Are you really interested?'

'I truly am.'

She sounded as if she meant it. Though he had not meant to launch into a lecture, it seemed he had done just that when, coming to a halt he looked back with astonishment at the distance they had walked. 'I did warn you I'd bore you.'

'You didn't. I was hanging on your every word. What's more I actually understood at least half of what you said. You make it all sound so obvious.'

'Well that's because it is, when you have the key, as I said.' Aidan grimaced. 'Sadly, what I've discovered is that while I'm very good at using the key to unlock the problem, I don't possess the creative vision, I suppose you'd call it, to actually discover the key myself. Studying here, in the shadow of some of the great, groundbreaking mathematicians, has forced me to acknowledge my limitations.'

'I think you underestimate yourself. You've explained it to me in a way I can understand, and what's more, you made it sound almost interesting.'

'That's an achievement, all right,' he agreed, laughing. 'Any time you find yourself with a spare hour or two, let me know and I'll bore you some more. You'd be astonished how much more sense the world makes when you understand the mathematics that underpin it, from nature to the artefacts in the Uffizi that you so despise.'

'Shh, that is our secret.' Miss Brannagh glanced theatrically over her shoulder. 'And I don't actually despise art, I just don't understand why people get so passionate about it.'

'Aren't you passionate about music?'

'Yes, but it is a personal pleasure. I don't feel the need to bore all and sundry on the subject.'

'Well that's me put firmly in my place.'

Her hand flew to her mouth. 'I didn't mean...'

'I'm teasing you.'

'Oh! We used to tease each other mercilessly

at home, but I'm afraid I've rather lost the knack, Mr Malahide.'

'Call me Aidan, and I promise to help you rediscover your ability to tease and be teased.'

'Then you must call me Estelle, and I would caution you to be careful what you wish for.'

He grinned. 'Oh, I think I'm prepared to take that chance. Now, here we are at last.'

Aidan watched her anxiously as they were seated in the rustic, verging on basic *osteria*, the proprietor raising his brows theatrically when he saw Estelle preceding him into the cool of the dark little room, silently mouthing *Bella*.

'As I said, it's an unpretentious eatery.'

To his relief, she saw the charm in the old-fashioned inn. 'I love it. It's the sort of place where you just know the food is going to be excellent.'

'There's not much choice. Not any choice, really. We eat whatever Signora Giordano has concocted from what was fresh in the market today. And we drink the wine from Signor Giordano's father's vineyard,' Aidan added, as the proprietor approached with a terracotta jug and two thick glasses. 'How are you, *signor*?' he asked, in Italian.

'God has spared me for another day,' Signor Giordano replied in his usual lugubrious manner, his attention fixed on Aidan's guest. '*Signorina*, you have brought the sunshine into our dining room this afternoon.'

He flicked a cloth over the already clean-scrubbed wooden table, before pouring the wine and rattling off the day's menu, beaming when Estelle asked for clarification, beaming even more widely when she smiled her approval.

'Your command of Italian is a great deal better than you led me to believe,' Aidan said when they were finally left alone with a basket of crusty bread, a dish of Tuscan olive oil and a platter of *pinzimonio*, raw vegetables which today included red peppers, cucumbers, radish and chicory.

Surveying the platter hungrily, Estelle merely shrugged. 'In essence Italian, French and Spanish are very similar.' She picked up a baton of peeled cucumber, salted it and dipped it in the olive oil before biting into it. 'Everything here tastes of sunshine.'

The oil glistened on her mouth. Fascinated, Aidan watched as she picked up her wine glass, took a sip, licked her full bottom lip, then carefully selected a slice of pepper, repeating the process. It had been so long since he'd experienced any sort of desire, it took him a moment to recognise it for what it was. Her kisses would taste of olive oil and wine. Making love to her would be a feast of sensation, a long, lingering delight of soft, giving flesh and hot, hungry lips and caressing hands. Not a duty. Not a means to a desperate end. A pleasure, pure and simple.

'Aren't you hungry?'

Appalled by the carnal turn his thoughts had taken, Aidan grabbed a piece of bread and tore it in half, sweat prickling his back, the physical proof of his desire pressing uncomfortably against his leg. 'Pacing myself,' he muttered, taking a swig of wine.

'*Affettati misti.*' Signor Giordano presented the next platter with a flourish. '*Buon appetite.*'

'Salami with fennel,' Aidan deduced, inspecting the platter. 'More salami, that one with green peppercorns. *Prosciutto*, naturally, and some *bresaola*, which is smoked beef—*signora* is serving us some real delicacies. May I help you to some?'

'You may help me to a little of all of it, thank you. How on earth did you discover this place? I would never have found it. Do you think they will mind if I come back alone?'

'Judging by Signor Giordano's reaction to you, I'd wager he'd happily keep the best table in the house free each and every day in the hope that you might turn up. It's the same in Café Piccioli where you have your breakfast. Did you know that the waiter reserves your seat for you? I saw him yesterday, before you arrived, shooing someone away who dared to sit down at your preferred table.'

'I didn't realise. I expect I over-tip hugely.'

'I expect that they would give you your coffee and pastry for free, simply to have you gracing the premises.'

Estelle coloured. 'I wish you wouldn't say things like that. Do you think I play on my appearance to get preferential treatment?'

'Of course not.'

She took a draught of her wine, placing the glass carefully on the table before fixing him with a firm gaze. 'I am not a piece of art to be stared and gawked at, you know.'

Wondering what particular nerve he had inadvertently hit, Aidan was surprised into a bark of laughter. 'I meant it as a compliment.' Seeing her unconvinced, he risked covering her hands with his own, across the table. 'You're right to reprimand me, though I stand by what I said.

Your beauty is quite dazzling, and whether you like it or not, people will be drawn to—to *gawk* at you. But I didn't invite you to lunch because I wanted to bask in your shadow. I was enjoying our conversation, and I wanted to get to know you better. It's the truth, Estelle, and if you don't believe me, ask yourself why I brought you here and not shown you off in one of the *ristorante* where the great and the good eat. Look around you. You will attract a few fleeting glances, but once the food is on the table, that's all people here are interested in.'

She smiled reluctantly. 'In that case, I shall eat here every day.'

'Don't you mind eating alone?'

'I'd become accustomed to it at Elmswood Manor. That is—was—my home in England.'

'It sounds very grand.'

'Some of it dates back to the reign of William and Mary, though it's been much adapted and altered over the years.'

'Have you lived in England long, then?'

Estelle, who had been staring down at her plate, frowning, stared at him blankly, so that he repeated his question. 'Since I was fifteen. I don't mind,' she added, 'eating alone—that's what you asked me—I don't mind it. I much prefer it, in fact, to eating with strangers.'

'And once again,' he said, wondering what she'd really being thinking about, 'that's put me in my place.'

Estelle's frown cleared. 'I don't mean you—though you are undeniably a stranger to me. Isn't it odd, I feel as if I've known you for far longer than an hour or so. But then that's most likely because I've talked more to you in this last hour or so than to anyone since I left England—made conversation, I mean, proper conversation, as opposed to the usual pleasantries about the weather.'

'Would you believe me if I told you I feel the same?'

'Surely you have made some friends here, after all this time?'

'Some of my fellow mathematicians are amenable enough. But I've preferred my own company, by and large,' Aidan confessed, surprising himself. 'Until now.'

'So have I,' Estelle said. 'Until now.'

A tense little silence ensued, as they smiled awkwardly, their hands resting on the table, just a few inches from each other. He wanted to touch her. Just to cover her hand with his, as he'd done a moment ago. It was almost as if he was compelled to touch her, drawn to her, as he had been from the moment he'd first set eyes on her.

'Finito?'

Estelle started at the proprietor's interruption, snatching her hands from the table. As Signor Giordano whipped away the empty plates with a flourish, she tried to collect her thoughts. What had just happened there? She realised it wasn't just Aidan's conversation she was enjoying, it was *him*. She hadn't ever felt like this before, but there was no mistaking it for what it was—attraction, and a very visceral, intense one at that, which was unmistakably reciprocated.

'Stracciatella,' Signor Giordan announced, setting the bowls down. 'Egg soup made with beef stock and thickened with ground almonds.'

Estelle picked up her spoon. 'It smells delicious.'

'Delicious,' Aidan echoed.

He smiled, and her tummy gave an odd little lurch in response. She smiled back foolishly, and their gazes held for a long moment, long enough for her tummy to flutter again, for her skin to prickle with heat. 'I must write this receipt down for my sister,' Estelle said, because she felt she had to say something. For heaven's sake, he really wasn't at all handsome. Though he did have the most irresistible smile. 'Do *you* have any siblings?'

'I have one older sister, Clodagh. She seems to think that gives her the right to organise my life, despite the fact that she has a husband and three children of her own.'

'But you adore her, really, don't you?'

'Oh, yes.' Aidan grinned. 'Never more so than when we're a thousand miles apart. Actually, I don't mean that. She has my best interests at heart, it's just that...'

'Her idea of what that constitutes and yours don't necessarily align?'

'There speaks the voice of experience. Is—remind me of your eldest sister's name?—is she cast in the same mould?'

'Eloise. And, yes, she is, in a way, though I can't blame her, for she had to stand in for our mother practically from the moment Phoebe and I were born.'

'Clodagh had to step into the breach too. Our mother died when I was a babe, not more than two years old. I hardly remember her.'

'Do you see much of her?'

His face clouded. 'Not so much these days.

She has three boys to raise, so she has enough on her plate. I tend to leave her to it. She lives just outside Wicklow, about fifty miles from Cashel Duairc.'

'Cashel Doo-ark?' Estelle mouthed, frowning. 'Dark Castle?'

'Brooding, or gloomy, would be a more accurate translation, though the name refers to a previous castle on the site.'

'Is it your home, then? Do you actually live in a proper castle?'

'Oh, yes, replete with a lake and turrets, battlements and even a dungeon. Pretty much everything save a moat.'

'And a resident ghost, no doubt?'

The wine he had been pouring slopped on to the table as his hand suddenly shook. Aidan set the jug down, mopping up the mess with his napkin. 'Too many to mention.' He took a draught of wine. 'Ah good, here comes our next course,' he said with palpable relief.

'Pappardelle sulla lepre,' Signor Giordano announced with a reverence which was entirely justified by the aroma rising from the plate, the gamey smell of hare mingling with wine, garlic and tomatoes.

Aidan was embarrassed, she decided. A mathematician ought not to believe in ghosts, but his dark and gloomy castle obviously harboured something that defied logic and reason. She longed to question him, but she didn't want to embarrass him further. Picking up her fork and spoon, the first mouthful of the hare *ragu* made her forget all about ghosts. Her toes curled with pleasure. *'Delizioso.'*

'I couldn't agree more,' Aidan said, smiling once again, raising his glass.

'You haven't even tasted it yet.'

'I wasn't referring to the dish.'

'Food can be delicious, wine can be delicious, but you can't describe a person as delicious, that's ridiculous.' Though what was ridiculous, Estelle told herself, was to blush at such an odd compliment.

His smile broadened, but he shook his head, refusing to be drawn, and the conversation turned to Florence and remained there, until they had both finished the pasta, and the plates had once more been cleared. 'Would you like cheese, an ice, coffee?' he asked.

'No to all, thank you very much. What I need is to walk off this excellent lunch.' She hesitated only briefly this time. 'Would you like to…?'

'Very much. Give me a minute to settle the bill.'

* * *

They made their way back to the Arno, walking along the riverbank as far as the Ponte alla Carraia, pausing in the middle of the bridge to look downriver. It was late afternoon and the sun was obscured by a heat haze, turning the river muddy and sluggish, the usually bright reflections of the buildings on the banks shimmering shadows. The air was damp, not so humid as to be unpleasant but languid, as if the sun were too sleepy to burn the mist away.

They retraced their steps on the opposite side of the river. There were fewer people about at this time of day, and their large lunch had made them both as lethargic as the afternoon, content to wander slowly, to gaze about them at the serene, confident beauty of the city. Estelle talked of her travels, reticent at first, made more garrulous by Aidan's obvious interest and his perceptive questions.

At exactly the moment when she was beginning to crave a cool drink, he suggested they stop and a little café seemed to appear out of nowhere. She sat beside him at the tiny marble-topped table looking out over the Arno, their knees brushing, her mood as serene as the city. 'Cashel Duairc. It sounds ridiculously romantic, your home. Is it very old?'

'Parts of it go back a few hundred years, but the current castle was rebuilt more recently. There's all sorts of papers, accounts and deeds in the attics. My father was always saying that someone should write a history of the place, but no one ever has.'

'How exciting. No, really,' Estelle said, in answer to his sceptical look, 'there were all sorts of documents in the attics at Elmswood Manor which we consulted to help with the restoration. The walled garden, for example, had fallen into a complete state of disrepair, and I discovered one of the original drawings, along with a map from around the time it had been laid out, allowing Aunt Kate to restore the garden to its original condition. Elmswood Manor is Aunt Kate's home,' she explained, seeing Aidan's confusion. I think I mentioned, she took the three of us in when we were orphaned. It's a long story, and beside the point. How lucky you are, to have such an archive waiting to be investigated.'

'You are serious! Should you like to be my archivist?'

'Yes, please! I am *fascinated* by old documents.'

'Good Lord!' Aidan exclaimed. 'No wonder the time has passed so quickly today, since we have far more in common than anyone would ever imagine, looking at the pair of us. We are both crusty academics, in our own way.'

Estelle chuckled, but shook her head. 'One cannot claim to be an academic when one is utterly uneducated. I know nothing of the classics, nor have any interest in them. Ancient history, it seems to me, is nothing more than stories and speculation. I've no intentions of visiting Rome, or any of the other popular ancient sites recommended in all the guide books. And I'm not interested in battles and wars or much in politics either.'

'I was force fed all the classics at school, and I came to much the same conclusion, that it was all speculation. Opinion tacked on to the few known facts.'

'But weren't some of the greatest mathematicians ancient Greeks?'

'Yes, but it's their work I'm interested in, not—oh, I don't know, philosophy, history or archaeology.'

'What has always struck me, reading history books, even recent ones, is how absent women are from the stories they tell. Of course they didn't take part in important battles, and they were not permitted to be politicians, but that doesn't mean they didn't play any sort of role. Take Aunt Kate. Will history take any notice of the key role she has played not only in preserving Elmswood Manor for Uncle Daniel's heir, but in restoring it to its former glory? To my knowledge, Aunt Kate doesn't keep a diary. My uncle rarely writes, and what she does with his letters I have no idea. The only evidence of her contribution will be in the account books and all the domestic paperwork—there, I told you you'd be bored.'

'On the contrary, I'm fascinated. Where is Uncle Daniel and why doesn't he write?'

'It's complicated.'

When she said nothing more, Aidan shrugged and set a stack of coins down on the table. 'Shall we?'

'Yes.' But Estelle made no attempt to move. 'I had started writing a history of Elmswood, but my time there is over now—by choice, I may add.' She got to her feet, giving herself a mental shake. 'And now I find myself collecting recipes for Phoebe while I traverse the Continent. It's my way of apologising for not taking her venture seriously. A practical reparation, of a sort. Any time you find yourself with a spare hour or two,' she said, 'feel free to assist me in my research.'

'Have a care, for I'm almost certain to take you up on that.'

He offered his arm, and it seemed perfectly in order, as they started walking, to tuck her hand into it. She had never strolled in this way with a man before, their paces matching, the skirts of his coat brushing against the pleats of her gown. It felt perfectly natural, yet it unsettled her at the same time. She was acutely aware of him as a man, of the difference in their heights, his solid presence at her side. For a woman of twenty-five who had been travelling around Europe on her own, she was remarkably inexperienced. Her instincts told her that she could trust Aidan, but could she trust her judgement? Was she being naïve? After all, she had been caught out before, in the early days of her trip. They had spent almost a full day in each other's company, but without anyone else to vouch for him...

'What is it, Estelle? You're frowning.'

'I was thinking how strange this is—our encounter today, I mean. If this was England and not Florence, we'd never even have dared to take coffee together.'

'Without an introduction, you mean? I'm very much aware of that. It's one of the reasons I didn't approach you before, though I wanted to.'

'I know, you said you were worried that I'd think you were accosting me. I admit I have been, several times, but I've become very adept at rebuffing unwelcome advances. I've learned that men seem to assume that any female of a certain age on her own is desperate for their charming company,' Estelle said sardonically. 'I knew you were not like that though, because when our eyes met that first time...'

'On Monday?'

'Was it only Monday?' She was blushing. 'You could easily have taken my looking at you as encouragement, but you didn't. Not that I was, though I was staring, and I don't. Not as a rule. Not ever. In fact you are an—an aberration.'

'You have an endearing habit of bestowing back-handed compliments.' He quirked a smile. 'But, speaking for myself, I'd very much like us to continue in this irregular vein—if, that is, you would like to?' He scanned her face anxiously as she hesitated. 'You wouldn't like to? In that case...'

'It's not that.'

'Then you're wondering what my intentions are?'

Blushing, she nodded. 'It is not for a moment that I think you dishonourable...'

'But you've encountered too many men on your travels who are?' Aidan ushered them into the shade of a tree. 'I've no intentions or expectations, save to enjoy more of your company if I'm permitted to. Just to be absolutely clear, and I hope you won't think me presumptuous, I'm not in the market for a wife, but I've absolutely no nefarious intentions either, I can promise you that hand on heart,' he said, suiting actions to words. 'I'm no seducer, I pride myself on being an honourable man, and despite the fact that you're travelling the world all alone, it's patently obvious that you're no adventuress. There now, have I cleared the air?'

'Yes. Thank you.'

'Then shall we call ourselves friends?'

'Yes, I'd like that.' She took his arm again and they walked on in silence, but halfway across the Ponte alle Grazie they stopped once more, this time distracted by the view. The falling sun cast a warm glow on the buildings on the opposite bank, making a golden haze of their reflections in the now still waters of the Arno. Estelle leaned on the parapet to watch as the shutters were being pulled down on the shops which lined the Ponte Vecchio. 'It's breathtakingly lovely, isn't it?'

'As a backdrop, but so is the subject.'

She turned to face him and her breath caught as their eyes met.

'May I see you again tomorrow, or is it too soon?'

She didn't hesitate. 'It's not too soon.'

He smiled. They stood together watching the sun sinking and the sky fading from gold to pink before they turned of one accord to continue over the bridge. He walked her to the door of her pension. They made arrangements to meet in the morning. When she bid him farewell, he took her hand, raising it to his lips, before pressing a kiss to her gloved fingertips. She rushed up the stairs to her room, pushing back the shutters to lean out, and he turned and waved. It was the perfect end to a perfect day.

Chapter Three

'I love to wander aimlessly like this, but I'm always a bit wary to do so on my own. Now I've you to chaperon me, I don't have to worry.'

Estelle smiled up at him, her eyes gleaming with humour, and Aidan exhaled sharply. He really had to stop thinking about kissing her. 'I'm a mathematician, not a prize fighter, I'll have you know.'

'And here was I thinking that beneath your coat there was a rigid wall of muscle, when it's just padding. I should have brought my parasol, at least then I'd have a weapon.'

He swore to himself as another part of him threatened to become rigid when she squeezed his arm playfully. He was acutely aware of her every touch—the brush of her skirts with the hint of warm limb beneath, the cushioned bump of her thigh or the sharp nudge of her shoulder, her fingers twined around his arm. Was it the same for her? She certainly made no attempt to maintain distance between them, but perhaps that was because she didn't notice! Yet in the café where they met this morning, when their hands were resting on the table, their fingers just brushing, there had been one of those moments when their eyes met and he was sure she felt that *awareness* of the contact that was both a pleasure and a pain because it wasn't nearly enough. He swore again, shaking his head at himself. He was a mature thirty-year-old, not an overeager juvenile.

Though he couldn't deny it was both a relief and a pleasure to learn that side of him wasn't after all quite dead. How long had it been since he'd felt so free of cares and glad to be alive? Not that he could remember ever feeling quite like this before, and besides, he didn't want the past to intrude on a day like this, with the sun shining, and with a woman so vibrantly full of life on his arm that he was able to persuade himself, just for now, that his slate had been wiped clean.

'Welcome back.' Estelle smiled at him again. 'You've no idea that you do that, have you? One minute you're here, the next minute, the shutters come down. Don't worry, I promise not to pry into your darkest secrets if you promise not to pry into mine.'

'I can't believe you have any.'

'I don't have any thoughts at all. Sure, didn't I tell you,' she said, thickening her accent just as he did when jesting, 'that I'm as empty-headed a female as any man could desire.'

'You've a very low opinion of my sex.'

'I've a very low opinion of those of your sex I've encountered on my travels. That's a very different thing. Yourself excepted of course—in fact, in future it would be easier if you just assume that you're the exception to every one of my rules.'

'Thank you kindly, but surely—Estelle, you must have encountered some more worthy specimens in three countries over the space of so many months.'

'You're right, I'm probably being unfair, but my experience has not been particularly positive. It comes of being single and female and—well, looking as I do.' She wrinkled her nose. 'People make assumptions—women too, to be fair—that red hair denotes a passionate nature would be to put it kindly, more crudely an indiscriminate one. Of course not all men are like that, I do know that. Certainly those on the list my sister gave me have been extremely respectful.'

'Diplomats, I assume?'

'For the most part, and all of the utmost good character. Why is it that good character seems to go hand in hand with boring character?'

'I sincerely hope that once again I'm an exception to your rule?'

'You are indeed, though I notice you didn't deny having something to hide when we were discussing dark secrets earlier.'

She was teasing, but her smile faded at his expression. 'Everyone has regrets,' Aidan said, 'I am no different.'

Would Estelle see him in a very different light if she knew the truth? Fortunately, he'd never know. There would be time enough to face up to the past when he returned to Ireland, but for now he wanted to savour this welcome respite, a chance to remember the person he'd once been, and to enjoy being that person again. It was just a pity that he'd not met her earlier, for the clock was already ticking on their day-old acquaintance.

'Don't look at me like that,' he said, covering her hand with his. 'My only recent crime is that

I've been less than assiduous in my studies this last month or so, and frittering away my time. I reckon I've been waiting on you turning up.'

'The fates must have conspired to bring us together then. Though I didn't realise it until we met yesterday, I've become rather bored with my own company.'

They had arrived in a little *piazza* on the outskirts of the old town. There had been a food market earlier, judging by the tatty bits of greenery that were strewn around. Water spouted from a worn lion's head into a small fountain in one corner. Estelle cupped her hand to drink from it, yanking it back when she remembered that she was still wearing her gloves.

'Here, let me,' Aidan said, making a cup of both his hands.

She hesitated only for a second before dipping her head and drinking. Her tongue brushed against his palm. He exhaled sharply. She stopped drinking. Their eyes locked. Water dripped down his fingers on to the cobblestones. A droplet glistened on the indent of her top lip. He brushed it away, heard her exhale as sharply as he had done. She stepped towards him. His heart was pounding. Her hand fluttered up to his cheek. He dipped his head, she lifted hers, and their lips met. Icy cold water, warm flesh. He felt dizzy with the delight of it, allowed himself a moment to relish the sheer pleasure of it, before stepping back.

Her face, shadowed by the brim of her bonnet, reflected his own feelings—wide-eyed, flushed, uncertain, as if she had imagined it. 'Estelle,' he said, then stopped, for she shook her head, and he had no idea what to say anyway.

'Do you like churches?' she asked. 'Not grand cathedrals but workaday churches, I mean, like that one, that smell of incense and candles and the congregation. Do you like them?'

At this moment, he reckoned if she'd asked him if he liked pickled herring he'd have told her it was his favourite food, but in fact he did like churches, the sort she'd described, very much. 'I do,' he said, taking her arm again. 'Shall we go and take a look?'

It was a lovely church, as far as Estelle was concerned, with no cavernous nave or fresco-adorned ceiling, but a simple affair with plain wooden pews, a scrubbed flagstoned floor, and a wooden altar. The icons on each of the side chapels were not painted by any master, though they were so old that the painted panels were cracking, but the flowers were fresh, and the church had the peaceful atmosphere of a place well used by the devout.

She wandered off on her own, trying to calm her racing pulses. She'd been kissed before. A good many kisses had been snatched from her or pressed upon her, during her early travels, before she'd become adept at spotting the warning signs, but she didn't count those as kisses. Received and never freely given, they had variously disgusted, repelled or angered her. But Aidan's kiss was very different. Firstly this, her first real kiss, had been as much her doing as his. She'd wanted him to kiss her, and he had duly obliged. Secondly, she was certain he wouldn't have, if he'd thought for a moment he was forcing himself on her. Which was why she wanted to kiss him again. That, and the fact that it had been too brief, that first kiss. It had made her feel as if she were flying and melting at the same time, and that was the most important reason of all.

Was it wrong of her to want to kiss him again? Aidan had been on the brink of apologising. Yet he had been the one to end it before it had really begun. He doubtless worried that he had taken advantage of her innocence. Which he hadn't because she'd wanted him to kiss her and he knew that, because otherwise he wouldn't have.

She was going round in circles. Exasperated, Estelle rolled her eyes at herself. For goodness sake, it was just a kiss! A delightful kiss, but hardly one fraught with danger, not in broad daylight in the middle of a *piazza*. A delightful moment in a delightful day that she refused to spoil by analysing it any further.

She'd made a full circuit of the church now, and joined Aidan where he was standing beside a rather battered harpsichord.

'Well,' he asked her, 'is it to your taste? The church, I mean?'

'Very much. In the cathedral of Santa Maria del Fiore, in any of the big churches in this city actually, you feel as if God is so remote as to almost not be present. Here, you feel He is so much more approachable, as if you could just sit down there and talk to Him. Do you think that's an odd thing to say?'

'If it is, then that makes oddities of both of us for I feel exactly the same. Clodagh fears that I'll return to Ireland a convert to Catholicism. I told her that it would be no bad thing,' Aidan said, 'for it would give me something else in common with the majority of my tenants. But my sister, though a liberal in many ways, is very much a traditionalist when it comes to the subject of religion.'

'Are you likely to become a convert?'

He shook his head, smiling wryly. 'That would require me to have strong feelings on the subject, and I don't. Look at this now. You claimed to be able to play almost any instrument, a church harpsichord should present no challenge.'

Estelle sat on the stool and opened the lid reverentially. The keys were worn, but when she struck some experimental soft chords, she discovered that the instrument was perfectly in tune. Her fingers twitched, feeling the connection, as if the harpsichord was begging to be brought to life. 'I shouldn't, not without permission,' she whispered.

'There's no one around,' Aidan replied, 'go on, I dare you.'

Bach's *French Suite* flowed from her fingertips to the keyboard, and she was quickly lost, playing her favourite movement, the fifth, meaning to stop there but finding her fingers flying on to the next and then the next as the music swooped and soared around the small church. She brought the seventh to a flourishing close, resting her hands on the keys and breathing deeply with the kind of intense satisfaction that only music could provide.

Aidan's applause made her eyes fly open. She blushed deeply. 'I'm sorry, I didn't mean…'

'Please don't apologise. That was quite breath-taking.'

'You told me you'd not a musical bone in your body.'

'Estelle, you made me feel as if I had heart-strings that were being plucked. You have a rare talent.'

'Raw talent, perhaps. I've never really had any lessons.'

'Then you're even more talented than I thought. You played for almost fifteen minutes without sheet music and as far as I could tell you didn't make one mistake.'

'I should think not, the number of times I've played that piece. We had hardly any sheet music when I was little, so the few we had, I played over and over again. That was one of them.'

'You'll think this sounds fanciful, but it was as if the music poured straight from your heart through your fingers and on to the keys and then into the air, filling the church with beauty.'

She stared at him, quite dumbstruck for a moment. 'That is possibly the loveliest compliment anyone has ever paid me.'

'I find that hard to believe. Anyone who has heard you play...'

'They are few in number. My sisters, mostly, so they're bound to think I'm good.' She closed the lid of the harpsichord, frowning. 'I wonder if that is why Phoebe opened her restaurant, because she needed some independent approbation of her cooking. I never thought of that before.'

'Perhaps you should play in an orchestra.'

Estelle shuddered. 'It was a family joke, that Phoebe would open a restaurant and I would establish an orchestra, but I never thought of it as anything other than a bit of fun. I don't like to play for strangers.'

'Then I'm extremely honoured.'

'You're not a stranger, I thought we'd agreed that yesterday.'

'We did, and now we've known each other almost two days, I suppose we should consider ourselves old friends. Look Estelle, what happened earlier...'

'Please don't apologise,' she interrupted hastily. 'You must know perfectly well that I wanted you to kiss me. There's nothing to apologise for, or to discuss. I'm twenty-five years old, Aidan.'

He held his hands up. 'But if we were in England...'

'I'm a woman of independent means, with a mind of my own and I'm not in England. I'm beginning to wish that we hadn't kissed now.'

'Well I'm not, despite the fact that I know we shouldn't have.'

'Oh. Good. Then why are we arguing?'

'I've no notion at all.'

'Can we forget about conventions and rules, and what we ought to do, and what people might say? Forget all about the real world for a little while?'

'You've no idea how much I crave that.'

There was the slightest tremor in his voice. She touched his arm tentatively. 'What did I say to upset you?'

'Nothing. Your playing moved me, that's all.'

She didn't believe him, but she didn't want to upset him further, and having agreed to forget about the real world, she didn't feel she had the right to enquire either. 'It was written for the organ, that piece. You don't get the full majesty of it on a harpsichord.'

His smile was grateful. 'You do know there's an organ here too?'

'It's quite usual for a church to have both. A

pipe organ is operated by a lever which works enormous bellows. It's very strenuous work and tends to be saved for high days and holidays, since it's difficult to find volunteers for the task. The rest of the time a harpsichord will suffice.'

'Are the bellows too strenuous for a feeble mathematician, do you think?'

'Aidan, you can't possibly mean—the harpsichord is one thing but I would not be comfortable playing the official church organ without permission. It would be sacrilegious.'

'There is no one to ask. Do you honestly think God would mind?' Aidan said, ushering her towards the instrument. 'I take it this lever is the bellows. How do I…?'

'Slowly!' Laughing, Estelle sat down, flexing her fingers. 'And regularly—like you're pumping water.'

She tested a chord, and it blared out, making Aidan jump and making her laugh more. She played a series of intricate scales, and then, with a theatrical flourish, the opening bars of Bach's most famous piece for the organ, the Toccata and Fugue in D Minor, before launching into the piece, playing it with a dramatic gusto that had Aidan, as she had intended, struggling to contain his laughter as he worked the bellows.

When she was done, collapsing over the keyboard herself in gales of laughter, he applauded with a gusto to match her own, calling bravo, and it was only when he ceased that the pair of them realised he was not alone in his applause.

'*Mi scusi,*' Estelle said, jumping to her feet, horrified.

But the priest smiled, extending his hand. 'I didn't know our humble organ could produce such a wonderful sound, *signora*. It was a pleasure to hear. Music is one of God's gifts and we can celebrate Him in many different ways. You seem such a nice young couple. Please, feel free to come in and play any time you are passing.'

'He thinks we're either married or engaged,' Estelle said with mock horror when they got outside.

'We are,' Aidan said.

'What!'

He grinned. 'Engaged in the business of being friends. What else!'

The next day, their meanderings brought them to another part of the city and another dusty little *piazza* where a few rickety wooden tables had been set outside an *osteria*.

'I think we might claim one of those,' Aidan said, 'what do you think?'

'I think you know perfectly well that you didn't need to ask,' Estelle replied.

The wine was rough, but the *ribollita*, a peasant soup made of stale bread, tomatoes and beans, Estelle pronounced delicious. 'More a stew than a soup, and very filling, which is just as well,' she said, eyeing the next dish with some trepidation. 'I didn't quite catch what this was?'

'*Lampredotto*. Tripe. I fear it's an acquired taste. I can just about manage a couple of mouthfuls.'

'I cannot contemplate even that.' She grimaced. 'What are we to do? I can't possibly send back my plate untouched. It would be the ultimate insult. I can imagine how Phoebe would feel.'

Aidan took a large glug of wine, before quickly tipping the contents of her plate on to his. 'Oh, no,' she protested, appalled, 'you'll be ill.'

'Ah but I'll have the compensation of feeling noble.'

'Aidan Malahide, you are a true knight errant,' Estelle said, quite seriously, 'let me pour you some more wine to help it down.'

He nodded, concentrating on the task in hand, and she concentrated on keeping his glass full. 'Not so bad,' he said when he had done, pushing his plate aside with a sigh of relief. 'I expect an Italian would feel much the same, confronted with crubeens and cabbage.'

'What on earth is a crubeen?'

'You call yourself Irish! A boiled pig's foot, of course. Have you really never tasted it?'

'Have you?' she asked, narrowing her eyes.

'I have it served every Saturday—to my old grandmother's receipt.'

'That is a fib!'

Aidan laughed. 'It is. My old grandmother, what little I remember of her, wouldn't have known the way to the kitchen. A woman with a strong sense of her own importance, and a strict proponent of the rule that children should be seen and not heard. Clodagh and I used to dread having to visit her. Once a month my father took us—she lived in a town house in Kildare itself, my father having had the presence of mind to forcibly relocate her from the castle when he inherited—or perhaps it was my mother's idea, I'm not sure. Anyway, for some reason my grandmother favoured me very much over poor Clodagh. At tea there would always be a big slab of cake and a glass of milk for me, while my sister was given water and a dry biscuit.'

'What on earth had Clodagh done to offend the old lady?'

'Nothing, she swears, and for myself, I didn't do a thing to endear myself to her either.'

'Save be your charming self.'

'At the moment, I'm a very full self. As a reward for my noble act I claim as my prize your company for a post-prandial walk, Miss Brannagh. The Parco delle Cascine is just a few steps away from here, on the banks of the Arno.'

'I would like that very much, kind sir. Without wishing to do your sister an injustice, I can quite easily see why your grandmother thought you so charming. Do you have any other relatives wrapped around your finger?'

'Oh, whole heaps of cousins on my mother and father's side. A few aunts and uncles too, scattered across Ireland and England. What about you?'

'There are cousins on my father's side, I believe, but none who would acknowledge us. When he married Mama they disowned him, and on her side—she eloped, and so her family disowned her too. My Uncle Daniel, my Aunt

Kate's husband, is Mama's brother and so my closest relative.'

'The mysterious absent uncle who rarely writes?' Aidan asked, steering her through a set of gateposts into the woodland park.

'The same. He is an explorer, and spends all his time abroad. Exploring.' Estelle made a face. 'To be honest, I've never quite understood what exactly that entails.'

'Haven't you asked him?'

'I've never had the opportunity. He married Aunt Kate when his father died, about twelve years ago, which was a couple of years before she took us in.'

'You mean he's never been back since?'

'The whole point of their marriage was to allow him to remain abroad. It is an arrangement that has suited them both very well, I assure you. Aunt Kate's father was the estate manager for many years, so she was ideally placed to take on Elmswood Manor, and Uncle Daniel never wanted the responsibility.'

'Good grief. Do you mean that your uncle and aunt have spent their entire married life living apart?'

'They have, and what's more have been very

content doing so. For my part, I think Aunt Kate and Uncle Daniel did a very sensible thing.'

Aidan caught the hand she had withdrawn from his arm. 'I didn't mean to imply any criticism, I'm sorry. I assumed—you see for me, the only reason to marry would be to have a family.'

'Actually,' Estelle said, wondering at the shadow that crossed his countenance, 'I happen to agree with you that it is the best reason, but that is not to say it is the only one.'

'You're right.' Aidan was himself again. Perhaps she had imagined it. 'Your aunt sounds like a very practical woman.'

'And the kindest, most loving—and in fact, she has always said that we three are the children she never had. She is only related to us by marriage, yet she took us in when none of our own relatives were in the least bit interested in our fate.'

'And you quite rightly won't have a word said against her. I'm sorry.' Looking down, seeing her eyes awash with tears, Aidan cursed. 'I've made you cry.'

'It's not your fault.'

Casting a glance along the deserted pathway, he pulled her to one side before producing a large handkerchief and dabbing at her eyes.

Half-laughing, she tried to bat him away. The handkerchief fluttered towards the ground and as she stumbled trying to catch it, Aidan caught her, righting her with a hand on each shoulder. 'Are you all right?'

'Perfectly.'

As he never wore gloves, she could feel the heat of his skin through the flimsy muslin of her summer gown. Her smile faltered as she met his eyes, and her heart skipped a beat, then began to beat far too fast. She closed her eyes. He kissed the teardrops from her lashes and she sighed. He whispered her name, and she opened her eyes, seeing the question in his, and she lifted her face.

Their lips met hesitantly. His short beard was surprisingly soft. He tasted of wine. His lips were warm on hers, and her heart was beating wildly. Anticipation and excitement edged with slight panic, for she had no idea what to do next.

As if he sensed this, he pulled her closer, sliding one arm around her waist, pressing little kisses to her bottom lip. She sighed, her apprehension evaporating, a liquid heat pooling in her tummy as he slid his other hand up her back, caressing the sensitive skin at the nape of her neck, teasing her lips apart with butterfly kisses, then moulding his mouth to hers, moving his lips gently. She followed his lead. As their kiss deepened, her body melted of its own accord against his. She clutched at his shoulder for balance, and beneath her lids, the world turned a flaming red.

When it ended, she gazed at him, dazed. Aidan's eyes were heavy, gazing at her in the same stunned way. There was a hint of auburn in his beard at the corner of his mouth she hadn't noticed before. She touched it, wonderingly, and he pressed his mouth to her open palm, and she caught her breath again, and it hung in the balance for a few seconds, the possibility of a second kiss, which she would have offered freely, before he smiled lopsidedly at her, setting her free from the circle of his arms.

And then they walked on, not quite as before, but in accord, because there was nothing to be said, passing a pyramid-shaped building which proved to be an ice house, and on, until the trees gave way to a *piazza* dominated by a fountain, surprisingly deserted. They sat on a bench in the shade, close enough for their bodies to touch, though they kept their gaze on the tinkling fountain. The park was silent, even the birds made drowsy and muted by the heat.

'I didn't think I was that sort of person,' Estelle said dreamily. 'The kind who kisses at the drop of a hat.'

Aidan gave a huff of laughter. 'The drop of a handkerchief, to be more precise. Ironically, until I met you, I thought I was no longer that sort of person. It just goes to show how resilient nature is.'

'What do you mean?'

'Nothing.' He reached for her hand. 'You do know, Estelle, that if we were in England—or Ireland—it would be quite wrong for me to kiss you.'

'I kissed you back.'

'You know perfectly well what I mean. You may be well travelled, but you're an innocent.'

'Not so innocent that I can't recognise that you have behaved like the honourable man I know you are, Aidan. Other men would have leapt at the offer of a second kiss, and probably pressed for a great deal more, whether it was offered or not. Not,' she added hastily, seeing his horrified expression, 'that I have been subjected to that, but there have been times when it could have become an issue, had I been a little less vigilant.' She sighed, fiddling with the strings of her bonnet. 'So please stop apologising. We agreed, didn't we, that we would make our own rules?'

'We did.'

Later, alone in her pension, realising she'd turned a page in her book without taking in a single word of what she'd read, Estelle cast her history of the Medicis aside. Today had been a revelation. Who would have thought that kissing could be so utterly delightful? Or more specifically, who would have thought that *she* could find kissing so utterly delightful? She had always found the idea of it frightening, a stormy expression of the unsavoury cocktail of hate and love which her parents felt for each other. And her actual experience, until she had kissed Aidan, had been distasteful. But kissing Aidan!

Jumping out of bed, she threw open the window to gaze out on to the *piazza* below. Kissing Aidan was like nothing she had ever imagined. For the first time, she understood how Phoebe's passion for the arrogant but charismatic Frenchman could have flared. When she discovered that her twin had taken Solignac as a lover, she had been shocked to the core—not, as Phoebe assumed, because she had behaved scandalously, but because she claimed to be passionately in love. This, Estelle had always assumed, was the one emotion all three sisters were quite immune to, and happily so, given the appalling example of their parents' tempestuous and ultimately miserable marriage. But Phoebe, thank goodness, had been cured of her passion for that French *enfant terrible*, and now that she'd got him well and truly out of her system, she had made a very sensible marriage much like Aunt Kate's, which allowed her to concentrate on her true passion, for her restaurant.

Aidan, unlike the despised Solignac, was a man of honour. A man who would never take advantage of her. A man she could trust not to overstep the mark, even if she wished him to. It was likely that, this wild, insistent desire to taste more of Aidan's kisses was a passing fancy, a fleeting passion of a very different nature than the one that had infected and driven her parents. Something to be relished, in fact, while it lasted. A little hiatus from the real world, and a much-needed break from worrying about the future.

Was she in thrall to Aidan, as Phoebe had been to her Frenchman? No, but she was enraptured, enchanted, fascinated and—oh, for heaven's sake, attracted! They were kindred spirits who had both been alone too much, but they were also ships that must inevitably pass in the night.

Estelle threw herself back on her bed. For the next little while, she could enjoy Aidan's company and his kisses for what they were. An interlude—an extremely pleasant one of say—a week—no, two weeks, before she left Florence for the next stop on her itinerary. Satisfied, she blew out her candle and lay back on the pillows, pressing her mouth to the back of her hand to relive today's kisses, and to imagine tomorrow's. If that was not being too greedy.

Chapter Four

Estelle peered at the plaque below the painting. '"Raphael, Portrait of Pope Leo X with Two Cardinals." With a spyglass in his hand too. Do you think he was short-sighted? He looks to me like a man who bears a grudge. I don't think I'd like to be in the cardinals' shoes.'

Standing beside her in one of the portrait galleries in the Uffizi, Aidan laughed softly. 'It does look as if they've brought him some very unwelcome news.'

'Are they standing or sitting?' Estelle peered closer. 'Either they are sitting, and that one at a very odd angle, or they are very short.'

'It's about fixing the perspective,' Aidan said, going on to explain, as he had with several paintings they had examined that morning, the mathematics and ratios behind the composition.

'Do you think Raphael understood all this?'

'Well da Vinci certainly did, and they were contemporaries.'

Estelle wrinkled her nose. 'I'm afraid it doesn't make me like it any more. I certainly wouldn't want it hanging on my wall. Which is just as well, since I don't have one, far less four to call my own.'

They made their way through the gallery stopping when the fancy took them to speculate, sometimes about the art, sometimes about the spectators of the art. It had been ten days since they had first met here, and they'd spent a large part of every one of those days together. Aidan had given up any pretence of studying. When he was with Estelle, the world was a golden place, with no past and no future to tarnish it. They talked of everything and nothing. Like him, she seemed content to forget the real world and to wallow in this one. There were still moments when unbidden memories caught him unawares, when he was reminded of the terrible burden he carried, but in Estelle's company, those were quickly banished, and if she noticed them—he knew she did—she made no comment.

Did she have her own secrets? It astonished him sometimes, alone in his rooms, thinking over the day, how little he really knew of her, but what did fact and history matter, when they understood each other on a more elemental level? Mind and body, there was a connection between them that grew stronger every day. They both knew perfectly well that it would have to be severed, and soon, and they both knew that the sensible thing would be to wean themselves off it. But instead, each day they fed the flames further, greedy for more, and never quite satisfied that they'd had enough.

She made him feel alive. She made him feel young. She made him feel new. He revelled in being the person she saw, not being the man he had become. With her, he could fool himself into believing he really was that person. Though there was a part of him patiently watching, ready to pounce when he was alone, that knew this was all a lie. No, not a lie, a dream. If only he never had to awake.

They had reached the Tribuna, the most popular of the galleries, where, despite the early hour, the usual assortment of people were sketching and staring. Estelle had joined a small group in front of one of the more infamous works featuring lasciviously nude women. It made him want to laugh, the way she tilted her head, wrinkled her nose, shuffled from one side of the frame to the other, attempting to see what so fascinated the others. She had no idea she was so transparent, and no idea it was one of the things about her which he found most endearing. For such an independent, seasoned traveller, she had a surprising innocence about her. She was not naïve, but she consistently underestimated herself. It made him fiercely protective, though he was careful not to let her see that. And careful, very careful, not to let the kisses they shared lead to anything more significant.

He wanted her. There wasn't a moment when he was in her company when he wasn't aware of her, and she of him too. They were forever brushing against each other, their fingertips touching on table tops, while their knees did the same, hidden from view. Her hand was always tucked into his arm when they walked. Their kisses were searing, heady, delightful. He couldn't get enough of her kisses, but he rationed them all the same, lest they lose their innocence. Such pleasurable kisses could so easily lead to more darkly sensual pleasures. Deeper kisses, more intimate caresses. Estelle would follow where he led. It was her implicit trust in him that made it easy to restrain himself—if frustrating.

And he did permit himself to speculate how it might be. Such fevered imaginings!

'If you were a painting, Aidan Malahide, I'd say that you were a man about to devour a most excellent dinner. You have a look of ravenous anticipation.'

'Do I?' he said, smiling. 'My appetite for art is certainly utterly sated. I think a coffee is called for. Shall we?'

Estelle took Aidan's arm, and he pulled her a little closer, as he always did, as they made their way to the Piazza della Signoria. The waiter waved them to what had been her table and had now become theirs, bringing coffee and pastries without asking. Above her, the sun shone from a perfect blue sky decorated with what seemed like impossibly fluffy clouds. Beside her, Aidan was idly surveying the promenade of tourists, artists setting up their easels, hawkers setting up their wares. He sat at an angle to the little table, stretching his legs out, leaning slightly back in his chair, his coat unfastened. His stomach was quite flat. There was a very pleasing breadth to his shoulders. There were any number of statues of naked men in this city, but until now, she'd never compared art to life. How would Aidan compare with Michelangelo's masterpiece over there? Aidan was flesh and blood, not cold marble. His skin would be warm. Smooth? Pale or tanned? She had absolutely no idea. Her experience of naked male flesh began and ended with statues, and until now, she'd had no inclination whatsoever to broaden her knowledge.

Estelle Brannagh! She reached for her coffee just as Aidan reached for his, and their hands brushed each other. He smiled at her, one of his slow, lazy smiles, and her breath caught, and her stomach fluttered as she returned his smile. He couldn't possibly have read her thoughts, but his gaze lingered on her, and something in his eyes made her hot under the summer gown she had so carefully chosen for today, and his fingers curled around hers, and he lifted her hand to his mouth and he kissed her fingertips. She'd taken her gloves off to drink her coffee, and the touch of his lips on her bare skin made her shiver in the most delightful way, and her shivering made his hand tighten on hers, and he kissed her fingertips again, his lips soft, warm. Dear heavens!

She blinked. He released her hand. A dog, one of those small, fluffy creatures with a coat so long that it almost completely obscured its feet, came racing towards them. 'It looks like a fur-covered ottoman on wheels,' Estelle said. 'Do you have a dog? I feel sure you must, for all castles should have at least one dog roaming the halls. A hound of some sort, perhaps?'

But Aidan seemed not to be listening to her. 'Ah, here comes the cavalry. Give me a minute.'

It took him three strides to catch up with the runaway lapdog, which he scooped up so suddenly that the creature's legs were still paddling the air. The two children who had been in hot pursuit took eager charge of their pet, thanking Aidan in careful English which became a stream of Italian when he responded in their own language. He knelt down on the cobbles to converse with the pair. A boy and a girl, twins, Estelle thought, or very near in age, and most certainly brother and sister. The boy hugged the dog while the girl attached the leash it must have slipped. The girl did most of the talking, while the boy soothed the dog, setting it carefully back on to the cobblestones, shaking his head furiously at something his sister said, launching into a speech that involved much gesticulating, while the little girl watched, her arms crossed, her expression so like Eloise listening to one of Phoebe's flights of fancy, that Estelle couldn't help but laugh.

When the trio were interrupted by a flustered mama, Aidan seemed reluctant to leave them. They talked on, the mother smiling, garrulous, now that she had her babes safe, stooping every now and then to kiss one or other, or to include them in the conversation, and Estelle felt such a yearning, she had to look away.

Aidan sat back down beside her, waving at the departing family. 'They're visiting from Rome, apparently. The dog was supposed to have been left behind, but the children smuggled it on to the coach and by the time it was discovered, it was too late to turn back. The children promised that it would be no trouble, but according to Mama it has been nothing but. I'm sorry, I didn't mean to abandon you for so long.'

'They looked like twins,' Estelle said, her eyes still on the departing family.

'I thought so too, but, as Carlo informed me proudly, it is because he is very big for his age.'

'You seemed very taken with them.'

'They were a nice family, obviously close.'

'I'd like a family like that. I mean I'd like what that woman had—to be the centre of some-one's world, to nurture a child—no, a host of children—and watch them grow.' Aidan looked as startled by the admission as she was herself. 'I don't know why I blurted that out. Ignore me.'

'It's a natural enough thing to want. I want it myself,' he said, with an odd little smile. 'But we can't always have what we want, can we? Cashel Duairc is crying out for a gaggle of children to fill it with laughter, turn it into a home, not a draughty castle. But it's not going to happen in my lifetime.'

'Why on earth not?' Estelle asked, both touched and taken aback by this confession.

'I told you, I'm not in the market for a wife.'

'Never? I thought you meant at the moment.'

'I meant never.'

His tone was clipped, his expression forbidding. Mortified, Estelle could think of only one reason for this sudden change in his mood. 'You need not worry that I have designs on you.'

His hand found hers under the table. 'I don't. Did I mention,' he continued after a brief silence, 'that I first came to university here when I was eighteen? When my father died, I was obliged to return home and therefore left before completing my degree.'

'So you came back to pick up the reins of your misspent youth when you turned thirty?'

He smiled weakly. 'I'm sorry to disillusion

you, but I never had a misspent youth. I was a very *serious* young man back then, and inheriting Cashel Duairc so unexpectedly made me even more so.'

'What happened?'

'To my father? He was one of the main investors in the project to build the Royal Canal, and I suspect an irritating distraction to the men charged with actually constructing the thing, for he was a bit of an amateur engineer. It was when he was inspecting one of the half-built bridges that he died—the scaffolding gave way.'

'Oh, Aidan, how awful, I'm so sorry.'

'He wasn't the only casualty, not by a long shot. Building canals—building anything—is a dangerous business. He was in the wrong place at the wrong time, is what it amounts to. It's a pity that he never got to see it completed. They invited me to the opening—one of my first official duties, after I inherited.'

'That must have been very difficult for you.'

'I was too busy to think, most of the time.'

'And so your studies were put on hold.'

'Abandoned for twelve years, would be more accurate.' Aidan picked up his empty coffee cup, frowned down at the cold grounds and signalled for another. 'As it turns out, the world hasn't been deprived of a mathematical genius after all. But my time here hasn't been wasted. I reckon I'll take some inspiration from my father and put my studies to more practical use in the form of engineering. There's no shortage of projects to keep me occupied.'

Estelle puzzled over this insight into his thinking while they waited for his coffee to be served. 'Occupied to the extent that there would be no room for a wife and family?' she asked when they were once again alone.

He hesitated, drinking his coffee in one gulp in the Italian manner. 'The structures I build will be my legacy.'

Was that an answer? She still couldn't understand why he was so set against marriage, but his words had struck a chord none the less. Aidan could not be a mathematician, but being an engineer was a practical alternative use of his talents. 'To follow your logic, if my continued single status denies me the opportunity of having a family of my own,' Estelle said, 'then perhaps I should consider helping other families raise their children.'

'Surely you don't imagine yourself as a governess?'

'Oh, dear heavens, no! I am far too independently minded for that. But establishing a school—now that is something I've not considered. Using my one talent to teach children to play musical instruments.'

'Estelle, tell me to mind my own business if you want, but isn't the obvious answer to your dilemma to find a husband rather than found a school, however laudable the motive? Look at you! You're beautiful, talented, clever, witty— you cannot possibly be short of suitors.'

'Oh, if I could content myself with marrying a man who was merely interested in fathering my children, not being a father to them, then I expect I could have settled down to raising my brood years ago. That sounds horribly conceited,' she added, grimacing, 'but I'm afraid I have a very romantic view of parenthood, and believe that children deserve both parents sharing an interest in their upbringing.'

'Is that romantic? It seems to me perfectly rational.'

'Ha, tell that to my parents!'

'From what you've told me, your parents set a terrible example, but they are not typical I assure you. If all you wish for is a man who wants a family...'

'Well, no, it's not as simple as that.'

'What else do you require? I'm fascinated. Go on, describe your ideal husband.'

'Oh, he is a perfect paragon of a man. Good company, a man who will share my life without wanting to dominate it. A man who respects me, and who doesn't simply lust after me, who truly listens to what I say, you know, and who makes conversation, rather than one of those men who simply spout their own views. A man who can see past the colour of my hair, and my figure, who doesn't think the sound of his own voice more important than his wife's—' She broke off, embarrassed. 'When I put it like that, it's clear my expectations are unrealistic, but a lifetime is far too long to spend in the company of a man I don't actually like and besides— Oh, it doesn't matter.'

'It clearly does.'

Estelle pondered. She and her sisters rarely talked about the past, for it was too painful a subject, and they were afraid of opening up old wounds. Being alone, first at Elmswood and then on her travels, had given her a great deal of time to reflect. Despite the fact that she had known Aidan for such a little time, and perhaps because their time was coming to an end almost before it had begun, it mattered to her that he understood her. 'In a nutshell,' she said, 'I want a marriage as different from my parents' as it is possible to have.'

'The fact that your eldest sister was forced to play mother from an early age, tells me that they were neither fond nor attentive parents,' Aidan said, choosing his words carefully.

'Nor particularly present for much of the time.' Estelle frowned down at her coffee cup, turning it around and around on her saucer. 'Mama was a beauty. Papa's role was to worship at her shrine. I suppose you would describe it as a tempestuous marriage.' She glanced briefly at Aidan before returning her attention to the coffee cup. 'My father was besotted with my mother and she with him, though not exclusively so. Their marriage was an endless cycle of passion boiling over into jealousy, resentment giving way to reconciliation. And all of it played out in front of their children, with absolutely no regard for the effect it was having. We used to peer through the banister rail at them, me and Phoebe, until Eloise dragged us away.'

'I didn't realise. I didn't mean to upset you. We'll talk of something else.'

But she shook her head. 'I might as well finish now I've started, if you want to hear it?'

'Of course I do, but I don't want to upset you any further.'

'It wasn't like that all the time. They preferred Dublin, and only came to the country when funds were short. We were happy enough left to our own devices, our little gang of three, or we thought we were. Looking back, I can see that we were quite neglected—out of sight, out of mind, you know?'

Aidan swore softly.

'My thoughts exactly,' Estelle said wryly, 'though to be fair, they neglected their tenants even more than their children and—and they didn't neglect all their children.' She pressed the heels of her hands together, bracing herself. 'I had a brother. Diarmuid was five years younger than Phoebe and I. The longed-for son and heir, the golden child—not only in our parents' eyes either, all three of us girls adored him. I haven't mentioned him before. I still find it hard to talk about him, even after all this time. He was only ten when he died.' She blinked rapidly. 'I struggle to remember what he looked like sometimes, how he smiled and that naughty laugh of his. He was a spoilt brat, but a very endearing one, when he chose to be. He'd be twenty now. I wonder sometimes, what he'd have made of himself—

though to be honest, I doubt he'd have had the inclination to make much of himself at all, for he was quite ruined. My point is, Aidan, that they were atrocious parents, to us girls and to poor little Diarmuid too.'

'They didn't deserve you.'

'No, they didn't. If we hadn't had each other, we three, and lovely Aunt Kate, we might have turned out very badly.'

'It is a tribute to the strength of character you must all have that you have turned out very well indeed.'

'Well, now, there's the rub, for I've yet to make anything of my life.'

'Estelle...'

'No, don't go singing my praises, for to date I've done nothing of merit save survive, and hordes of people have done that in much worse circumstances. I didn't tell you all this to make you feel sorry for me or even to impress you, I told you because I wanted you to understand why I won't compromise when it comes to finding a father for my own children. Children need to be loved, Aidan, they need to be cared for, they need certainty and stability, not turmoil. What they don't need is a mother and father who are so passionately in love with each other that they feel obliged to act out *The Taming of the Shrew* twice a day in front of them. Do you see?'

'Only too well, and I couldn't agree more, trust me.'

'I must do, for I've told you far more than I meant to.'

She watched him anxiously, dreading any sign of pity, but when he spoke, there was only warmth in his voice, and in his eyes, something approaching tenderness. 'I'm glad you did. I feel I understand you much better now.'

'Is that how you view me, a puzzle to be solved?'

'A beautiful conundrum? That would certainly explain why I can't stop thinking about you.'

Colour flooded her cheeks. 'And now I am no longer a mystery, your interest will pall.'

'On the contrary, I am already certain that you're going to be very difficult to forget.'

'Aidan, I...' But the polite disclaimer died on her lips as their eyes met. 'I feel exactly the same, believe me.'

'I know.' He pulled a handful of change from his pocket and pushed back his chair. 'Shall we get on with making the most of what little time we have left, then?'

* * *

Time had grown wings since she met Aidan, Estelle thought. It was already almost a week past her self-imposed deadline. They had spent the afternoon exploring the Boboli Gardens, and had climbed from the amphitheatre, past Neptune's fountain and up the stairs to the highest point. It was late afternoon, and the gardens were clearing, leaving them alone, sitting on the grass side by side in the shade of the cypress trees. Florence was spread out below them, a mass of red-tiled roofs, with Brunelleschi's Duomo, and Giotto's Campanile highlighted against the dramatic backdrop of the Chianti mountains.

'I like your gown,' Aidan said. 'I don't think I've seen it before.'

'I didn't think you noticed my clothes.'

'I notice everything about you. What is this colour—mint green? You favour it, you've another gown the same colour, though the sleeves are different, a puffier shape, and it has emerald ribbons. I prefer the lemon. Though my favourite of your gowns is the pale-blue one with the lace trim.'

'It's a little too tight for comfort.'

Aidan's smile became wicked. 'In my opinion

it fits like a glove, since it shows your figure off to perfection.' He held his hands up, laughing. 'Or maybe I'd better not express any opinion.'

She was blushing, laughing, and because it was Aidan, not at all offended. 'Have you any other observations to make about my toilettes?'

'Oh, any number, but I won't embarrass either of us by sharing them. Are you looking forward to your trip away tomorrow?'

'Honestly? I wish I hadn't agreed to go to Siena with Lady Gertrude.'

'The wife of our most senior diplomat in Tuscany. Her invitation is quite an honour. You must go.'

'It would be considered very rude of me to refuse.'

'And foolish. You will travel in style, and sleep in comfort.'

'I have only met her once, but she seems very amenable. And I'll only be gone a couple of days.'

'I'll miss you.'

'And I will miss you. Will you resume your studies while I'm away?'

Aidan shook his head. 'I think my studying days are behind me.'

'And your sabbatical year too, will be over soon.'

His smile faded. 'Let's not talk of that.'

Estelle plucked a blade of grass. It was wiry, even this early in the year, the soil already parched. 'I'm thinking that Venice will be the next major destination on my trip.'

'When? Have you made plans?'

'Not yet.' Though she should have, long before now. 'When I get back from Siena though, I was thinking...'

'That it was time you moved on.' Aidan stared out at the view, but bewitching as it was, she had the distinct impression he was seeing a very different landscape. 'You're right, of course,' he said, nodding to himself. 'And after Venice, what then?'

Estelle shrugged. 'Perhaps I'll just keep wandering on into another sunset and then another, and never go back to England.'

'You don't mean that.' He turned back towards her then, covering her hand with his, his expression a gentle rebuke. 'You're not a wanderer at heart, Estelle. You're a woman that needs a place to call her own. A home.'

His words brought a lump to her throat, for they showed an understanding of her character that even she hadn't quite recognised. 'I also need a purpose. I owe it to Eloise as well as myself, to do something productive with my funds.'

'I'm not sure I understand.'

'My independence was not a legacy from my parents, Aidan, it was Eloise's doing. When she married Alexander, it was part of the arrangement, that she could make settlements on both Phoebe and I.'

'Arrangement? You mean the marriage contract?'

Estelle plucked another blade of grass, twisting it around her finger into a ring.

'Forgive me, I didn't mean to pry.'

'Isn't it strange how, despite spending many hours in each other's company, we've avoided discussing our circumstances?'

'The real world, you mean? I thought that's what we both wanted.'

'It is. Only—my sister, Phoebe, bought me a little globe in Paris. It's a glass dome with a model of the city in miniature inside it. I sometime feel that you and I are living in our own glass dome, isolated from the world. I don't want to leave our little private bubble, but I must, I've wasted enough time. I have to get on with the rest of my life now.'

Estelle pulled the grass ring from her finger, casting it aside. 'Eloise's marriage of convenience has turned out very well. She and her husband have proved an excellent match. They have a little girl now, and they are working together on a vast project to modernise his lands. After Eloise was married, Phoebe wasted no time in putting her windfall to use.'

'Her restaurant?'

'Yes. There were a few twists and turns along the way, but she succeeded—is now succeeding beyond her wildest dreams. She's actually married too now. A business arrangement, not a love match, and like Aunt Kate, she and her husband were living apart for a time, though according to her latest letter, he recently returned, and she seems very happy to see him.'

'Good Lord! When you told me that your parents' marriage was destructive...'

'But we learned from it, all three of us.'

'And then there was Aunt Kate,' Aidan said, looking much struck. 'Was she the role model for your sisters' marriages?'

'Are you imagining her as a sort of scheming wedding planner?' Estelle burst into a peal of laughter. 'If you could see her, you'd understand why that is so funny. In fact she was very much against Eloise's marriage at first, even though it was proposed by my Uncle Daniel.'

'So he is the scheming wedding planner?'

'Ha! If he was, then perhaps he could find me a husband like Eloise's—for in my view, she has the perfect marriage. But he had nothing to do with Phoebe's marriage, she arranged that all by herself and now he—oh, it doesn't matter.'

'You told me, oh, aeons ago, on the first day we met in fact, that your time at Elmswood Manor was over—by choice, you said. But it's been your home for nigh on ten years, Estelle, wouldn't it make sense for you to return there, regroup, consult your oracle of an aunt on your future?'

'No.' She picked up another strand of grass and began to weave it into another ring. 'I've had five years to think about the future, Aidan—five whole years of more or less living in limbo while my sisters got on with their lives. I've not been entirely useless. Latterly, just before I took up my travels, I was looking after Elmswood for Aunt Kate, but now suddenly I'm twenty-five!' She cast her second attempt at a grass ring aside impatiently. 'Perhaps we were right after all not to talk of the world outside our little glass dome, it's too depressing. What will you do while I'm in Siena?'

'Miss you?'

'Don't say that.'

'It's the truth.' He leaned in, pressing his cheek to hers, pushing back her bonnet, smoothing her hair. 'When you leave Florence, the spell you've cast over me will lose all its power, and I'll go back to the real world, and you—you'll go on to work your magic somewhere else, spellbind some other lucky fellow.'

'I don't want to spellbind any man, I thought you understood that.'

'I do. I meant— Ach, I don't know *what* I mean. Let's not spoil the day.'

'You're right.' She nuzzled her cheek against his, the smooth skin, the contrasting roughness of his beard, sending a frisson of pleasure rippling through her tummy. 'Let's not.'

Their lips met, and their kiss was gentle, an apology, smoothing away the rough edges of their discord. Then it changed as the desire which all the little touches during the day kept simmering beneath the surface broke free from its leash. Their kisses deepened, their tongues touching, and their hands drifting, from shoulder to back, to waist. They fell back on to the grass, still kissing, and Estelle ran her fingers through Aidan's hair, and he smoothed his hands from her waist, down over her flank. She could hear herself making odd little noises, panting, pleading, as their kisses went on, deep, delicious, heady kisses, and she instinctively rolled closer to him.

But as she did so he moved away, as ever, the one to show restraint. She could see, from the dazed look in his eyes, that it took a huge effort, but she also knew that later, when her body had ceased protesting, she would be grateful for it.

'We'd better get you back. You've an early start ahead of you,' he said.

She nodded, her body aching, throbbing, crying out in protest, but following his lead because, innocent as she was, she knew that it would be madness not to.

Chapter Five

Aidan realised, as soon as he saw the crest on the hand-delivered letter which arrived the next morning, that Estelle's removal from the scene and this polite but firm summons were connected, no mere coincidence but evidence of a co-ordinated plan. It would appear that their behaviour had not gone entirely unnoticed by her local surrogate guardian. He supposed he'd been naïve to imagine they were unobserved, for Florence was awash with Englishmen and women with as much interest in the activities of their fellow countrymen as they had for fine art.

His instincts were to consign the instruction disguised as an invitation to the fire, but in the end he relented, and went in order to preserve Estelle's illusion that her life passed free from scrutiny, hoping to persuade the letter's author she was not at risk.

And knowing that to do so, he'd have to agree to terminate their relationship. Which they'd all but agreed they'd do of their own accord anyway, yesterday in the Boboli Gardens. Their idyll was coming to a premature but timely end, just as it ought to. Time to quit the glass dome, to use Estelle's rather whimsical analogy. The fact that he didn't in the least want it to end was clear evidence that it should.

Sir George, Minister Resident and the most senior British diplomat in the Grand Duchy of Tuscany, did not honour him with his presence, but the man assigned the delicate task of sounding him out was no minion. Aidan thought at first he was misreading the veiled suggestions and hints. When it became clear that he was not, he was incredulous. 'Am I to understand that you have been checking up on me?'

'Merely verifying your suitability as a companion for Miss Brannagh,' the nameless man replied, with a bland smile. 'You will be delighted to know that the results of our enquires were very positive.'

'Indeed! May I ask in what way?'

'In every way, Mr Malahide. Financial health,

estates, reputation. Given your personal circumstances, it was obvious that your intentions towards Miss Brannagh could only be genuine and honourable.'

Aidan gritted his teeth. 'What circumstances?'

The man offered him a conciliatory smile. 'I understand it has been almost three years since you were afflicted by tragedy. A long time for a man to be alone, sir, if you will forgive my commenting on such a personal matter. Especially a man in his prime, as you are.'

'Who the devil have you been talking to? What business is it of yours?'

'You are upset.'

'Damn right I am. I'm bloody furious.'

'Understandably so,' the man answered with another of his conciliatory smiles. 'However, our primary concern is Miss Brannagh's welfare. Ours is a temporary and quite unofficial responsibility of course, for she is fully of age and perfectly entitled to make her own decisions. The Earl of Fearnoch made it very clear that we have no *legal* status.'

'What the devil has the Earl of Fearnoch to do with the matter?'

For the first time, the diplomat looked put out. 'He is married to Miss Brannagh's sister.

A most respected man in diplomatic circles—I had the honour to meet him myself once, several years ago. An intrepid type. You were not aware of the connection?'

'I knew that Miss Brannagh's sister was married to a man of influence.' A great deal of influence, it seemed, and probably far more than Estelle realised.

'Indeed. Though his interest in Miss Brannagh, as I said, has no legal basis he has, quite rightly, a natural concern to do as much to keep a young woman travelling on her own as safe as it is possible to be. Which is where we come in, Mr Malahide. As we see it here, we have been invested with a duty of care towards Miss Brannagh while she is in Tuscany. A duty we intend to discharge diligently.'

Aidan struggled to control his temper. Though he would happily have discharged his right fist into the face of the supercilious oaf before storming out, he owed it to Estelle to do no such thing. 'So now you've vetted me and failed to find me wanting, you're keen to know what my intentions are?' Taking a deep, calming breath, he unfurled his clenched fists. It was, after all, precisely what he'd expected. 'I'll spare you the trouble. When she returns from her very conveniently arranged trip to Siena, Miss Brannagh will continue on to Venice. Alone, I need not add.'

'And you, sir? Will you resume your studies?'

'My future plans are none of your business, since your *duty of care* will have been fully discharged upon Miss Brannagh's leaving Tuscany,' Aidan said curtly. His return home loomed, but he would deal first with losing Estelle. 'I would prefer that you kept this encounter of ours from her. She thinks herself free to come and go as she pleases, and would not take well...'

'...to the discovery that her elder sister has sent an invisible chaperon to accompany her on her travels.' The diplomat smiled thinly. 'We shall consider the matter closed, Mr Malahide. I am sorry to have offended you, but you must understand, though we are in foreign climes, it is our duty to uphold British values. Such intimacy as you and Miss Brannagh have developed would never have been tolerated back home, unless formal overtures had been made.'

'Getting to know one another when the promises have already been made and it's too late to change your mind,' Aidan said sardonically. 'The British rules of courtship are somewhat perverse, don't you think?'

* * *

The nameless man made no attempt to rebuff Aidan's criticism, and the meeting ended with his surprising assurance of his best attempts to provide his assistance in any future matter, should it be required. Aidan left the building in an odd mood, restless, uncertain, confused, and unable to pinpoint why he felt any of those things, as he walked aimlessly in the heat of the afternoon. Though he and Estelle had tacitly agreed that what they called their friendship must come to an end, they had not set a firm date. The outcome of his strange encounter with officialdom was that their parting needed to be finalised as soon as Estelle returned from Siena. Otherwise, the wheels of diplomacy would turn, and he didn't doubt that she would be summoned for a more explicit warning off. He didn't want that. She'd be mortified and angry, hurt by what she'd see as her elder sister's lack of trust in her, and quite unable to understand her very natural concern. And so their little idyll must end before that risk became reality.

The idea that he would never see her again was like a punch to the gut. Every fibre of his body rebelled against it. But they could not continue as they were, he knew that. Estelle had to move on. He had to return to Ireland and face the reality that he had temporarily escaped.

Ireland. Aidan's stomach gave a sickening lurch. He didn't want to think about Ireland, though he'd have to, and soon, for his sabbatical was nearly over. Heading for the nearest café, he ordered a coffee and stared morosely at a scrawny cat sunning itself on a window ledge. This year had been exactly what he'd hoped for, at first. The bright light of Tuscany, the red-tiled roofs of Florence, the busy *piazze*, the food— all had served to make him forget home. And the university too, had been the distraction he'd needed, for he'd had to wrestle hard to get his rusty mind working again and he'd thoroughly enjoyed the challenges of trying to catch up with more than a decade of progress in his field. Then just when that distraction was starting to pall, and his thoughts were once again turning, bleakly, to home, along came Estelle.

He drained the thick black coffee in one gulp and signalled for another. He'd thought of her as a diversion, their time together as an interlude, but this afternoon it had been made clear to him that others saw it very differently. So it must end. The conclusion was inescapable. As was his own next move.

Ireland. As the diplomat had pointed out, and as Clodagh told him when he gave her the chance, it had been almost three years. Time to put the past behind him. It appeared that the Florentine tittle-tattlers observing him with Estelle had assumed he was doing exactly that, thinking their friendship a courtship, assuming that promises had been secretly made. It was ridiculous of course, Estelle didn't want a husband any more than he wanted a wife. Though ironically, what the pair of them wanted more than anything was a family.

He stirred a lump of sugar into his second coffee. The image of the little boy and girl and their dog, in the Piazza della Signorina popped into his head and he recalled the wistful expression on Estelle's face as she watched them. It was an expression of yearning he was horribly familiar with, and he knew, only too well, the bitter consequences of such heartfelt dreams not being realised.

'We can't always have what we want,' he'd told her at the time, though he'd given her no clue as to the pain and devastation lying behind the trite little phrase. He thought he'd stopped wanting the impossible. He had come to Florence to find an alternative, and he had one now,

dammit, in his decision to build something—not a family, but a few bridges, a canal or two maybe. So why was he even wasting his time thinking about this most painful topic? He was a mathematician. The logic was incontrovertible. Nature was the variable in his equation for happiness, one that he had no control over. He would never risk testing it again.

Never? Even if it meant that there was a tiny chance that he and Estelle could have what they both wanted? Aidan groaned. A mathematician, he called himself, and here he was, defying logic. But he was also a man, thinking not with his head, but with another part of his body entirely. He didn't want to bid Estelle farewell. He wanted them to continue living in their little glass dome, forgetting all about the real world, and while he was indulging in this little fantasy, why not admit that he ached, yearned, agonised with the desire to make love to her. Just once. Just once, to let their kisses be the beginning and not the end of things. He wanted to lie naked with her. To kiss every bit of her delectable body. To watch her eyes become lambent as he touched her, roused her, feel her tighten around him, slick, hot as he entered her…

Aidan cursed viciously under his breath.

Mortified and impatient with himself, he threw a handful of change down on the table before making for the banks of the Arno. His mind raced, trying to order the various elements of his dilemma into a new equation, one that would miraculously produce the desired result. But by the time he reached the entrance to the Parco delle Cascine he had given up. What Estelle wanted and what he wanted coincided but could not be reconciled, and that was an end to it. When she returned from Siena, the day after tomorrow, they must say their goodbyes and put an end to their little idyll.

'So, it sounds like it was an enjoyable trip, then?'

'Yes, it was.' Puzzled by Aidan's somewhat abrupt interruption of the Siena anecdote she'd been recounting, Estelle steered their steps towards a bench in the shade of the amphitheatre of the Boboli Gardens, with a view to the Neptune fountain. 'You don't seem yourself, Aidan. Did something happen while I was away? Have you received some bad news from home?'

'No, nothing like that.' He stretched his legs out in front of him, ran his fingers through his hair, then sat up again, squaring his shoulders.

'The days felt longer. It brought home to me how very much I've enjoyed our time together.'

'You know I feel the same.' Truth be told, Estelle thought, beautiful though Sienna was, she had been counting the minutes until she returned, from the moment she left Florence. She sighed. 'But we both know it will have to come to an end at some point.'

He dug the toe of his shoe into the hard-packed earth. 'I think sooner, rather than later, would be best. In six weeks my sabbatical year will be over. I'll probably head back to Ireland when you leave. Florence won't be the same without you.'

'I'm thinking that I might curtail my travels too. It's time I went home, faced the music, so to speak, made a start on the rest of my life.'

'Your idea of establishing a school of music? You could always return to Ireland and set it up there. There's a sore need for education of every kind.'

'Back to the old country,' Estelle said, in an exaggerated brogue.'

'I would be happy to let you set it up on my estate, gratis.'

'You know, if it were not for the fact that you are dead set against marriage and I refuse to entertain having a husband I want to kiss, then you would be the paragon I've been searching for and I wouldn't have to set up a school.'

'Estelle...'

'I was teasing, Aidan.'

'I know. It's not that.' He picked up a stone that he'd dug up with his toe, turning it over in his hand before letting it fall back into the dust. 'Even if you did find your paragon, there's no guarantee that nature would co-operate with your desire for a family.'

'Co-operate? That's a very strange way to describe the most natural process in the world.'

'Then I'll put it in mathematical terms. Any equation which contains a variable has an unpredictable outcome. In your case, nature is the variable in your recipe for a perfect husband. Suppose you find someone who is more interested in being a father than a husband, who likes you but doesn't adore you, who respects you but doesn't revere you—do I have all that right?'

'I couldn't have put it better myself, but...'

'Suppose you find him, Estelle, and you get married. Remember, the only reason you married is to have children, but nature doesn't co-operate, as I said, and you can't have children. You'll have failed.'

'I don't think I'd see it as a failure, precisely, though I take your point.'

'My point is that you would see it as failure, eventually, and you'd be utterly miserable. Trust me, I know.'

She stared at him, shocked to the core as realisation dawned. 'You're speaking from experience.'

He paled, but met her gaze unflinchingly. 'Yes, I am.'

'You're married,' she said, beginning to shake.

'What? No, God no, Estelle, I'm not married. Not any longer. But I'm not the bachelor I led you to believe. I'm a widower. My wife died almost three years ago.'

The blood which had drained from her face now flooded her cheeks with colour. 'Oh, Aidan, I'm so sorry.' Her hand instinctively reached for him, but he shook his head, stiffening, and she withdrew it immediately.

He shifted on the bench, creating a space between them. 'Being with you these last few weeks has made me feel like a new man—or rather, I suppose, I've remembered the man I used to be. It's not that I've been lying to you, but while I've been with you, it's been very easy to forget.'

'I wondered why you were so set against marriage. It never occurred to me...'

'That I was set against trying again? With good reason,' he said heavily. 'You see, in some ways I had what you say you want—the ideal spouse. A woman from the same background as me, who wanted the same things as me. We got on. We shared a dream. But when the dream wasn't realised— I swear to God, Estelle, I wouldn't wish that on anyone.'

'Oh, Aidan! What happened?'

'It's a sorry tale, but I'll tell you if you can bear to listen.'

'Of course I can, though I don't want to upset you further.'

He smiled crookedly. 'You confided in me that morning we saw the children with the dog, it's only fair that I return the favour.' He stared off at the fountain for a moment before turning back to her, visibly bracing himself.

'I was twenty-two when we met in Dublin. I'd already been in sole charge of Cashel Duairc for four years, and I was ready to settle down and start populating a nursery. My wife was born and raised in County Wicklow, just next door to Kildare, and on a very similar estate to the Cashel Duairc lands. We were well suited, as I said, and of one mind when it came to wanting a big family. A perfect match, everyone said.'

Estelle felt a mortifying twinge of envy. What had she looked like, this perfect wife? she wondered, immediately chastising herself for being so venal. The poor woman must have died tragically young. Aidan must have been heartbroken.

'And so we were duly married,' he continued, fortunately oblivious to her thoughts. 'And we were happy enough at first. But when there were no signs of children after a year or so my wife began to fret—she wanted children so badly, you see. Don't get me wrong, I was every bit as anxious as she was, but I thought we just needed to be patient. But time passed and we were still not blessed. And my wife blamed me.'

'Oh, Aidan, that's so unfair.'

He shook his head impatiently. 'The reason we married was to have a family. It was what brought us together, and my failure to deliver what I promised drove us apart. A marriage without children was a sham, she was forever saying, and I couldn't argue with her.'

Why not? Estelle thought indignantly. It took two to have a child. Why did he assume the burden of guilt? But Aidan's eyes were troubled, and she knew, having witnessed her parents' behaviour, that in a marriage nothing was ever black and white.

'It was awful, watching her going through the cycle of hope and disappointment every month, knowing that I was to blame. She kept it hidden from everyone else. She was good—very good—at maintaining appearances,' Aidan continued. 'It was like an obsession with her, and every time she was disappointed...' His shoulders shook. He cleared his throat. 'Whether the fault lay with me at that point, I still don't know and I don't care. I begged her to speak to someone, her mother, my sister, anyone, but she refused point blank.'

Estelle, her heart twisted with pity, couldn't begin to imagine how wretched he must have felt. And his poor wife too—though to blame Aidan—but she knew nothing of such matters, nor of the raw emotions which drove a childless wife. Several things about him fell into place. The moments when he had seemed to disappear into himself. His coming here to Florence, his sabbatical from real life, where he'd been happy in his youth. And his taking refuge in the world of mathematics too, where order and logic reigned, where outcomes were reassuringly predictable. Now he had given her the key, in the form of his poor deceased wife, she understood him. Guilt, regrets, a tragic loss and a barren, blighted marriage. Looking at him, she could see what it had cost him to bare his soul, for he looked positively haunted.

'I can't imagine how you must have felt,' she said helplessly, 'what it must have done to you. I'm so very sorry. How did she die, Aidan?'

'There was an accident.'

'An accident?'

He nodded. 'I'll probably never know exactly what happened. It's irrelevant now, for what's done is done.'

'I understand,' she said, which she did. She didn't like to dwell on her parents' accident either, though secretly, she was rather morbidly curious about this one. 'May I ask what her name was?'

'I prefer not to talk of those days. It's been almost three years. Life goes on,' Aidan said grimly, 'as my sister never tires of telling me. It's why I came here. And since I met you I've come to believe she might be right.' Though his smile was forced, there was warmth in his eyes when his gaze met hers. 'I *never* talk of those times, Estelle, I told you only because I don't want you to make the mistake I did. You can't bend nature to your will.'

She shivered, for his heartbreaking history had twisted her dream into a nightmare she had never considered. 'It's a tragic irony, isn't it, that nature is most bounteous where she is least desired. There were families on Papa's estates who had ten, twelve, fifteen children, and who could barely afford to feed one mouth. The workhouses must have been full of such poor wee souls, and the orphanages too, when the women nature favoured eventually died as a result of her over-generosity. I'm sorry,' she added, grimacing, 'that's hardly the point you were trying to make.'

'No, but it does beg an important question. If there are already more than enough children in the world in desperate need of a home, why not reduce their number rather than add to it?' Aidan said. 'It's simply never occurred to me, to look at the problem that way.'

'I'm not sure what you mean. Are you suggesting, that I raise orphans or foundlings? It's an excellent idea, but aside from the fact that I doubt very much any orphanage would contemplate handing a child into the care of an unmarried woman, I'm firmly of the opinion that any child deserves both a mother *and* a father.'

'An opinion I share, as you know.'

'Why are you looking at me so strangely?'

'I'm not sure, it's probably an absolutely lunatic idea, but there's a chance that you and I might be the perfect solution to each other's problems.'

'What on earth do you mean?' Estelle demanded, looking utterly perplexed.

'I'll explain,' Aidan answered, though he was already wondering if he could or indeed should. Was he a genius or a madman? He needed time to think. Jumping to his feet, holding out his hand. 'Come on, we'll take a walk up to the viewpoint.'

To his relief, she did as he asked, following him through the amphitheatre and up the slope. He was aware of her studying him, bemused by his sudden change of mood. She was probably thinking his brain had been addled by his confession.

Was it? Even the severely curtailed version he'd shared with her had stretched his self-control to the limits. Thank the stars Estelle hadn't pressed him for details. He still couldn't bring himself to say *her* name. The salient facts, even though they revealed only a small part of the sad, sordid story, would be enough, he hoped, to give her the benefit of his torrid experience. A salutary lesson that she could digest when they parted.

But what if they didn't have to part? What if there was a way for them to be together? He hadn't dared to consider such a possibility, because he had ruled out the one obvious solution. The solution which, ironically, half of Florence seemed to think he'd already proposed. But he had ruled out that solution for the wrong reason—or rather, looked at the problem from the wrong angle. It wasn't that he didn't want to marry, it was that he didn't want to risk failure. If he could guarantee success, then it changed everything.

No, not quite everything, for ironically, the attraction which had brought them together in the first place was, as far as Estelle was concerned, a barrier to them spending their lives together. She probably wouldn't even consider what he was about to suggest. Was it then wrong of him to suggest it at all?

They had reached the top of the hill. Aidan took off his jacket and spread it on the grass for Estelle to sit on, taking care not to sit too close to her. It was thankfully quiet up here, for most people baulked at the climb. Decision time. He could choose to say nothing, and bid Estelle farewell. If he spoke, there was a chance that she would take extreme umbrage, and never speak to him again. But there was a tiny chance that she might actually consider what he had to say.

'I beg you to put me out of my misery,' Estelle interrupted his mental debate. 'You look like you are trying to decide whether to jump off a precipice or push me instead.'

Aidan gave a bark of laughter. 'What I'm actually debating is whether we should jump together. A leap in the dark.'

'Towards what?' she asked, laughing. 'For heaven's sake, spit it out!'

'You can't just spit out a proposal of marriage.' There was a brief, tense silence. 'Except I just have.'

'Very funny,' Estelle said.

'I'm deadly serious.'

'You don't want to get married. The very first day we met, you told me that you weren't in the market for a wife, and after hearing what you said this afternoon, Aidan, I perfectly understand why.'

'I don't want to take a chance on marrying

again, if it doesn't result in having a family. But if I could guarantee that it would, that's a different matter entirely.'

'Forgive my inability to follow your logic, but I don't understand a word of what you're saying.'

'That's because I'm making a mull of it.' Because now that he'd thought of it, he desperately wanted to succeed. He took a calming breath. 'Nature is a variable that I can't control. Adoption is the solution. Remove the risk and guarantee success by adopting a family, just as you suggested, from an orphanage or a workhouse. It's the perfect solution—from my perspective, at any rate.'

'I can just about see that, and I'm delighted to have helped, but I don't understand why you think that it necessarily means that we should get married.'

'Because if you asked me to describe my perfect wife, it would be you. You're good company. You listen to what I say and make conversation rather than spouting your own views. You don't think the sound of your own voice is more important than mine.'

'Stop it, those are my words.'

'And very sensible ones too. A lifetime is too long to spend in the company of someone you don't like—your words again, and I couldn't agree with you more. I know you were teasing when you said that I was your ideal husband, but I'm not teasing when I tell you that you are my ideal wife.'

Was he really serious? Eyeing Aidan askance, Estelle concluded that he was. Her head was reeling. She had barely had time to take in the fact that he'd been married before, and now he was proposing to marry her. Marry Aidan! It was an absolutely insane idea, and she shouldn't even be considering it. But if she didn't, what then?

'I *was* teasing,' Estelle said, 'when I said that you are my ideal husband, I mean. You are ideal, in every respect, save one.'

'You want to kiss me.'

'I want to kiss you.'

'I understand why it's a problem. Is it an insurmountable one?'

Estelle frowned, twining her fingers together, remembering a rhyme that one of the kitchen maids had taught them as children. *Here's the church and here's the steeple.* 'Phoebe had a passionate *affaire* with the man who trained her in Paris. We had a falling out over it. Fortunately she came to her senses. Do you think that we will do the same?'

'Come to our senses, you mean? We have said all along that our undoubted mutual attraction is, to use your own phrase, an aberration for both of us,' Aidan said, though his voice lacked conviction.

'One we'll inevitably grow out of,' Estelle said, 'when we leave Florence for the real world?' Though right at this moment, she couldn't imagine it. Despite the life-changing significance of their conversation, she was acutely aware of his every move, even when her mind was concentrating on other things.

Aidan sighed, shaking his head. 'I want to agree with you, because I want you to agree to marry me, and the more we discuss it, the more it seems to me to be the perfect solution. But it's too big a decision to leave room for regrets. We're talking of a lifetime's commitment, of our children's lives, not only ours.'

'I know. And don't you think that because we want this so much, it will make it easy to set aside this inconvenient longing?'

He laughed. 'You'd think so, but nature isn't rational. Despite all we've talked about, and all that is at stake, all I have to do is look at you, and I want to kiss you.'

'Then don't look at me.'

'Estelle, be serious.'

'I am always at my most flippant when I'm at my most serious. I have a terrible habit of making jokes at the most important times.'

'Do you mean you *are* considering my proposal?'

'You haven't actually proposed. No,' she added hurriedly, 'I beg you not to get down on bended knee just yet. I need to think.'

She tried to imagine herself packing up her trunks, leaving for Venice, leaving Aidan behind for ever. Would there be another man who came close to what she wanted from a husband? She was twenty-five years old—how many more years did she plan to waste on what was, in all likelihood, a fruitless search? He had been married before, married at a very young age, because he wanted to settle down and have a family. Solid proof that he wanted exactly what she wanted, and that he was that increasingly rare thing, a man committed to marriage. In the years since his wife died there had been no other woman. He hadn't said so explicitly, but he'd been very clear that she, Estelle, had brought him back to life.

It was an accident, not an illness that had taken his wife. What kind of accident? she wondered, momentarily distracted. A carriage accident? Had this perfect but nameless wife of his fallen from a turret? There were bound to be turrets in the castle. More likely it was something very mundane. She was probably thrown by her horse. All of which was beside the point. Never mind the first Mrs Malahide, the question was whether she wanted to be the second?

She did. Very much. Eyeing Aidan from under her lashes, she felt something very like a pang of longing. Of course she would much prefer to be the first Mrs Malahide, but second was not necessarily second-best.

It was very tempting to simply discount her feelings for him. The kisses they had shared had never frightened her, but they were only kisses. Aidan had always ensured they were only kisses. But if Aidan was her husband, he would want more than kisses and frankly, the way she felt when he kissed her, she was pretty certain she'd want more than kisses too. And then where would they be?

She couldn't risk it.

But she didn't want to say no.

She really rather desperately wanted to say yes.

But she couldn't say yes, unless…

'Aidan, what if *I* was to think logically? What we need to do is—how did you put it—eliminate the variables.'

'I'm not with you.'

'Our inconvenient longing. We need to eliminate it.'

'How do you propose to do that?'

Was it too much to expect? She had to ask or walk away. 'Ban it?' She grimaced. 'I mean, agree to make our marriage platonic.' Aidan's jaw dropped, and Estelle began to panic. 'I know it's a lot to ask…'

'It makes horribly good sense.'

'I know. Do you think it's possible?'

'Do you?'

A platonic marriage with *Aidan*! Her senses screamed denial, but Estelle was determined to think with her head. 'If it meant that we could both have our heart's desire,' she said staunchly, as much for her own benefit as his. 'It would be a sacrifice worth making, don't you think?'

'Estelle, it would also mean that we would

both be accepting that we would never have children of our own.'

'Forgive me, I thought you had already accepted that.'

'I had, but you...'

'Until this afternoon, I had more or less given up on the possibility entirely. I've been trying to reconcile myself to the idea of teaching music, Aidan. Adopting is so much closer to what I have always wanted.'

'But it's still not the same as having your own flesh and blood.'

'You have managed to reconcile yourself to that.'

'There's a big difference between having tried and failed, and never trying. Perhaps you need to take some time to think about it. Write to your sisters. Go back to England, talk it over with them. To make a decision like this without due consideration, would be unwise.'

More or less exactly what Aunt Kate had counselled Eloise to do. Her decision to marry Alexander had been discussed for weeks and weeks. But Phoebe had married in haste and in secret and, according to her latest missive, she was very happy. 'It would take for ever for me to write home and wait on replies. You're due back in Ireland in a few weeks. And what's more,' Estelle said, 'you have just proposed to me without any sort of prior consideration at all. Besides, we *are* considering. We've been considering for the last hour. In fact it seems to me that we have been extremely logical and rational in making what most people would describe as a very emotional decision.'

'Good Lord. Estelle Brannagh, are you saying that you are willing to consider accepting my hand in marriage?'

'I'm saying that I have considered it, and—and I rather think I will accept.'

They stared at each other, struck temporarily dumb, before their smiles dawned, and they broke into laughter. Aidan got to his feet, helping her up, keeping her hands in his. 'We should wait, consider for longer. It's such a leap in the dark...'

'I prefer to think of it as a leap of faith. I don't want to wait. I've been waiting for years to get on with my life. Let's start straight away, Aidan.'

'What do you mean?'

'Let's get married here in Florence. I'm sure it can be arranged. Lady Gertrude is not without influence and I'm sure would be delighted to help.'

'Actually, I recently met someone on the diplomatic team who I'm pretty sure will expedite matters, if I ask him. Are we really talking about getting married?'

'When we met today, I thought we were going to be saying our goodbyes.'

His fingers tightened on hers. 'Instead we are welcoming a whole new chapter in our lives. Are you absolutely certain?'

'I am, but I think it would be wise to wait a few months before contemplating adopting our first child. It will be an opportunity to accustom ourselves to each other properly in Ireland.'

'Yes indeed. That makes excellent sense. We must take every step to ensure success.' His smile tightened. 'I never thought I'd get a second chance. I won't let you down, I swear. I'll do my very best to make you happy.'

'I don't doubt that,' Estelle said, confused by the fervent note in his voice. 'We've made each other happy, these last few weeks, I see no reason why that should change. We might be husband and wife, but we'll still remain friends.'

'The difficult part will be restricting it to that.'

She waited, but whatever debate he'd been having with himself seemed to have been resolved. His brow cleared, and above them, the sky had cleared to a brilliant blue, the few remaining clouds puffy white, like a child's drawing. 'We should go,' Estelle said.

Aidan nodded. Their eyes locked, and she stepped closer to him, and though it had only been two days since they had last kissed on this very spot, it seemed like two months and she ached to kiss him again, and she could see her own wanting reflected in his eyes. Their lips met, lingered. And then they drew apart.

'Did we pass or fail?' she asked, fighting the urge to throw herself back into his arms.

He smiled, tucking her hand into his arm. 'Though the mathematician in me tells me it's not possible, I'd say both.'

Chapter Six

They left Florence immediately after a hastily arranged marriage ceremony performed under special licence. The many weeks at sea provided Estelle with ample time to reflect on their impulsive decision, for there was little else to do, save to watch the crew attend to their duties and watch the sun rise and set on the distant horizon.

At first she was assuaged by doubts. What had she done? Why had she acted so hastily? The decision to tie herself for life to a man she'd known only a few weeks had made perfect sense when they were bathed in the rosy glow of the Florentine sunshine, but as the weather turned grey and cold, her memories of Florence began to seem like a mirage. The wind filled the sails, sending the ship scudding far too quickly across the sea, and she felt a sense of rising panic. Ireland, the country of her birth, looming ever nearer, felt like a strange and foreign land.

Thinking of her sisters and Aunt Kate had a calming effect. They had all made a similar leap of faith, and they had all found their own form of contentment in their marriages. It was too late for regrets. Slowly but steadily, Estelle's doubts gave way to anticipation. She was glad she'd managed to keep them hidden from Aidan who, as their voyage drew to a close, had seemed increasingly distracted.

'Of course not,' he said, when she braced herself to ask him if he was regretting their impulsive decision, taking her hand, pressing it reassuringly. 'The fact I've been away a year is just sinking in. I'm just fretting about all the things I'll need to attend to as a matter of urgency.'

Including introducing her as his wife, Estelle thought. She would be the second bride he had brought home to Cashel Duairc. It was inevitable that she'd be compared and contrasted to the first, outwardly perfect Mrs Malahide. Was Aidan worried that she would come up short? It would be naïve of her to imagine that those who had known and cared for his first wife would embrace his second wholeheartedly. Would they see her as a usurper? Was that what he was anxious about?

Negative thoughts! She made a conscious effort to banish them. She and Aidan understood each other. Yes, there were lots of things they didn't know about each other, but when it came to the important things, the ones that really mattered, they were of one mind. She was making a leap of faith, but she was not alone. They were in this together.

Mid-July 1832—County Kildare, Ireland

They were in this together. Estelle reminded herself of this fact as they completed the final leg of their journey in a coach and four, but as the horses sped towards Aidan's ancestral home, she was horribly aware of how alone she really was. She had written to her sisters and Aunt Kate informing them of her change in circumstances, giving them her new address, but asking them to honour her decision as she had theirs, not to consider visiting until she and Aidan had settled into their new life as man and wife.

She was a wife in name only, but in the eyes of the law she was Aidan's property. She would be living in a country she'd left ten years ago, without any friends or relations of her own that she knew of. She'd be the chatelaine of a castle whose previous incumbent had been Aidan's first choice, the woman he'd still be married to, had she not died so tragically young. Estelle didn't know how she had died. She still didn't even know the poor woman's name. She had tried, on board the ship, to return to the subject of his first marriage, but Aidan had made it clear that their one conversation was the beginning and the end of the subject. Perhaps he was right, after all. Today was the first day of the rest of their lives in Cashel Duairc. She should be looking forward to that, not glancing back nervously over her shoulder.

Estelle wiped the condensation from the carriage window. It was raining. The height of Irish summertime, she thought wryly, peering out at the light smir that made a haze of the last dregs of evening light. How long before they arrived at the castle? She dragged her gaze away from the view from the carriage window and the question died on her lips as she caught sight of her new husband, sitting stock still, his hands clasped tightly together on his lap, gazing blankly into space, his expression unfathomable.

'Aidan?'

He started, blinked. 'Sorry, I must have dozed off.'

It was an odd little lie, for his eyes had been wide open. 'I was wondering how much further we had to go?'

'Not far. We're just about to cross the bridge.'

He spoke without looking out of the window, but the words were no sooner out of his mouth when the carriage slowed into a sharp turn. 'How did you know?'

'I was born and raised here. This place is in my blood and my bones.' He forced a smile, edging closer on the seat, putting his arm around her shoulders. 'If you look out now, you'll get your first glimpse of your new home.'

Butterflies fluttering in her tummy, Estelle pulled down the glass and gazed out, exclaiming with astonished delight at what she saw. Cashel Duairc, perched on the edge of a bluff on the other side of the river, dominated the skyline. It was a castle out of a child's storybook, picturesque and grandiose, forbidding, haughty, and alluring. Built of grey granite, there were square turrets and cone-shaped towers. Battlements lined every rooftop while Tudor-style chimneys vied with the towers for attention. There were an astonishing number of leaded windows.

'It's not nearly as old as it's intended to look,' Aidan said, resting his chin on her shoulder, 'around a hundred years, most of it, though there are parts that date back centuries.'

'How many rooms are there?'

'I've never counted them. A hundred? I use very few. Some of them have been closed up for decades.'

'And is there really a dungeon?'

'There are certainly cellars, cut deep into the escarpment.'

'Dark Castle,' Estelle said, as the horses slowed again to turn off the bridge, through a set of gateposts and on to a steeply rising carriageway. 'I imagined something gloomier.'

'The name referred to the original, much smaller castle, which was used as the foundations for the core of this one.'

'Oh, and there's the lake you mentioned!' Estelle exclaimed, 'and there's an island too, with its own tower. How lovely.'

Aidan returned to his own side of the seat. 'It might look romantic but the tower is in an unsafe state of repair, which is why I've declared the island out of bounds. I don't want anyone injured by falling masonry.'

'That's a shame. Perhaps you could make that your first engineering project, to restore it. It looks like a perfect spot for a picnic. I can picture us rowing out there in a little boat...'

'It's a folly, not a pleasure garden,' he snapped. 'A monument to someone's vanity, it should be left as such as a salutary lesson to us all. In any event, there is no little boat and therefore no way to access the island.'

'I wasn't being entirely serious,' Estelle said, hurt by his autocratic tone. 'In any case, I'd forgotten this is Ireland, the Emerald Isle where the rain never stops falling. We're not likely to get a lot of picnic weather.'

Aidan said nothing in response to this olive branch, instead turning his back on her to stare morosely out at the view. He was nervous about returning home, Estelle reminded herself. Worried about whether she would pass muster? It was a bit late in the day to be asking herself that question!

'Did you notice the knotted serpent on the gateposts?' Though he kept his eyes on the window, he reached for her hand. 'There's another above the main door, and a good few sprinkled around the cornicing of the more formal rooms.'

'A family crest?' Estelle asked, grateful that whatever had triggered his abrupt mood change had dissipated.

He snorted. 'It is indeed, though it actually belongs to an English noble family, and my great-grandfather borrowed it without permission. My father fought a long-running battle with the last Duke, who instructed him to remove them all. My father did not take kindly to being told what to do, and won the day by dint of outlasting the man. His son, it seems, has other battles to fight, and so the misappropriated serpents remain in situ. Ah, here we are at last.'

The carriage came to a halt. For one absurd moment Aidan wanted to instruct the coach driver to turn around and head straight back to Dublin Bay. The euphoria which had carried him through his wedding and the first days of their voyage had long since worn off. In the last few weeks at sea, he'd had plenty of time to question his decision, plenty of time to agonise over whether he should have revealed more of the truth to Estelle. He came to the uncomfortable conclusion that he had not done so because he didn't want to feed her curiosity. He didn't want to have to answer awkward questions. He didn't want her to uncover the whole truth because then she would almost certainly regret having married him.

Given that, ought he have married her in the first place? He was besieged by doubts. Estelle thought she knew him. He thought he'd changed. He'd been so sure that he could make a fresh start, that bringing her here, his new bride, so utterly different from his first, would change everything at a stroke. But he was starting to wonder if anything had changed at all. Here was the castle just as he'd left it, and inside it, the ghosts and the painful memories waited for him. And here he was, not made anew at all, the weight of guilt and despair already looming like a black cloak, ready to envelop him as soon as he stepped out of the coach.

He gave himself a shake. It was understandable that he was having doubts, but the trick was to recapture the confidence he had developed in Florence, that he could start afresh. With Estelle, he could have all he'd ever wanted and all he thought he'd never have. All he had to do to safeguard it was to ensure the past remained buried. If he did that, then his future and the future of the family he so desperately wanted was secure.

But looking at her, clearly bracing herself for the coming ordeal and trying not to let him see, other doubts assailed him. She was intelligent, and she was intuitive, two of the many things which had drawn him to her. Attributes that would pretty much guarantee she would discover he'd not told her anything approaching the truth about his first marriage. He knew she'd been less than satisfied by his vague account, for she had tried to reopen the subject on the voyage. Little wonder, given he had not even explained the exact nature of what had been euphemistically dubbed the accident. He'd shut down her questions. Had that been a mistake? Wouldn't it have been better to hear the truth from him, rather than piece it together from the speculation about the demise of the first Mrs Malahide which the arrival of the new Mrs Malahide would undoubtedly resurrect?

The truth? His heart began to pound. The carriage floor loomed up to meet him. No one knew the truth save him and *her*, and the dead cannot speak. If Estelle ever knew the truth, she'd flee. He cursed vehemently under his breath. He was married. This was the first day of the rest of his life. He'd take it a step at a time. No point speculating, he'd simply have to deal with situations as they arose. The carriage door was flung open. The first step, quite literally, was to get out. 'Ready?' he asked Estelle.

She pinned on an extremely unconvincing smile. 'Ready as I'm ever likely to be. Are you?'

'Yes,' he said, pleased to hear that it sounded convincing, starting as he meant to go on. He would walk proudly up those steps with Estelle by his side. His wife. His second wife. She couldn't be more different from the first. And he—yes, he was going to make damned sure he was different too. He already was, thanks to Estelle. He'd *been* different, with her, in Florence. The trick was to hang on to that man, to remain that incarnation of himself, and forget about the one he had been previously. He had ruined one woman's life, he wasn't going to ruin another.

Helping her down from the carriage, he pressed her hand in what he hoped was a reassuring gesture. She was making a determined and touching effort to subdue her own very natural nerves, smiling bravely up at him, though everything here was alien to her. He smiled back rigidly, tucking her hand into his arm and pulling her closer than he'd allowed himself to do since they were married. 'Be yourself,' he whispered into her ear, 'that's all I ever ask of you. Be your bright, lovely self, and you can't fail.'

Her cheeks flushed. 'Aidan! Thank you.'

'Welcome to Cashel Duairc.' He planted a kiss on her lips. She exhaled sharply, and his senses jumped to life, and for a long moment they were entranced, as they had been from the first, gazing into each other's eyes, remembering Florence, and it restored his confidence, just as he'd hoped it would. Then he released her, and she gave an embarrassed little huff of a laugh, and they turned towards the steps.

'Aidan! It's good to see you—and looking so well too.'

'Finn, may I introduce you to my wife. Estelle, this is Finn Connolly, my estate manager and my oldest friend.'

'Mrs Malahide, it is an honour and a pleasure to meet you.' Finn bent over Estelle's hand with an exaggerated flourish.

'Mr Connolly, how do you do.'

'You're Irish! Mind you, I should have known the minute I set eyes on you. You're far too lovely to come from anywhere other than the Emerald Isle.'

'And you're far too charming to be anything other than a Kildare man.'

'Finn here says a lot more than his prayers, to coin a phrase,' Aidan said, his smile fading as, over his friend's shoulder, he saw his housekeeper making a belated appearance.

'Mrs Aherne.' His heart sank. 'May I introduce you to my wife. Estelle, this is our esteemed housekeeper, who I'm sure will be a great help to you as you settle in.'

'How do you do, madam?' The woman dropped a shallow curtsy. 'You must excuse the informal welcome. I had intended to have the staff lined up in a guard of honour to welcome you, as is the custom, but Mr Connolly was adamantly opposed to the idea. I only mention it to reassure you that *I* did not intend to show any lack of respect.'

It was a perfectly pitched reminder that Estelle was not the first bride he'd brought home. Was it deliberate or obtuse? He never could tell with the damned woman, and it was obvious that Estelle was wondering the same. 'I'm sure my wife is relieved not to have to face such an ordeal after our long journey,' he said. 'I know I am. I assume you have carried out my instructions regarding the rooms?'

'Everything is as you requested, sir. Shall I take madam up? I believe your dresser has not yet arrived, madam. Are we to expect her imminently?'

'Oh, I don't have a dresser,' Estelle said.

'Then you will be wishing to send to Dublin for one, madam. I know of a reputable agency, it is the one that Mrs Malahide used. That is to say, the first Mrs Malahide.' A dull flush mottled the housekeeper's throat. 'Beg pardon, madam.'

'Well, the second Mrs Malahide prefers to dress herself,' Estelle said, stepping into the breach, casting Aidan a worried glance. 'I would, however, very much appreciate it if you would arrange a bath for me.'

'Have one of the chambermaids wait on my wife,' Aidan snapped. 'And then you may inform Cook that we'll take dinner in the library.'

'That was a bit harsh,' Finn muttered, watching Estelle follow in the housekeeper's wake. 'Though I completely I understand why you find her continued presence here an unwelcome link with the past. Would it not be easier to just move her on?'

'I can hardly dismiss her,' Aidan said, rubbing his eyes. 'Apart from the awkward connection, I can't fault her as a housekeeper, though

I have to confess, it's beyond me too, why she stays. She knows I'd give her an excellent reference since I've told her so several times.'

'Perhaps it's a misplaced sense of loyalty. Regardless, it's to be hoped that your wife has a thick skin. I presume you told her what to expect.'

'I thought it best not to prejudice her against Mrs Aherne.'

'Aidan! This is me you're talking to. The woman constantly harps on about the good old days. You'll need to warn Estelle.'

'I will. I just need to find the right moment.'

Finn eyed him speculatively. 'What *have* you told her?'

'She knows all the salient facts,' Aidan said, horribly aware that he was prevaricating, and Finn knew it. 'Which reminds me, I appreciate you sparing us both the staff line-up.'

'To be honest, I did worry that your wife would be insulted by the lack of formality, but given the circumstances that gave rise to the last guard of honour…'

Aidan winced. 'The funeral. I don't need reminding.'

Finn patted his shoulder awkwardly. 'Your household has grown considerably smaller in the last three years, what with you deciding to live like a hermit. You'll need to think about taking on quite a few more indoor staff, assuming that your wife intends to open the house up properly again. I was thinking it might be a good idea for you to host a party, show off your lovely bride. And she is lovely, Aidan, as good looking a woman as I've seen in many a long year. Put yourself back out into society again. It's about time.'

'Do you think anyone would come?'

'Why the devil wouldn't they? You shut yourself off from the world, Aidan, not the other way around. Yes, it was an extremely difficult time for you, it generated speculation and ill-founded rumour, but it's been three years. All that has died down, life moves on. Time you did too.'

'That's what Clodagh thinks. 'You don't think that holding a party to celebrate my new marriage…'

'…will cause all the rumours surrounding your first one to resurface? Frankly that's much more likely if you keep this wife hidden away. Give them something different to talk about.'

'Perhaps you're right.'

Finn grinned. 'I nearly always am.'

'What about estate business? Anything I should be concerned about?'

'Nothing urgent. You're a good landlord and people know it. We've no shortage of available labour, there are lots of people migrating from the west. Times are awful harsh there, I hear.'

'You're managing to find them all gainful employment?'

'Not all, but as many as I can.'

'You're a good man, Finn. I'm lucky to have you.'

'You are. Now that's enough of business. I've managed for the better part of a year, I can manage a few more days. You concentrate on making your wife feel at home. She's very different from the first one, I'm thinking.'

'She couldn't be more different.'

His friend nodded thoughtfully. 'A breath of fresh air, exactly what you deserve, though with hair that colour,' he added, grinning, 'I reckon there will be a few squalls too.'

Aidan laughed. 'Your reckoning is quite out. I've never seen Estelle out of temper.' Though he had seen the fire smouldering within her when she played music. And when they kissed. Estelle's kisses were like the colour of her hair, fiery, flaming his blood...

'I can see you're itching to go and join her, and I don't blame you.' Finn slapped Aidan's back. 'It really is good to see you, and looking more like your old self to boot. Congratulations.'

Estelle opened the door and found herself in a large square room. Covered bookcases occupied one wall, a large oval gilt grille providing a window into the contents of each. The walls were dark green, the ceiling painted a lighter shade of the same colour, the cornicing gilded. Crimson velvet drapes covered the windows. Two wingback chairs upholstered in the same colour sat facing each other across a fire, and in the middle of the room, a small mahogany table was set for dinner.

Aidan, who had been peering out of the window, turned to greet her. 'You found your way. I was starting to think about sending out a search party.'

'Luckily I had a guide. I hope I'm not late. The journey from my bedchamber felt only marginally shorter than our journey from Florence to here. I must say this is a lovely room.'

'All the more so now it is graced by your presence,' he said, ushering her over to one of the wingback chairs. 'I like your gown.'

'Emerald green, for the Emerald Isle,' Estelle said. 'I thought it was appropriate.'

'The colour suits you. I don't think I've seen it before.'

'It was too hot in Florence to wear it.' Like her, Aidan had bathed and changed. Like hers, his smile was a little forced. 'It was Niamh who showed me the way here. She is one of the chambermaids. She's relatively new to Cashel Duairc, like me. If I must have a personal maid, then I would be happy if she were assigned the role, if you don't mind.'

'Why on earth would I mind? You must do as you see fit. Simply inform Mrs Aherne to make it so.'

'I got the distinct impression Mrs Aherne disapproved of my forgoing a proper dresser.'

'Mrs Aherne has rather entrenched views on what is right and proper.'

'I suspect she doesn't think that I am either right or proper, Aidan.'

There was a brief silence. 'You know how it is with old-fashioned servants, they don't like change. She's a very good housekeeper.'

'I'm sure she is.' And very loyal to her previous mistress too, judging by the several pointed remarks she had made about how the first Mrs

Malahide liked things to be done. She wouldn't mention it though. Aidan, who couldn't be anything other than aware of this fact, was obviously embarrassed by it. Mrs Aherne was simply the first of many people she'd have to win over.

'I'm glad you asked for dinner to be served in here tonight. It's cosy.'

'You'll have worked up quite an appetite if you've been wandering the corridors,' Aidan said, visibly relaxing at this change of subject.

'I shall need a map if I'm not going to get lost.'

'I'll have Finn draw one up. *He* for one will be delighted to be of service to you. He's quite smitten.'

The emphasis was not lost on her. Estelle smiled. 'I suspect Finn convinces every woman he meets that he is smitten by them.'

'I see you have his measure already.' A gust of wind rattled the window panes, followed by a sudden flurry of rain. Aidan pulled the curtains closed before indicating that they take the seats opposite each other by the fire. 'Like me, Finn was born and raised here. He's a good friend, and an excellent manager, as was his father before him.'

'Estate management seems to run in families.

Aunt Kate's father managed my Uncle Daniel's estates. Talking of families, can we expect a visit from your sister Clodagh?'

'She'd have been camped out on the doorstep waiting to welcome us if I'd not had the good sense to pre-empt that. As you can imagine, she's extremely eager to run the rule over you, in a protectively sisterly way.' Aidan grinned. 'You'll be relieved to know that I put her off. I told her that I wanted you all to myself for a couple of weeks.'

'Thank you! Though I'm looking forward to meeting her, I would rather not do so until I have had some time to settle in.'

'Are your rooms comfortable? Do you have everything you need? There was no time to have them redecorated, and besides, I thought you'd want to choose your own colour scheme.'

'My rooms are perfectly comfortable, thank you very much. I certainly can't fault Mrs Aherne on her housekeeping.'

'My bedchamber is located across the corridor.'

'So Mrs Aherne informed me.'

'No doubt she informed you that I moved out of the master suite some years ago.'

'No, she didn't, though I can understand why

you would have done so after—' Estelle broke off, shrugging helplessly. 'In any case, I appreciate your thoughtfulness. I wouldn't have been comfortable in the master suite, for obvious reasons.'

'No more would I.'

'We haven't really discussed how we will set about being married, have we?'

'I rather thought we'd learn as we go along.'

'Yes, but oughtn't we to think about how we present ourselves to the world? And to your family, come to that. When Eloise married Alexander, they pretended it was a love match.'

'No. Categorically not.'

'I wasn't suggesting that's what we should do,' Estelle said, mildly insulted by his vehemence, 'but I do think we ought to talk about it.'

A discreet tap at the door interrupted them. While Aidan took the tray, replete with a bottle of champagne on ice and two glasses, from the footman, she wandered over to the bookcases, pretending to peer through the lattice at the content. They were both on edge, she as much as he. Despite what he'd said, Aidan must be every bit as conscious as she was that this was the second time he'd brought a bride home. This was why she'd suggested a period of adjustment before they even considered adopting the first of their children. It wasn't that Aidan had changed, it wasn't that she didn't know him, for goodness sake, it was simply an awkward situation that had to be managed.

'Was it a mistake, ordering champagne?' Aidan asked. 'I thought we should mark the occasion.'

'No, I think it's an excellent idea. We certainly have something to celebrate. The first day of our new life together.'

'Then why the frown?' He set down the glass he'd been filling. 'Come here.'

'Ah, I thought it wouldn't be long before you started ordering me about. We've not been in this castle—' She broke off, crossing the room to join him. 'Sorry, I told you…'

'That you are your most flippant when you are at your most serious. Or most apprehensive. Is our leap of faith starting to feel like too much of a leap in the dark?'

'No, but it's uncharted territory for me. I've never been married, Aidan, you have.'

'But not to you. There will be a queue of people eager to draw comparisons with my first marriage. We must not fall into that trap.' He touched her cheek lightly. 'You asked me how we should present ourselves to the world? As we

are. I don't want us to pretend. I want the world
to see us as exactly what we are, a newly married couple happy to be in each other's company.
And once we're satisfied that's exactly what we
are, we'll move on from being a happy couple
to a happy family.'

'Oh, yes.' Estelle beamed. 'Now that is something I'd gladly drink a toast to.'

Aidan's smile warmed. 'Just be true to yourself. You've already made one conquest in Finn.
He thinks you're a breath of fresh air. This is
your home now, and I want you to be happy
here, to make it your own. Throw out every stick
of furniture, paint the walls cherry pink, I don't
give a damn. In fact I'd positively encourage you
to change as much as you see fit.'

Giggling, she took the glass of champagne
Aidan offered her. 'I don't see how we can either of us be comfortable if I've thrown out all
the furniture, but I appreciate the sentiment.'

He chinked his glass to hers. 'Here's to the
future.'

'To the future.' Estelle took a sip of the icy
sparkling wine. 'Do you remember the first time
we drank champagne together?'

'That snooty restaurant on the Arno. I should
never have insisted on eating there. The food

looked like a work of art, and unfortunately tasted like one too. And as for the champagne...'

'Barely a bubble, and so sweet it made my teeth ache. We climbed all the way to the top of that bell tower afterwards, do you remember? I got dizzy.'

'And I was terrified that you were going to tumble over the parapet.'

He had pulled her into his arms. She had clung to him, to steady herself at first and then simply for the pleasure of clinging to him. And they had kissed. The memory of that kiss hovered between them now, dispersed only when their lips met and clung, and they hesitated, but only for a moment, before they melted into the sweetest of kisses.

Long and lingering, tasting of champagne, the kiss soothed her doubts and roused her senses. Her eyes drifted closed, she raised her free hand to his face, relishing the smoothness of his cheek, the slight roughness of his beard, and his hand on the exposed skin at her nape. And when it ended, they stared at each other, smiling. Reassured, Estelle felt a renewed surge of excitement and confidence. Everything was going to be fine, how could it fail to be, with Aidan at her side.

* * *

'Good heavens,' Estelle exclaimed as Aidan ushered her into a huge salon, the furniture looking like strangely shaped lumps under its protective holland covers. 'Is this another drawing room?'

'A ballroom.' He opened a set of shutters to reveal a set of tall French windows leading to a terrace with steps into the gardens to the rear of the castle. 'There should be a piano in here somewhere. It was my mother's.'

'I've found it.' Estelle excitedly pulled the cloth aside before lifting the lid, but her smile faded as she ran her fingers over the keys. 'Oh, dear, it's horribly out of tune.'

'Not surprising when it hasn't been played for many years. I'm sorry, it should have occurred to me when I wrote to Mrs Aherne from Florence, to ask her to have someone take a look at it. I'll see what I can do.'

'No, let me deal with it, I need to get on good terms with Mrs Aherne.'

Estelle wandered around the room, pretending to admire the cornicing and the twin fireplaces, though after two hours of admiring similar cornicing and fireplaces in a vast array of unused rooms, she was beginning to understand the housekeeper's pointed remark about Cashel Duairc mourning the loss of its mistress. Aidan had closed up most of the formal rooms, presumably when the first Mrs Malahide died. As the morning had progressed, as he led her through the seemingly endless procession of rooms, he'd become increasingly morose. He'd prefer to be out and about in the fresh air checking on the health of his estates, she thought guiltily.

'I can't see us needing to use this room any time soon,' she said, joining him at the window, 'but I'm wondering if it would be prudent to have a room made ready to receive morning callers?'

'The announcement in the press said we wouldn't be at home to visitors for a couple of weeks, but I expect there will be cards left. As you've seen this morning, there's a bit of work to be done to get the house fit to receive guests. I've been somewhat out of the habit of socialising.'

'You told me as much, when we first met, though I must admit I hadn't appreciated you'd cut yourself off quite so severely.'

Aidan kept his eyes fixed on the garden. 'A hermit, Finn said I'd become.'

'Mrs Aherne will be delighted to know that the rooms will be put to use again. I think she must have been bored, with so little to keep in regimented order.'

Her quip failed to raise a smile. Aidan leant his forehead against the glass. 'Mrs Aherne is actually a distant relative of my first wife. I'm sorry, I should have told you before now.'

Estelle's mouth fell open. 'You most certainly should.'

'My father left the previous housekeeper a pension in his will, and I had never replaced her. The castle was much as it is now, actually, when my first wife arrived here. It was she and Mrs Aherne between them who redecorated and repurposed many of the rooms.'

'I see now why Mrs Aherne is so eager to have them restored to use.'

'When she came here, I understand she had fallen on hard times. There was some scandal attached to her. I've never known what it entailed, though I do know there's never been a Mr Aherne.'

'She must have been very grateful to your wife for coming to her aid and offering her the post of housekeeper.'

'Extremely. And slavishly loyal as a result, as you'll have noticed yourself.'

'You don't like her, do you?'

'The boot's on the other foot. She'd much rather it was me who had died.'

'I think she's rather in awe of you, but I don't think she dislikes you.'

Aidan snorted. 'She can't open her mouth without reminding me that things are not how they were.'

Estelle wrinkled her brow. 'She is the same with me, but I don't think it's deliberate. In fact I'm sure it can't be, for she blushes painfully at each gaffe. If she actually disliked you, she'd have left your employ by now.

'I don't know why she hasn't.'

'If she really had fallen on such hard times, she'll be grateful to you as well as her former mistress, for rescuing her.'

Aidan smiled crookedly. 'She's a strange way of showing it.' He pushed himself away from the window, rolling his shoulders. 'Finn reckons we should throw a party. What do you think?'

'What kind of party?'

'Drinks, supper, meeting and greeting, you know the kind of thing.'

'Not really,' Estelle confessed. 'Must we? I'm

not particularly eager to be put on display like an artefact you collected on your Grand Tour.'

Aidan burst into laughter. 'I can just picture you in a glass case. We can decide later about the party. It looks as if the rain might be going off.' He opened the French window. 'I'll just take a look.'

'What you mean is, you've had enough and you're anxious to be outside talking to Finn about the harvest.'

Smiling sheepishly, he stepped outside, and Estelle began to wander around the room again, peering under the covers of the objects which were strewn at random across the floor. A spectacularly ugly mahogany side-table with bowed legs topped with the carved head of a sabretoothed hound, and talon-like feet made her shudder. Outside, Aidan was staring fixedly at the sky. She spotted something she had missed earlier leaning against the wall, hidden behind a big lump of a cabinet. Pulling the cover from it, Estelle gave a yelp of satisfaction. A harp. Running her fingers along the strings, she was pleased to hear that it needed only a little adjustment.

'What the hell are you doing?'

'Aidan! You frightened the life out of me.'

He was standing in the window, his face ashen. 'Where did that come from?'

'It was hidden behind that cabinet.' She stared down at the instrument, realising with dawning horror who it must have belonged to. 'I'm so sorry. I'll put it back.'

'Don't touch it!'

She stared at him in astonishment. 'For heaven's sake, Aidan, it's a harp, a harmless instrument.'

He was staring at the instrument as if it was the devil incarnate. 'This was her doing! She deliberately left it there, knowing I'd eventually stumble upon it. She left it there to taunt me.'

'Your dead wife?'

'Mrs Aherne.'

'That's preposterous. You need to calm down, you're being quite irrational.'

'Really? If you know how attached my wife was to that harp, then you'd know it couldn't have been anything other than deliberate, to leave it there. Get it out of here. I never want to see it again.'

He stormed off, leaving Estelle utterly at a loss but Mrs Aherne, when summoned, eyed the harp with almost as much horror as Aidan had.

'What's that doing still here? It should have been packed up and sent back with the rest of her things. I can't imagine how we missed it. I'm terribly sorry, madam, Mr Malahide must have been very upset to see that.'

'He was. I didn't realise that his first wife was musical.'

'She was certainly fond of this harp.'

'My husband has just informed me that his first wife was a relative of yours,' Estelle said diffidently. 'I'm afraid I wasn't aware of the connection until now.'

'I did wonder, madam, but it wasn't my place to tell you.' The tell-tale flush was mottling Mrs Aherne's throat. 'It obviously makes things more than a little awkward.'

'Not least of all for you. Would you mind my asking why you have stayed on, all this time?'

The housekeeper ran her hand over the frame of the harp, her eyes fixed on the floor. 'There was no one to look after him, when she died. No one who knew how he liked things done.' She looked up, a sad little smile quivering on her lips. 'He endured some dark times. I know what it's like to feel that the world has ended. I couldn't do much, but I could at least see that he was left to grieve in peace.'

'But you were grieving too,' Estelle said, touched.

Mrs Aherne nodded. 'He's uncomfortable with me being here, I know that. I'm clumsy with my words, I say things that remind him—I don't mean to, but I can't seem to help myself. Aoife was such a presence.' The housekeeper snatched her hand from the harp. 'But there, he has you now, madam, and you're a breath of fresh air.'

'That's what Finn said.'

'Did he? Well, he's right. When the master wrote to tell me he was bringing a new bride home, I thought to myself, that's your time at Cashel Duairc up. If the master can move on, then so can I. I was going to offer to stay on until you were settled and had found a replacement, but perhaps it would be better if I leave sooner rather than later?'

'Of course that's entirely up to you, but if you'd like to stay for a trial period, see how we get along?'

'That's very generous, but I think I'd rather not. You'll be having a party, I take it? Well then,' Mrs Aherne said, after Estelle nodded, 'I'll stay for that. I arrived here not long after Aoife's bridal party. It's only fitting that I leave after yours. Now, if you'll excuse me I'll go and see if I can find a crate to have the harp packed up in.'

'Ee-feh,' Estelle mouthed. She finally knew the mysterious first wife's name. Aoife. Before her parents died, one of the more resilient governesses they had employed to look after their daughters had been fascinated by Irish folklore, the Irish language and the traditional songs. Bridget had taught Estelle and her sisters next to nothing of arithmetic, grammar or geography, but there had been many pleasurable hours listening to her tales of fairies and giants, joining in the chorus of her ballads and laments. Aoife had been one of their favourites, because she was a warrior princess. The name came from the Irish word for beauty.

Byron's lines came into Estelle's head.

She walks in beauty, like the night
Of cloudless climes and starry skies.
And all that's best of dark and bright
Meet in her aspect and her eyes.

A woman called Aoife must have been a rare beauty. She would have hair the colour of a raven's wing and eyes of midnight blue. She would be fairy-like, as delicate as gossamer, with the smile of an enchantress.

Aidan had endured rather than relished this morning's tour. There had evidently been ghosts lurking in the corner of every room. She'd watched him brace himself as he opened each door, listened to him describing it in wooden tones. Which room got sun when, which room was easier to heat, which room subject to damp. Practical information, but he'd provided no sense of the lives that had played out in these rooms. Save the ones that had been closed up for decades, she remembered now, the ones he remembered from childhood.

Some of the larger, formal rooms were more recently decorated than others. Aoife's doing, she knew now. She had a taste for pomp and ceremony, for traditional furnishings, a preference for appearance over comfort. There had been no sign of any portraits of Aoife. The family portraits were hung on the wall of the long corridor on the first floor of this, the main wing. There was one of Aidan as a babe in arms with his parents and toddler Clodagh. In another, painted just after his father died, he was eighteen. But there was nothing more recent of Aidan, and nothing of his first wife. Surely there would have been a wedding portrait?

She could ask Mrs Aherne. Poor woman. It was odd that Aidan so completely misread her intentions. Odd that Aidan had so completely lost his temper at the sight of that harp. It was a very lovely instrument, no wonder Aoife had been so fond of it. Estelle's fingers itched to tune it, but the very thought of playing it was sacrilege.

Instead, she set off to tour the bedrooms, opening doors at random, refusing to acknowledge to herself what she was looking for, hoping that someone would come to find her if she had not returned by dinner time. Aidan wanted her to be herself. She had absolutely no desire to step into his dead wife's shoes. She was a stranger, a usurper, barely even Irish, and her predecessor, who died so tragically young, must surely be a saint in the eyes of those who had known her, for one could not think ill of the dead. Estelle would not allow herself to be compared unfavourably to a saint.

The master suite was in the central wing of the castle, facing out over the river. There was no mistaking it for what it was, a grand affair comprising two interlinked bedrooms flanked by dressing rooms with a view not of the gardens but of the river. The knotted serpent, the conceit of Aidan's great-grandfather, was embossed in gold on the ceiling of both chambers. But both rooms were empty and stripped of all furniture. Her footsteps echoed on the bare boards. If the first Mrs Malahide had occupied this suite with her husband, no trace of her remained. It was as if her very presence had been expunged.

Aidan's first marriage had ended in tragedy. He and his wife had been desperate for children. When she died, he'd locked up most of the castle, and by the sounds of things, locked himself away here, for two whole years. In Florence, he'd come alive again, he'd told her, thanks to her. She'd thought he meant he'd recovered his joie de vivre. She hadn't realised he meant he'd been all but dead and buried here.

But all that was going to change. Not overnight, that was too much to expect, for one thing there were bound to be other echoes of the past like that blasted harp lurking still. On reflection, Mrs Aherne's offer to leave was a godsend.

Estelle studied the master suite with a fresh eye. The rooms would make an excellent nursery suite, with ample room for a day and night nursery. Were they too far from her own bed-chamber? She wanted to be able to hear her little ones if they cried out in the night. She'd suffered terrible nightmares for months when they first moved to Elmswood Manor, though Eloise was always on hand to soothe her. Thinking back, she wondered if her elder sister ever got a full night's sleep in those early days when they were first orphaned.

The children she and Aidan adopted would also be orphans. Funny, it hadn't occurred to her to make that link before. How she would love them. Estelle wrapped her arms around herself, smiling. This was why she and Aidan had married. She would remind him at dinner. Talking about the future would make him forget all about the past.

Chapter Seven

The next day, the Irish weather grudgingly decided to acknowledge that it was indeed summer. Bright sunshine flooded through the leaded glass panes of the breakfast parlour, lifting Aidan's mood. The damned harp was gone, and soon Mrs Aherne would be joining it, he had been astounded to discover. Last night, over dinner, they had talked of the future. Estelle was full of plans, her enthusiasm infectious. It had been unrealistic of him to expect her simple presence to act like a magic wand. What he had to do was reclaim the castle, fill it with new memories of his new marriage, so that he was no longer confronted by the ghosts of the old one every time he entered a room.

His musings were interrupted by Estelle peering uncertainly round the door, her face brightening when she saw him. 'Good morning, Husband.'

'Good morning, Wife.' Aidan set down his coffee and went to greet her. His wife! She smiled at him, and his spirits soared. Her glorious hair was loosely fastened in a knot on top of her head from which a vibrant tress was already trying to escape. She was wearing one of his favourite gowns, the pale-blue one with the lace trim that she claimed was too tight, but which was, in his opinion, quite perfect.

'What is it? Why are you looking at me like that?'

'I'm trying to persuade myself that you're real and you really are here. Did you sleep well?'

'After the permanent bustle of Florence, I can't get used to the quiet of the Irish countryside.'

She reached up, smoothing her hand over his freshly shaved cheek then down to his beard, a gesture that never failed to make his pulses jump. He caught her hand, pressing a kiss to her palm. She swayed towards him, her eyes wide, her mouth curving into the most sensual of smiles. It was impossible to resist the urgent need to taste her lips. Putting his arm around her waist, he pulled her closer, and she lifted her face for the kiss they both craved.

She tasted so sweet. Their kisses were so achingly familiar, so ardently missed. He kissed her hungrily and she kissed him back just as hungrily, melting into his arms, her breasts crushed against his chest, sending the blood rushing to his groin, making him so hard so quickly that he groaned with the effort of keeping a respectable distance between them, forced to break their kiss as he did so, startling the maid who was hovering uncertainly in the doorway.

'Begging your pardon sir, madam, but I have brought Mrs Malahide's tea.'

Estelle flushed scarlet. 'Thank you.'

'Cook told me to ask if you would like some ham with your eggs, or there's sausages if you would prefer, or some of her blood pudding, which she says to tell you is fresh made and much tastier than it sounds.'

'Please tell her that I'd very much like to try that. No, leave the tea, I can pour it myself.'

'My sisters and I drink a great deal of tea,' Estelle said, when the maid had left and they were seated at the breakfast table together. 'It's one of the things I missed the most when I was travelling. I don't want to sound like one of those awful people one meets abroad who talk very loudly about how superior everything is in England, but until yesterday morning, I hadn't tasted a decent cup of tea since I left London.'

'I take it you've met Cook,' Aidan said. 'You're probably not aware of what a privilege it is to be allowed to sample her famous *drisheen*, but I assure you, it is.'

'Yesterday afternoon, I decided to brave the kitchens, and I'm very glad I did. The fact that I've a hearty appetite endeared me to her. Having a sister for a chef, and a notebook full of receipts from foreign climes made her wax lyrical. I am thinking of trying a few of them out on our party guests, what do you think?'

'You've decided that a party is a good idea?'

'I'm not exactly looking forward to it, but I'd rather get it over with sooner rather than later and put an end to all the speculation.'

'What speculation?'

'Who is the new Mrs Malahide, what does she look like?' Estelle said, taken aback, for he had snapped at her. 'What did you think I meant?'

'Nothing.' Aidan took a sip of his coffee, making a concerted effort to smile. He had to stop looking for trouble where none existed.

'Whatever they are imagining, they're going to be pleasantly surprised.'

Estelle opened her mouth to speak then changed her mind. He knew what she was going to ask, it was the obvious question. Did she look very different from *her*? Thankfully she did not ask, but it pained him, to see her guarding her tongue, knowing it was his fault she did.

'I was a single lady traveller when you met me. They will be expecting one of those earnest women who reads excerpts from her journal. Although the Florence section might be a bit rich for their blood.'

Aidan laughed, as she had intended him to. 'Shall I draw up a list of guests?'

'Yes, please. I was thinking that we should have it on your birthday, which is three weeks away.'

'Why not? Here's your breakfast.'

'That was delicious.' Estelle poured herself the last cup of tea and buttered the last bit of toast, frowning over at Aidan's plate. 'You didn't eat very much.'

'I never do, at breakfast.'

'It's rather odd, isn't it, how little we know about each other's daily lives? I don't even know if you'd prefer to take breakfast alone, in future. Or in silence. Eloise is like a bear with a sore head in the morning, if you talk to her before she's had at least two pots of tea. Phoebe and I, on the other hand, are both morning people, but if you prefer not to chatter over the breakfast cups...'

'I like it.'

She raised her brows sceptically. 'Really?'

'I'm not used to it, but that doesn't mean I don't enjoy it.'

'I hadn't realised you'd been quite so alone. Since she died. Your first wife. I mean, the castle has been more or less closed up, you told me yourself that you'd got out the habit of socialising and—I hadn't realised...' Estelle trailed off awkwardly '...how lonely you must have been.'

Lonely. Her death had released him from one level of hell only to place him in another. He remembered sitting here, in this room, the morning after the funeral, looking at her empty chair and feeling relieved that the day wasn't going to begin with recriminations or worse, pleas, only to be immediately swamped by guilt, for it was his fault she wasn't there. He'd been lonely for a long time before she died. He had been beyond grief, but overcome with regret.

'I'm sorry.'

Aidan blinked. 'Sorry for what?'

'You don't like to be reminded, and I seem to do nothing but remind you,' Estelle said. 'It's only that I know so little about her, and I want to make things different, but I'm not sure how. I want us to be happy, Aidan. I don't want to let you down.'

'You have no idea how impossible that is.' Nor any idea how terrified he was that the boot would be on the other foot. He pushed his chair back, irritated by his self-indulgence. This wonderful woman was his wife, for heaven's sake. 'Shall we go outside, make the most of the sunshine?'

'Haven't you got a hundred other things to do?'

'A thousand, but every one of them can wait, for there's nothing I want to do more than to spend the day with you. What do you say?'

'I say, yes, please.'

Outside, Aidan was himself again and Estelle was accordingly more herself too. She read him some snippets from the letters she'd received that morning, her sisters and Aunt Kate having written in response to the missives she had sent from Florence.

'And she wishes me luck, sends her love, and looks forward to meeting you in due course,' she concluded, tucking Eloise's letter back into her pocket with the others.

'She sounds remarkably sanguine about your news,' Aidan said. 'In fact they all did.'

'Oh, they will all have countless questions, but they'll save them until they can ask them in person. Though I have to admit, reading between the lines, I suspect that Eloise has dispensed reassurance.'

'Your silent guardians in Florence reported back?'

'It looks like it. I shall have words with Eloise when I see her. You don't sound surprised. Do you know something I don't?'

Aidan shrugged. 'It seems an obvious conclusion, that's all. Shall we take a walk?'

They spent the rest of the day outside in the sunshine, talking, reminiscing, laughing, and Estelle relaxed, for Aidan was just as he had been in Florence, and the spark between them was just as bright as it had been in that city too. Cashel Duairc had extensive parklands, swathes of rolling green and shady groves, with the river forming one boundary, the edge of the lands belonging to the tenant farms on the other. They would be expected to host a party for the tenants, she learned, separate from the one to introduce her to the local gentry, but Aidan seemed disinclined to talk about either, and Estelle was perfectly happy to consign them to her list of future worries.

Though the kitchen garden was extensive and well maintained, the formal gardens seemed to her rather sad-looking. 'If you don't mind my saying so,' she said as they strolled through what looked as if it had once been a rather lovely parterre, 'your garden looks like one owned by a man who cares for vegetables and nothing else.'

'Does it? I must admit, I've never taken much of an interest in it. My mother created much of it, and when she died—well, you see what has happened.'

Aoife was not a gardener then, Estelle noted. 'I enjoy gardening. My Aunt Kate is a keen gardener, and we girls helped with the restoration work at Elmswood.'

'I remember now, you said something about finding the plans for a walled garden. Would you like to restore these gardens? No one has touched them apart from my mother, I promise.'

She wouldn't be treading on his dead wife's toes, he meant. 'I'd like that. Do you know if any of the original plans still exist?'

'If there are, they'll be in the attics in the west wing. I know that secretly it's the only reason you married me, to get your hands on all those fascinating old documents.'

'May I have a look for them?'

'If getting covered in cobwebs rummaging around in a dusty old attic makes you happy, then please do. We have a walled garden here too, you know. Would you like to see it?'

'Yes, please.'

Aidan led the way across one of the few remaining paths of the parterre, towards a row of succession houses. 'Tell me more about Aunt Kate.'

'Why don't you tell me how you imagine her.'

'A matriarch,' he said promptly. 'Stern, a little like Mrs Aherne, but with a tender heart.'

Estelle gave a peal of laughter. 'You couldn't be more wrong. For a start, she's only eight years older than Phoebe and I.'

'But that means she was—good grief, twenty-three when she took you in, have I that right?'

'Exactly right.'

'I imagined her an old spinster when she married your uncle. To have taken on three girls at such a young age—I see now where you got your own intrepid spirit from.'

'Oh, we were used to fending for ourselves, we three, from a very young age.'

'Yes, but not literally, surely? I know your parents were often absent, but they must have left someone in charge.'

'We had governesses some of the time, but they left as soon as they could find a better situation—and to be honest, it would have been difficult to find worse—or they left when Papa persistently failed to pay them. I did tell you, Aidan, that my education had been neglected.'

'Neglected! Do you mean to tell me that there were times when the three of you were left in the care of the servants?'

'The servants who were left behind, for Mama and Papa took most of them to the Dublin town house. You know, put in such stark terms, I'm inclined to agree with you, we are rather intrepid to have survived such an upbringing.'

'You make light of it, but it's appalling.'

'Looking back, yes, it is, but we knew no different. Is this the walled garden?'

'As you can see, it's lacking a full complement of walls. A project for you, if you wish it. Shall we sit over there, in the shade?' The stone bench was mottled with lichen. 'Here, let me.' Aidan stripped off his coat. 'There, I don't want you to ruin my favourite dress by sitting on moss.'

'I'm not sure I can sit down after eating that enormous breakfast.'

'I'm sure Cook would love to try some of the recipes you gathered for your sister. If the weather holds, we could set up a little table here for lunch, and pretend that we're back in Florence.'

'I wonder if she'll be able to lay her hands on some tripe, I know how much you enjoyed it the last time.'

'I feel terribly guilty for eating so much of it,' Aidan said, grinning. 'This time, I'll leave the lion's share for you.'

'You are too thoughtful. It tasted even worse than Phoebe's grass cake.'

'No! Is this a speciality she serves up to the gourmands of London?'

Estelle giggled. 'It was one of the first cakes she ever made. I think we were only six, perhaps seven at the time. She said it was a very special cake, but though we tried for hours, neither Eloise nor I guessed the ingredient which made it so very special. My sister has a penchant for trying out odd combinations, some more successful than others. A legacy of having to conjure food from an empty store cupboard.'

'Are you teasing me again?'

Regretting that she'd said this much, Estelle shrugged. 'We never starved, thanks in part to Phoebe, and we were always well dressed, thanks to Eloise, who could make a ballgown worthy of Almack's out of a pair of old curtains. And thanks to me, we were never short of entertainment.'

'You are a very gifted family.'

'Sadly, my talent is a great deal less practical than my sisters'. Music doesn't put food on the table.'

'No, but it feeds the soul.' Aidan stretched his legs out in front of him, putting his arm around her shoulders. 'I'd rather listen to you play than eat one of your sister's dinners any day of the week.'

'You say the nicest things,' Estelle said, surrendering to the temptation to put her head on his shoulder.

'I do, don't I?'

* * *

Estelle woke with a crick in her neck. The sun had moved round so that the walled garden was completely in the shade. Easing herself upright, she studied Aidan, who appeared to be sound asleep. His lashes fanned his cheek, and a lock of hair had fallen over his brow, making him look tousled and much younger. His long legs were stretched out in front of him, the leather of his breaches pulled taut against his thighs. He had wrapped his arms around himself in his sleep. She leaned in, watching his chest rise and fall, feeling his breath on her cheek. There had been no need for her to ask, this morning, if he had slept well. The shadows beneath his eyes told their own story.

She wanted to snuggle back down beside him, but she didn't want to wake him. Besides, snuggling was not meant to be part of their arrangement. Though snuggling was hardly passionate, was it? Heaven knew, between them, she and her sisters had witnessed her parents sharing far more intimate moments than any child should see, but she couldn't remember anything remotely like snuggling. Wheedling, on her mother's part. Cajoling on her father's. But snuggling? No.

Which meant that snuggling with Aidan, as far as Estelle was concerned, was permitted. Maybe even required, in these early days, when their path was still a little rocky, when they needed to remind themselves of how happy they had been in Florence. Did this morning's kiss count as snuggling, for it had started with a hug, hadn't it? She studied his mouth. His lower lip was much fuller than his top lip. When he kissed her, his beard wasn't at all tickly or scratchy, and it wasn't soft, precisely, but it made her lips tingle, adding something to the kiss, making sure she didn't forget that he was a man. As if she could forget! When he kissed her, it made her insides hot. It made her restless, and sort of anxious, and this morning, when he kissed her, she hadn't wanted him to stop kissing her, though he did. He always did.

Was it unfair of her, to expect him to be the one to rein in their kissing, to ensure that it never led to anything else even though she was increasingly intrigued and curious and sometimes downright rather desperate to experience the something else? She wanted him to touch her breasts. If they were fully clothed, and if that was all he did, would that be permitted? It was she who had insisted on a platonic marriage.

Did that mean she could bend her own rules, provided they didn't bend to breaking point? If Aidan touched her breasts, would he expect her to touch him? She shivered, trying to imagine him sprawled on the bench but without his shirt and waistcoat.

She was ogling! Ogling her own sleeping husband. Mortified, Estelle jumped to her feet. She would take a closer look at this walled garden, see if she could discover any trace of its former glory, and leave Aidan alone to sleep unmolested.

Clambering on to one of the ruined walls at the far side, she spotted a huge dog on the other side at the same time as it spotted her. Lolloping over to her, its long tail wagging gracefully, the hound's fur was dark grey flecked with white, the tips of its ears a much darker colour.

'Hello there,' Estelle said, jumping down to the other side of the wall and holding out her hand. The dog whined, licking her fingertips. 'You're a lovely boy.' Kneeling, she checked the silver tag on the large leather collar. 'Oh, I do beg your pardon, Hera, you're actually a beautiful girl. I wonder who you belong to?'

'Finn.'

Estelle jumped, for she hadn't heard Aidan approach. 'Finn?'

'Finn looks after her. I don't know what the hell he's thinking of, letting her loose. Come away from her.'

'But she's clearly friendly, Aidan.'

He jumped down from the wall. 'She's not permitted to be in the castle grounds.'

Shocked, as much by his tight-lipped expression as his harsh tone, Estelle stood up, releasing her hold on the dog's collar. Hera immediately took off. 'You frightened her. What is wrong with you, Aidan, don't you like dogs?' He was staring at the rapidly retreating dog. 'Aidan?'

He jerked around, stared at her for a moment as if he had no idea who she was, before striding off in the opposite direction. Bewildered and hurt, Estelle picked up his coat from the bench, shaking the dried moss from it before making her way despondently back to the house.

An hour later, when there was no reply to her tentative knock on his bedchamber door, she entered the room. Guiltily, she took a look around, but the only personal items on display were his brushes on the dressing table, his razor on the shaving stand. There were no pictures on the walls, no miniatures on the bedside table, only a book, the history of the Medici family which she had lent him.

Still holding his coat folded over her arm, she sat down on the end of the bed, smoothing the dark-red silk counterpane. Their kiss at breakfast seemed like days ago. Their kiss at breakfast had restored her optimism, it had restored Aidan to himself, but both had quickly vanished when Hera appeared.

Come away from her. He'd reacted to the wolfhound and the harp in exactly the same way, as if he was seeing a ghost. A ghost playing the harp. A ghost petting the dog. Aoife. Hera was Aoife's dog. It was so blindingly obvious, she couldn't think why she hadn't realised straight away. The look on Aidan's face should have told her. It was a sure fire way to blight his mood, she was discovering, to make any mention of his dead wife, transforming him into a man she barely recognised.

If he could bring himself to answer a few simple questions, then she'd be able to do as he bid her and consign the woman to the past. Why was it so impossible for him to talk? In Florence, the day he'd proposed, he'd been painfully frank, but ever since then, he'd been simply pained each time she tried to broach the subject.

Had he been frank with her? She was certain he hadn't lied to her, but there were so many things he hadn't said, she couldn't help wondering if there was more to his wife's death than a tragic accident. And the changes in his mood were so extreme! Even in Florence, he'd had these moments of disappearing into himself, but they were silent moments of contemplation. His temperament had never struck her as volatile.

She didn't understand him. Was it too early to expect to? She had ample evidence of how much it hurt Aidan to talk of his first wife, but she couldn't understand why. The woman had suffered, but so had he, and he'd had the extra burden of putting a brave face on to the world. For two years he'd mourned her, alone here at Cashel Duairc, it was time to move on. His sister said so. He had said so, when he'd proposed. Didn't he realise that by failing to put action to words he was putting their whole future at risk? Those moods of his, didn't he realise the effect they would have on a child? For heaven's sake, they were already upsetting her, making her think goodness knew what.

She had to put an end to it. No matter how

much she loathed the idea, she had to confront him, make him listen to her worries and answer some of her questions. But the very idea of it made her feel sick. Perhaps she was being premature. She'd give it a few more days, and see if things settled down.

'Am I disturbing you?' Aidan peered round the parlour door. 'Oh, Mrs Aherne. Do you mind if I borrow my wife for a moment?'

'Of course, Mr Malahide.' Mrs Aherne dropped a curtsy. 'If you'll excuse me?'

'We haven't finalised the...' the door closed, leaving Estelle alone with her husband '...changes to the green drawing room,' she continued flatly. 'Which I intend to make into a small dining room. We can't keep eating in the library, it's not good for the books, and the grand dining room is far too big for two. There is another dining room in the east wing, but there is no direct route from there to the kitchen. It took me ten full minutes. I can't imagine whoever thought it was a good idea, but I'm not fond of eating stone-cold food. So if you've no objection, Aidan...'

'You actually timed the walk from the kitchen to the dining room?'

'Did you want something? I'm very busy.'

'And understandably feeling a bit neglected. I'm sorry.'

'What for?'

'These last two days, I've been occupied with estate business.'

'There's no need to apologise. You've been absent for a year, you must have a hundred things to do. I've not exactly been kicking my heels, sitting around waiting for you to pay me attention, I've found plenty to do.'

'I hope Mrs Aherne is being supportive.'

'We're getting on like a house on fire, which is more than I can say for you and me. I've been sitting opposite you at dinner these past two nights and you've barely spoken a word to me.'

'I know.' Aidan ran his fingers through his hair. 'There's a host of things requiring my attention, and I've been struggling to catch up, that's all.'

Struggling to catch up, and nothing to do with his peculiar reaction to the dog, Estelle thought sceptically. 'You could have explained that.'

'I could have. I should have. I've been feeling guilty for leaving so much in Finn's hands.' He was smiling, but it didn't reach his eyes. 'Let's have a cup of tea, and you can tell me what you've been plotting with Mrs Aherne.'

'You don't drink tea.'

'I'll consider it a penance.'

She was obliged to laugh. 'It's cold.'

'Even better, I deserve to suffer.' He made a show of surveying the room. 'You've made quite a few changes here.'

He wasn't going to say anything about his behaviour. Which meant she was going to have to bring the subject up. 'I like it because it's cosy, and it gets the morning sun, when it shines. It's not been used in a very long time. I didn't think you'd mind.'

'I'm happy for you have your own little sanctuary here.'

'Aidan?'

Her tone made his attempt at a smile stall on his lips.

'I know you don't wish to discuss your first wife…'

'No, I don't.'

'I understand that, but frankly, it would be foolish of us to pretend that she wasn't mistress here for five years.' He said nothing. 'I don't even know what she looked like. There's no portrait of her anywhere.'

'No, there's not,' he said in a tone that made it clear he had made sure there was not.

'You even haven't told me her name.'

'She's dead, Estelle. She has nothing to do with us.'

'Aoife,' she exclaimed impatiently. 'Her name is Aoife. Can't you bring yourself to say it?'

He went completely still. 'Ah, now I see. You've been using Mrs Aherne to find out things behind my back.'

She gazed at him in shock. 'Do you really think so little of me?'

'I didn't mean you to take it that way.'

'How else am I supposed to take it? You are accusing me of being disloyal.' Shock gave way to outrage. 'How dare you!'

'Estelle, don't look at me like that.'

But once unleashed, her temper had her in its grip, fuelled by two days of walking on eggshells and a growing sense of frustration at her own reticence. 'Her name was Aoife,' she said. 'She had a dog called Hera. She liked to play the harp. She had a very different taste in furnishings from me. That is about the sum total of the facts I know of her. I don't even know how she died. I could easily have asked Mrs Aherne but I didn't Aidan, because I've been hoping you would tell me.'

'What good would it do? She's dead!'

'Dead, but not buried it seems. You see ghosts in every room, but I've never seen a place stripped so bare of a person. It's like you're trying to pretend she didn't exist.'

'I wish to hell that she had never existed. I wish to hell I'd never set eyes on her. I wish to hell she'd leave me alone.'

He looked so wretched that her spurt of temper died as quickly as it had flared. 'But she won't, Aidan, and I don't understand why.'

He eyed the door, contemplating his escape, flexing and unflexing his fingers, before giving a shuddering sigh. 'The last year, maybe more, of our marriage, it was a living hell.'

She wanted to put her arms around him and tell him to say no more, but she had waited so long for him to speak, she forced herself to stay silent.

'She refused to talk to anyone about her— our situation. None of her woman friends, certainly not Clodagh. I think she thought if she talked about it, it would make it real or—to be honest, I don't know what she was thinking half the time. She was so unhappy, we both were. It was clear to me that we'd never have children, that whatever happened, we couldn't go on as we were, but—' He broke off, squeezing his hands tightly together. 'As I said, she wouldn't listen, she wouldn't talk to anyone, she certainly wasn't ready to admit defeat. Whenever I suggested it, she became completely overwrought.'

'So you continued to help her put on a front,' Estelle said softly.

'What else could I do? Perhaps I should have tried harder to make her face reality, but I'd failed her so badly in this one vital thing, I couldn't bear to let her down again, not when this was something I could do. In the grand scheme of things, keeping up appearances wasn't a lot to ask.'

'Oh, Aidan, you didn't let her down.'

'I did.'

Her instinct was to contradict him, but he was so determined to shoulder the blame that she feared any attempt to mitigate it would turn into an argument. He'd confided in her, he'd bared a little of the darkness in his soul. That was more than enough.

Aidan unclasped his hands, flexing his fingers. 'I'll take that cup of cold tea now.'

Estelle forced a smile. 'I'll let you off. This time.'

'There won't be another.' He pulled her into his arms, hugging her fiercely. 'Against the odds, we've found each other. I'd be an errant fool to ruin our chance of happiness.'

Heartsore at what he'd told her and moved by the raw emotion in his voice, she smoothed her hand over his hair. 'That's not going to happen. We've not even been here a week. Don't be so hard on yourself.'

'I won't let you down, Estelle.'

'It's no wonder you're finding it difficult to adjust, being confronted with such dreadful memories.'

'No longer. We'll put it all behind us now.'

'Yes.' A weight had lifted from her shoulders. She understood completely now why he didn't want to discuss it. She didn't need any more answers. All she needed was this, his arms around her, dissolving the distance that had grown between them in the last few days. She tightened her embrace, nestling closer.

Aidan nuzzled his cheek against hers. 'Do you realise that it's nine weeks and six days since we first encountered one another? And nine weeks and three days, since we first spoke?'

The contrast of his smooth cheek and his beard was having its usual effect on her senses. His fingers were stroking the skin on her nape under her hair. 'Then today is a very special day.'

'How should we mark the occasion, do you think?'

She curled her fingers into his hair. 'I'm sure we can think of something appropriate.'

He kissed her neck, then her throat. His eyes were lambent, reflecting her own desire. 'I don't know about that, but I can certainly think of something utterly inappropriate. I know we shouldn't but...'

'We definitely shouldn't,' she said, 'but will you kiss me regardless?'

'Regardless? It is never, ever anything other than a pleasure.'

He kissed her, but it was a teasing kiss, his lips just brushing hers. And then he kissed her again, butterfly kisses along her bottom lip, his fingers stroking the skin at the back of her neck. And then he moaned, pulling her tight up against him, and kissed her again and the pulses which he had set fluttering began to thrum. She clung to him as their tongues touched and their kiss deepened, their mouths clinging, hungry for each other, the kiss seemingly endless, and yet still not enough.

She ached for more. Her body was alive with longing, yearning to be touched. When Aidan broke the kiss, breathing raggedly, her mouth sought his and it started again. Their kisses grew wilder. She was dimly aware that they had staggered backwards, that she was leaning against the door.

He touched her. His hands on her back, on the curve of her bottom, sliding up to her waist. His hand closed gently over her breast, and as his fingers brushed lightly against her nipple, she moaned. His other hand covered her other breast, and his fingers teased her nipples to an aching peak, the pleasure so intense that it made her whimper. She barely registered that they were no longer kissing, aware only of his touch sending waves of pleasure coursing through her body, of the throbbing tension building between her legs, of his ragged breathing and her own shallow, rapid breaths, and the desperate desire that he not stop, so unprepared for the sudden lurching conclusion that she flailed wildly, clutching at his arms for fear of falling, only half-caring if she did, as the hot, liquid pleasure pulsed inside her.

'Estelle, I swear I didn't mean— I'm sorry, I should have stopped. I've gone too far.'

Reluctantly, she opened her eyes. Aidan's pupils were dark pinpoints, his lids heavy. A bubble of elated, slightly hysterical laughter escaped her. 'I have no idea where *I* have gone.' She straightened, pushing back her hair, which had come undone, still dazed by the turmoil reverberating inside her. 'I've never experienced *that* before.'

Aidan shook his head, his smile crooked. 'You've no idea, have you, that you're testing my powers of restraint to the limits.'

She was, rather late in the day, mortified. 'It was my fault. I asked you to—regardless, that's what I said, but I shouldn't have. It was selfish of me.'

'Shush. You'll be offering to return the compliment in a minute.'

'Ought I to?'

'No! I was teasing you.'

She put the backs of her hands to her flaming cheeks, but every bit of her seemed to be on fire. 'I simply *abandoned* myself, expecting you to ensure that we did not break our agreement and you did, but you must be feeling—' She broke off, at a complete loss. 'I don't know what you must be feeling.'

He swept her into his arms. 'You've no idea how adorable you are.'

'How naïve, you mean,' she muttered, her face pressed into his chest.

'Innocent. There's a big difference.'

'So innocent I have no idea how I would go about returning the favour.'

He gave a shout of laughter. 'Please don't take offence, it's just that I find your somewhat unique way with words endearing.' Setting her at arm's length, he waited until she met his gaze. 'There's no equation that needs balancing in this case, Estelle. Believe me, it was every bit as delightful for me as I hope it was for you. You've no idea.'

'I really haven't, Aidan.'

He laughed softly. 'That's not what I meant, but it doesn't matter. You know you can trust me, don't you?'

'I do, and I know it's unfair of me too.' She hesitated, but guilt forced her to continue awkwardly. 'When we decided to get married, it was my idea to insist that it was in name only.'

'For very understandable reasons.'

'Yes, but I didn't think it would prove to be so difficult to adhere to.' She smiled sheepishly. 'Perhaps if we argued a bit more, I might be less tempted to lead you astray.'

He let her go, his face clouding. 'The whole point of us marrying, Estelle, was to provide a safe haven for our children. Discord between us is not something to aspire to.'

'I was *teasing.*'

'I *know*!' He smoothed out the furrow between his brow with his thumb. 'I think we both need a little bit of time on our own to reflect.'

After he had gone, Estelle sat down at her desk, but the writing in her notebook was a blur. Absent-mindedly, she poured a cup of cold tea, screwing up her face when she took a sip. Throwing herself down on a more comfortable chair, she closed her eyes, reliving the extraordinary delight of—was there a name for what she'd felt? What had happened between them, was that lovemaking? No. She was woefully ignorant, but she was not completely uninformed. They had not made love. Besides, she hadn't for a moment felt passionate, not in her parents' sense of wanting to scream and shout and taunt and provoke. She'd felt the most sublime pleasure, and then sheer bliss. And she'd felt safe. And what's more, she believed Aidan when he said that he hadn't wanted more. His delight in her delight was unmistakably real, in the way he looked at her, as if he couldn't quite believe what had happened, as if she was the one and only person in the world. And for a moment, a perfect moment, that's how it had been, just as it had been before.

She had been right to marry him. She had been naïve to expect everything to be perfect from the start, but he had come to her of his own volition and explained his strange moods, She now understood why it was going to take time for them to adjust and why she had to stop asking questions because all they did was rouse the ghost Aidan was trying so desperately to bury.

He thought her curiosity morbid. It had been at first, but if she really had wanted to know more about Aoife, she would have asked Mrs Aherne. What she really wanted to know was why *Aidan* seemed rather morbidly obsessed with his dead wife. *Why* did he find it so difficult to lay her ghost? Aoife had been dead almost three years, and he'd spent the first two here in the castle, more than enough time to accustom himself to her absence. He felt guilty for not doing more to help her, and though he must know, rationally, that there was little he could have done, he probably wouldn't have been at all rational at the time.

But three years had passed, and Aidan still couldn't bring himself to say his wife's name.

Was that odd? And his reaction to the harp, and to poor Hera, wasn't that rather extreme? If he'd been in love with Aoife, she could understand his wretchedness, but he hadn't been in love with her, and in any case, a man still mourning his beloved dead wife did not make love to his second wife with such obvious pleasure.

Not that they'd made love. Made up? No, that had horrible overtones of what her parents had constantly done. They'd bonded. Reaffirmed. Reunited. Until she'd made that silly joke about arguments being useful, that is. She really needed to think a bit more before she spoke, though that did not come at all naturally. Estelle sighed. Had Phoebe and Eloise had the same problem? She smiled at the very notion of Eloise trying to guard her tongue. She owed both her sisters a letter. She could ask their advice about the party.

Sitting back down at her desk, she pulled a sheet of notepaper from the drawer and selected a pen. Onwards and upwards.

Aidan stood at the edge of the lake. The waters were intensely blue today, under a perfect summer sky, the gentle breeze just enough to cause a few wavelets to ripple on to the little stretch of shore where the boat used to be moored. He sat down on the grass verge, digging his boots into damp gravel, his hand automatically searching for and finding the iron ring which they'd used for tying up. His grandfather had put it there. A chunk of rust came off in his hand. He cast it into the water. The lake had always been a source of happiness. His father had taken him out fishing in the boat, and taught him and Clodagh to sail there, when the wind was right. In the summer they'd swim, all three of them, sometimes wading in from this little bit of shore, sometimes from the island, other times diving in from the boat. His father's teaching methods had been basic but sound, tying a rope around their waists and making them jump in after a very elementary demonstration of what to do with their arms and legs. It had been one of the many things he'd dreamed of doing with his own children, though he'd jump in with them, and not leave them floundering. Now he could make his dream a reality, with the family he and Estelle would make together. That's if he could ever bring himself to go into the lake again.

As if the weather had read his thoughts, a cloud scudded over the sun, turning the ruined tower and the island into a dark silhouette just as his eyes were drawn to it, making him shudder. It had been October, that last journey out to the island. The skies had been appropriately leaden, the wind blowing in stiff gusts. The heavens had opened on the journey back. When they returned to the house for the wake, he remembered the steam rising from the wet wool of the men's clothing. Those of them that came.

The cloud moved on. The sun blazed down once more on the island. They used to cook the fish they'd caught on a fire in the ruins of the tower, he and Clodagh and his father. He could see the spot from here. The other, more sacred spot, was not visible from anywhere on the shore. It was set in a little hollow, quite private, completely peaceful. Was she at peace? Was it too much to hope, that she'd leave him be?

In the distance, a dog barked and the hairs on the back of his neck prickled. Another possession of hers he should have returned, but her family would have none of poor Hera. He rolled his eyes at the taunting irony of the name. Goddess of marriage and childbirth. The dog adored her mistress. It would have been kinder to have got rid of her, Finn had said, for the wolfhound was miserable with him. But even in his shock and grief, Aidan hadn't been able to stomach that, and Finn said she'd settled well enough now. If only she hadn't found Estelle.

Estelle. He'd been home less than a week, Aidan reminded himself. His plan was to make new memories, he reminded himself, picking up a handful of pebbles to throw into the water. Like this morning. He hadn't any notion of kissing her when he sought her out to apologise. But she'd been as relieved as he, to put an end to the coldness that had been insidiously developing between them, and when they'd kissed, it had reminded him of why he'd been so sure, that day in Florence when he proposed, that this time, he'd get it right.

He'd lost himself in kissing her, just for a few perfect moments. It was as much her sheer delight in kissing that went to his head, as the taste of her and the touch of her. She was such a sensual creature, though she had no notion of it, and heaven knew, it was a miracle that she could be even half as abandoned, from what she'd told him of her childhood. To kiss, to touch, for the satisfaction of simply kissing and touching—just remembering was making him hard, and though she'd never understand, being hard was enough for him. A simple, primal affirmation.

Estelle. He said her name softly to himself

like a talisman. He'd spoilt the moment. She'd been glowing, so frankly, delightfully sated, and he'd spoilt it, snapping at her over a silly joke, when one of the things that he liked so much about her was the way she spoke without thinking.

He dropped his head in his hands, cursing. If he wasn't careful, he'd leach the spirit out of her. Had it been wrong of him to marry her? He'd been so sure they could be happy, but he was doing a fine job so far of making her unhappy, and she was so valiantly struggling to succeed.

He owed it to her to try harder. And to tell her the whole truth? Ah, no! He'd already told her more than enough. No more! Aidan got to his feet and headed off in the direction of the stables. From now on he really was done with looking over his shoulder. He had a lovely wife, and it was time that he concentrated on making sure she didn't live to regret marrying him.

Chapter Eight

They had settled on Aidan's birthday as the date for their wedding party, with the party for the estate tenants and staff to be held the following night. Just over a month after their arrival at Cashel Duairc, the day had finally arrived, and the castle was a hive of activity. Seated at her desk in her little parlour as the afternoon drew to a close, Estelle checked her list for the tenth time that day, but everything seemed to be in hand. She had taken responsibility for most of the arrangements herself, for Mrs Aherne, with whom she had established a comfortable relationship, had not had the heart to remain at Cashel Duairc for the party, and had departed, relieved and eager to start her new post, at the end of the previous week.

Estelle was determined to ensure that the

ghost of the first Mrs Malahide did not intrude tonight. This was her party, and she was going to put her stamp on it—with some assistance from her sisters. Cook had been delighted to try out some of Phoebe's suggestions for the supper which would be served. Tonight, Estelle would wear the evening gown Eloise had sent her.

She was looking forward not to the party itself, but what it represented, establishing her as Aidan's wife, confirming she and Aidan as a happily married couple, a significant step in their journey towards becoming parents. Things had settled down between them. Though there were still times when Aidan was morose and distant, his mood never lasted more than a few hours, and it was easier, Estelle had discovered, to ignore these minor aberrations which were, after all, part of the natural process of adjustment. They breakfasted and dined with each other, but spent much of the day apart, Aidan on estate business, while she concentrated on putting the house in order—her order!

They were admittedly careful with each other, a fraction too polite, not quite as entirely at ease in each other's company as they had been in Florence. They were learning their new roles, concentrating on practicalities, mak-

ing a conscious effort to play the companion-
able husband and wife they had contracted to
be, proving themselves, as Estelle thought of it,
as ideal future parents. By tacit agreement there
were no more kisses, though the absence made
them both strain towards each other in different
ways, a hand on the shoulder or a hand clasped,
the brush of an arm or a leg as they passed each
other, fingers touching when they handed something over.

Pushing her list aside, Estelle left the parlour
to make one final check upstairs. The party was
to be held in the Gothic Salon. Second only to
the ballroom in size, the vaulted ceiling was
painted white with the ubiquitous serpent coated
in gold leaf coiled at the intersection of the main
ribs. Standing beneath it, Estelle thought, was
like being under a particularly large umbrella, or
an Arabian tent, an illusion which was enhanced
by the gold-flocked wallpaper and heavy curtains. The room had been cleared of most of its
heavy carved furniture, the remaining side tables, sofas and chairs pushed back to the walls to
allow their guests to circulate. She had decided
not to draw the curtains and to risk leaving the
windows open, for the weather was still balmy.

In the grand dining room every leaf of the

table had been inserted, so that it stretched almost the full length of the room. Cook had been delighted with Phoebe's suggestions, and far from taking offence, had seemed genuinely honoured to have a famous chef think her worthy of attention and capable of executing her personal receipts. No one in the whole of Ireland would be able to boast as Cook would now be able to, that they had served up dishes that rich Londoners were paying through the nose to sample.

Retiring to her bedchamber, Estelle bathed and changed into the gown which Eloise had sewn for her. Made of ivory silk, it had puffed sleeves and a deeply ruffled hem, the whole embroidered with tiny leaves and flowerheads picked out in silver and gold. It reminded her, as she knew Eloise had intended, of a much-loved, though much simpler gown, her eldest sister had made her for her eighteenth birthday. She was very nervous. Seated at the dressing table, watching Niamh carefully threading a silver ribbon through her hair, her hands shook as she dabbed perfume on to her wrists.

'There, madam, if you don't mind me saying so, you look stunning.'

A light tap at the door sent Niamh scurrying

to answer it, and Aidan peered round the door. 'Am I allowed to come in?'

'Of course. You can go, Niamh, thank you, and don't wait up.'

The maid left, and Aidan stepped into the room and gave a low whistle. 'Is that the gown your sister sent?'

Estelle gave a twirl. 'She has excellent taste, don't you think?'

'I think that the people of County Kildare will be saying that I am the one with excellent taste when they meet you.'

It was the first time she had seen him in evening dress. His tailcoat was black with a shawl collar, the fashionable nipped waist suiting his lithe form, as did the plain black trousers. A white waistcoat with gold buttons fitted neatly over his flat stomach, and a plain starched cravat showed off his tanned face and neatly trimmed beard. 'You look rather magnificent yourself, if you don't mind my saying so,' Estelle said, crossing the room to join him. 'What was it that brought you here?'

'I have something for you. A surprise.'

'What is it?'

'It wouldn't be a surprise if I told you.'

'It's your birthday, not mine. In actual fact I

have a surprise for you. It's downstairs, in my parlour.'

'Oddly enough, that's where I have just placed my surprise for you. Shall we?'

'Let me get my gloves.'

'Bring them with you, but don't put them on yet.'

Aidan caught her hand, lifting it to his lips, pressing a kiss to her palm. She felt the flick of his tongue, and her breath caught in her throat. He smiled as he let her hand go. 'It seems abstinence makes the body grow fonder. I'm thirty-one years old today, far too old to be brought to boiling point by hand kissing.'

'It's because we have been simmering for weeks.'

He gave a bark of laughter. 'Simmering! You and your unique way with words again. Come away out of this room, woman, before I forget myself.'

Smiling, she followed him on the circuitous journey to her parlour, where he made her close her eyes before leading her in. 'I can't imagine what you have hidden here, for I've been in and out all day, and I would have noticed if...'

'I had it brought in just now while you were dressing. You can open your eyes now.'

She gazed in silent wonder at the harpsichord which stood in the centre of the room. 'Oh, Aidan!'

'We had to move some of the furnishings to accommodate it. I don't know if you'll want to keep it here, or have it moved elsewhere.'

'No, it's perfect where it is.' She touched the instrument reverently. The case was made of mahogany inlaid with walnut, simple but elegant. She opened the lid, carefully positioning the prop, and ran her fingers over the keys. 'It's utterly beautiful.'

'They said you'd want the underside of the lid painted, that most ladies preferred something more ornate, but I thought…'

Estelle smiled, shaking her head. 'Your instincts were right. I much prefer this.'

'Go on, try it out.'

'I'm dying to, but there's no time. Our guests will be arriving any minute.' But she couldn't resist, and was already seated. 'Now I know why you told me not to put my gloves on. I'll keep it brief.'

'Bach,' Aidan said when she had finished. 'Minuet in G Major, I do believe. It sounds as if it's in perfect tune.'

'You are quite right, it is. You have a good ear for someone who sings like a distressed Wicklow lamb.' She sighed, closing the lid. 'It's a magnificent instrument. My gift is going to look very insignificant compared to this. Close your eyes and hold out your hands. There, you can look now.'

'Estelle! Is this the globe that Phoebe gave you? I can't possibly take it.'

'I want you to have it. I had Aunt Kate send it from Elmswood. See, there is Notre Dame Cathedral. I wanted to commission a similar one of Florence, but there was no time.'

'I will look at Notre Dame and think of the Duomo. And I'll look at the Seine and think of the Arno. And instead of the Pont Neuf, I'll imagine you and me standing on the Ponte alla Carraia watching the sun go down as we did that first day. Do you remember?'

'How could I possibly forget.'

He set the globe down carefully on a side table. 'I'll put this in my room later. Thank you.'

'Happy birthday, Aidan.' She pressed a kiss to his lips. A fleeting kiss, it was meant to be, but their lips clung, and his hand went around her waist, and hers around his neck. And then the doorbell clanged.

'At last! Have you any idea how much forbearance I've had to show in order to stay away for these last few weeks? I'd have thought that you'd want to introduce your nearest and dearest to your new wife before the masses, but Finn was quite adamant you wanted to be left in peace. Noel will be with us in a moment, I ran ahead. Are we first to arrive? I hoped we would be.'

'Clodagh, it is good to see you.' Aidan surprised his sister by giving her a hug. 'You're looking well. Estelle, this as you'll have gathered is my sister Clodagh.'

'Goodness, you look very like your brother.' Estelle dropped a curtsy and extended your hand. 'How do you do?'

'How do *you* do?' Clodagh took Estelle's hand, smiling warmly. 'I am very glad to meet you at last. You won't mind my saying that you are very different from Aoife.'

'Clodagh!'

'Everyone will be itching to compare them, Aidan,' she retorted, 'there's no point pretending otherwise. So it's a very good thing indeed that Estelle is so very different.'

Aidan had almost persuaded himself that Finn was right when he said that tonight's guests would be far too interested in meeting Estelle to talk about his first wife, but here was Clodagh, talking about her before she'd even taken her cloak off. 'I don't think that's a subject Estelle wants to dwell on, tonight of all nights,' he said through gritted teeth.

'Estelle isn't offended, are you Estelle?' Without waiting for an answer, Clodagh continued, 'No, I thought not. Your dress is quite lovely. Paris?'

'My sister, actually.'

'Your sister! My goodness, she is very talented, and you wear it very well, I hope you don't mind my saying. You are quite voluptuous, aren't you? Cook will be pleased to have someone who actually eats the food she puts on the table. Aoife was one of those women who claimed that looking at food made her full.' Clodagh beamed. 'I think Estelle and I are going to be the best of friends. Ah, here is Noel. Come and be introduced to Aidan's surprisingly ravishing new wife.'

'I'm sorry,' Aidan said, when Clodagh had taken herself and her long-suffering husband off to inspect the arrangements. 'My sister has all the tact of a Dublin docker.'

'I liked her, and what she said is perfectly

true. It's only natural that people will attempt to draw comparisons.'

'They'll be wasting their time. There is no comparison.'

He'd worked so hard these last few weeks to keep his doubts about this party under control. Seeing Estelle throwing herself into the arrangements, determined to make her mark on both Cashel Duairc and local society, he'd persuaded himself that Finn was right, that no one would be interested in the first Mrs Malahide when faced with the second. But what if the old rumours began to circulate? Ought he to warn her? No, that would put her on the alert, and there was still a chance she might hear nothing untoward.

Down in the hallway, the arrival of the next guests took the decision out of his hands. 'Forget my tactless sister,' Aidan said. 'Be yourself, and you can't fail to charm everyone.'

Several hours later, Estelle had run out of reserves of charm. The last of their guests had left half an hour ago. Clodagh and Noel, who were spending the night, had finally retired. She'd sent the servants to their beds, postponing the clearing up until the morning. Aidan had muttered something about locking up.

She perched on the parapet of the narrow balcony which fronted the Gothic Salon, gazing out at the gardens. The moon was a quarter full, casting an eerie light on the lake, while the ruined tower was nothing more than a dark shadow. She'd discovered a rusty iron ring on the shore down there a few days ago, where a boat had once been moored. It was a shame that it was no longer there, for even if the tower was too dangerous to permit a visit to the island, it would be pleasant to take a sail on the lake.

'I assumed that you'd gone to bed.'

'I needed some fresh air after all that socialising.'

'Good idea.' Aidan perched down beside her. 'I think it's safe to say that went well, thanks to you.'

'Although there were moments when I felt like I was being inspected like a prime piece of horseflesh. "Now I know what he sees in you, m'dear,"' Estelle mimicked. 'Addressed for the most part to my cleavage, not my face. One of the so-called gentlemen actually pinched my bottom.'

Aidan's brows snapped together. 'I sincerely

hope you are not being serious, or his own bottom will feel the full weight of my boot.'

'I'm joking,' she lied hastily, seeing his thunderous expression. 'There were, however, a few not-so-subtle attempts to discover my pedigree. "Brannagh. I'm not sure that's a name I've come across. Would that be a family from the west?" That kind of thing. Thankfully no one seems to have encountered my parents. I suppose I could have confounded them with talk of my sister, the Countess of Fearnoch.'

Aidan reached for her hand. 'You must know, from the number of invitations we've been promised, that you stole the show. I was proud of you tonight, Estelle. I heard one comment over and over again that I agree with wholeheartedly. I'm a very lucky man.'

'Why thank you, Aidan, what a lovely thing to say.'

He lifted her hand to his lips. 'It happens to be true.'

Now that the party was over, she could see that he also felt a weight had fallen from his shoulders. Clodagh's tactless if true remarks had set him on edge, and for the whole time they'd stood in the hallway receiving their guests, she sensed him poised to intervene at the slightest hint of a reference to his first wife. *'So glad to see that Aidan has finally put his tragedy behind him'* and *'You are not at all what we had imagined'* had been the closest anyone had come in his hearing, as far as she could tell. But she had been aware, when circulating alone, of conversations abruptly changing tack. And one mysterious reference, overheard, to the tragic loss of the first Mrs Malahide as being inexplicable.

Now, however, was not the time to mention any of those things, not when Aidan seemed finally able to do what he so fervently wished, to consign his first marriage to the past. A huge wave of relief made her aware of just how worried she had been. It was quickly followed by a gust of happiness, bringing a beaming smile to her face. 'This finally feels like the first day of the rest of our lives,' she said.

'I do believe it is,' Aidan said, returning her smile. He got to his feet, pulling her into his arms, burrowing his face into her neck, holding her so tightly she could hardly breathe. Estelle wrapped her arms around his waist, sighing with contentment. 'It's a beautiful night. Look at the stars. I know it's trite, but they really do look like sparkling diamonds in the sky.'

'I think the brightest star in the heavens has fallen into my arms.'

She lifted her head, smiling up at him.

'Trite,' he said sheepishly, 'but also true.' And then, to her utter relief, he kissed her.

It was a slow, sensuous kiss, leading to another, and then another, leading very quickly to burning, searing, scorching kisses. Kisses that had been far too long suppressed. They clung to each other, lips and hands, kissing wildly, deeply, endlessly. There was no control in their kisses, no savouring, but a hunger, a craving that would not be satisfied by kisses alone, a primal need to lose themselves in each other, that excluded all else.

They kissed, and she clung to him, and he pulled her tight, his hands on her bottom as they half-stumbled, half-staggered back into the salon. The hard ridge of his arousal sent a deep shiver through her. He wanted her as much as she wanted him. He kissed her neck. His hands cupped her breasts. Her nipples ached. She undid the buttons of his waistcoat, feeling the heat of his skin through his shirt, and wanting more. He shrugged himself out of both his coat and waistcoat. He loosened the fastenings of her gown, enough to expose more of her breasts, pressing hot kisses on to them, making her moan, making her want still more.

She managed to wriggle out of her gown. She tugged his shirt free, running her hands over his skin. Smooth belly. Rippling muscles. Rough hair on his chest. Hard nipples. He shuddered when she touched them. She touched him again, because it fed the heat inside her when he shuddered.

He loosened her corset, pulling her chemise down. For a moment he stared, mesmerised by her breasts, his breathing fast, shallow, then he dipped his head, took one of her nipples in his mouth. He sucked and she shivered, and he sucked again, and she felt herself tightening, tingling, edgy with need, craving to surrender but desperate to cling on. And wanting more.

He lifted his head, said her name, and she feared he would come to his senses. She didn't want either of them to come to their senses, so she kissed him again, using her tongue, her hands on his back, pressing her bare breasts against his chest, sliding her hands down, to the taut slope of his buttocks, tilting her hips, excited by his hardness, heedless of everything but the driving need for more.

They dropped to the floor, still kissing. She

was on her back. He lay on his side beside her. Kissing. He had lost his shirt. She couldn't get enough of his skin, the smoothness of it, the rough hair on his chest, the way his muscles rippled under her caress, the dip in his belly. He slid his hand under her petticoats, hesitated, moved up when she arched up towards him. She couldn't keep still, kissing, touching, mouth on mouth, skin on skin, she was on fire with sensation. When he slid his fingers inside her she cried out with the sheer delight of it, and when he touched her, stroking, thrusting, sliding, she cried out, a harsh sound she barely recognised, tumbling suddenly, uncontrollably, over the edge, her muscles tightening around him, her hands clutching at his shoulders, saying his name over and over, And when he let her go, she instinctively pulled him towards her, wanting the weight of him on top of her, wrapping her legs around him, though there were still trousers and petticoats and pantaloons between them.

He lay for a moment on top of her, then he rolled away on to his back, his chest heaving. 'There's only so much a man can take.'

She had never felt more alive. Her blood fizzed. Her body was positively singing, making no effort to disguise her delight. 'I didn't know that this was what I was missing.'

Aidan gazed at her for a long moment, looking quite stunned. And then he laughed, pulling her on top of him, kissing her, a long, slow kiss. 'Neither did I.'

Clodagh and Noel were still abed, leaving Estelle to have breakfast alone with Aidan. 'Isn't it a lovely day?' she said pouring her tea.

He glanced out of the window, where the sky was overcast, leaden with rain that was not yet falling. He grinned. 'Beautiful. All the same, I think it might be prudent to think about moving tonight's banquet into one of the barns.'

'Oh, no, let's keep it *al fresco*, I'm sure the sun will come out. I must admit, I'll be glad when tonight is behind us. Two parties in two days is more than I've been to in two years.' Estelle wrinkled her nose. 'Or perhaps five. I'm not really much of a party-goer.'

'One of the many reasons I was so proud of you last night. You're actually quite shy, though you cover it up well.'

'I hide behind my role as the family comedienne.'

'You became the entertainer because you couldn't cook or sew.'

Estelle set her cup down, taken aback. 'I didn't know I was quite so transparent.'

'I'm just fiendishly observant.' Aidan pushed his empty plate away. 'Estelle, about last night...'

'Must we talk about that? Can't we put it down to celebrating our successful launch into County Kildare society?'

'I agree, there was an element of that, but we very nearly lost all self-control.'

'And I'm well aware that I am the one who said we had to control our urges in the first place.' She swallowed the last of her tea. 'The problem is, if you must have it, that I am finding I *want* to lose control with you. And when I do, it is so very delightful that I can't help wanting to do it again. Now I've embarrassed you.'

'I'm not embarrassed, Estelle.'

'Your face is red.'

'It might be, but not because I'm embarrassed.'

'Oh.' Her cheeks flamed, but not because she was embarrassed either. They gazed at each other across the table. If she made the first move, he would follow her lead. But he would not make the first move. Damn, why did he have to be so honourable! 'Do you think it's better to resist or submit? Which do you think is most likely to make us become indifferent sooner?'

'That is what is known in a court of law as a leading question.' Aidan got to his feet. 'I've a host of things to do before tonight. When Clodagh and Noel finally appear, have someone fetch me, I'll be in the estate office.'

He made to kiss her cheek, caught himself, shook his head ruefully and left. Smiling inanely at the closed door, it took a maid returning for the breakfast plates to rouse Estelle. Outside, the clouds were starting to clear. Informing the maid that she'd be in her parlour when their guests came down, she made her way there and pulled her latest list purposefully towards her. But she couldn't settle.

The glass dome had gone from her side table. Aidan must have taken it up to his bedchamber. She sat down at her harpsichord and began to practice scales. Now that Aidan had finally buried his ghosts, the future positively sparkled. True, she still didn't quite understand what, precisely, had made him so edgy last night, what he was so patently worried would be said. The most likely explanation was that he didn't want the shadow of his first wedding party to eclipse his second. Estelle moved up an octave and played another scale. In fact that was so obvious she didn't know why she was looking for another reason.

Aidan was happy. She was happy. Lying in bed last night, she had tried to imagine what it would have been like if they had really made love. Try as she might to frighten herself with the idea, all she'd felt was intrigued and rather delightfully excited. Would it be so wrong after all? Was it possible that lovemaking, rather than a weapon of destruction, was a weapon of peace? Could a weapon be peaceful?

No matter. She launched into one of her favourite happy pieces of Mozart—'Say Goodbye', from *The Marriage of Figaro*. Last night had brought them closer together. This morning, in the aftermath of last night, they had been newly at ease with each other. More aware of each other too, but in a wholly new way that was intimate, exciting, to be savoured.

She came to the end of the song. Was it possible that she'd been wrong to assume their desire for each other would ultimately tear them apart? They were so very, very different from her parents. She liked and cared for Aidan, for a start. She didn't like to see him upset and she most certainly didn't like being the reason for his distress. So they were not in love. In like? She laughed softly to herself. They were not in love, but she really did want to make love to him. After last night, a platonic marriage had very little appeal. It was all very well to give up something one had never had, but now she knew what she was missing—goodness, and what she was depriving Aidan of too.

'Sophistry,' she sang, drawing the word out into a scale.

'You're full of the joys this morning,' Clodagh said, popping her head around the door. 'I'm so sorry not to have joined you for breakfast. May I come in?'

'Of course, please do. Would you like me to have Cook make you something now? Some eggs or...'

Clodagh shuddered. 'No, nothing, thank you. I must say, you've made this into a very comfortable room. It was the receiving room in my father's day.'

'It gets such excellent light in the morning. Do you mind?'

Clodagh laughed. 'Goodness, no. I've never envied Aidan this place you know, it's far too big for my liking. What a delightful harpsichord.'

'It only arrived yesterday.'

'Aidan's doing?' Clodagh ran her hand over the burr walnut. 'I heard you were musical.'

'Do you play?'

'No, I'm tone-deaf, like our father. Do you mind if I sit down? Just between us, I'm expecting, which is why I can't face breakfast. I didn't like to mention it in front of Aidan. My brother probably thinks I'm past breeding age. To be honest, I thought I was myself. The news came as quite a surprise. I was thinking, when we were driving here, how marvellous it would be if he or she had a little cousin roughly the same age. I can tell from the way you're blushing that you think I've been far too forward. I talk too much and think too little beforehand, as you'll have gathered.'

'You mustn't apologise for that, for I do the same myself. It comes of having two sisters.'

'I've always pined for a sister. And you are a twin, I believe. What is that like?'

'Lovely and painful both.'

Clodagh clapped her hands together. 'I just knew I'd like you the moment I set eyes on you. I can't tell you how happy I am that Aidan has finally put the past behind him. I've been nagging him for ever to get married again.'

'So he told me.'

Clodagh laughed. 'I'm sure he did. I'm so glad he waited until he found you, you're perfect for him. I hope you didn't pay attention to any inappropriate muttering last night? I did my best to stamp it out. Last night was your night, no need for any spectres at the feast, so to speak.'

'I was aware that there was some talk of his first wife, but only when our guests thought I was out of earshot.'

'It was inevitable, I suppose. I mean, Aoife was so young, with her whole life ahead of her, and she and Aidan seemed so happy. It seemed inexplicable that she would choose to take her own life.'

Estelle's hands fell on the keyboard, making a jangling chord. She felt the blood drain from her face. 'She took her own life?'

'You didn't know.' Clodagh looked stricken. 'Oh, dear heavens, I'm so sorry. I assumed Aidan had told you.'

'You were clearly wrong,' Aidan said from the doorway.

'Don't look at me like that,' Clodagh snapped. 'I'm sorry, Estelle, I can see I've given you a shock, but I can't believe you didn't know. For goodness sake, Aidan, she could have heard it from any one of your guests last night. What would it have looked like…?'

'Our guests had the decency not to discuss the painful subject. Unlike you, sister dear. I came to tell you that Noel has ordered the carriage.'

'Already! That man, he'd have himself carried out from his own funeral before the service ended, just to avoid a crush at the church door.' Clodagh got to her feet. 'I am truly sorry to have sprung that on you. I do hope you won't hold it against me. I've very much enjoyed my little stay at Cashel Duairc, it's been far too long in the making. Now if you'll excuse me, I'd better go and get my cloak.'

Chapter Nine

Aidan and Estelle stood together on the carriageway to wave Clodagh and Noel off. As soon as the driver raised his whip to set the horses in motion, Aidan's fixed smile faded. Giving her a curt nod, he made to turn on his heel, but Estelle grabbed his arm.

'Where are you going? You must know we have to talk about this?'

'I know nothing of the sort.'

'Aidan!'

He rounded on her. 'Why the hell can't you stop raking up the past?'

She reeled at the vicious tone of his voice. 'I do nothing of the sort.'

'You leapt at the first opportunity to interrogate my sister. You couldn't wait to get her to spill the beans.'

'For someone who prides himself on having a logical brain you are behaving utterly illogically, Aidan. I haven't interrogated anyone on the subject of your previous marriage, not even you. In fact I've done my level best to forget that you had another wife. You're the one who's obsessed by her, not me. If you had told me yourself that she had died at her own hands, I'd have thought it both shocking and tragic, but I'd have been more than happy to let the subject drop, believe me. The fact that you couldn't bring yourself to tell me makes me wonder why on earth not?'

The colour drained from his face. 'What do you mean by that?'

'You can't talk about her, you can't say her name, you can't even bear the sight of her dog. Do you feel guilty for marrying me?'

'No!'

'Are you still in love with her?'

He looked quite sick. 'How can you ask that?'

'Because I can't think of any other reason for this obsession.'

'It's not an obsession.'

'How else would you describe it?' Estelle said, tears stinging her eyes. 'This morning we were so happy, and now you're almost unravelling in front of my eyes.'

'You are overreacting. I was shocked to hear my sister speak so lightly of a tragedy.'

'How did she die, Aidan?'

He took a visible breath. 'She drowned.'

Estelle's hand instinctively went to her heart. 'Oh, Aidan—'

But he cut her short. 'I don't want your entirely misplaced sympathy. What I want is for us to focus on why we married in the first place.'

'That is so unfair! I have not lost sight of why I'm here, you're the one blinded by whatever emotion is eating away at you,' Estelle exclaimed.

'I don't have time to bandy words with you. In case you'd forgotten, we have another party to host.'

Without another word, he turned his back and walked off. Belatedly realising where she was, and mortified lest any of the servants had overheard them, Estelle fled for her room, where she locked the door, threw her hairbrush against it, threw herself on to the bed and gave way to a flood of tears.

Aidan threw his pencil down in disgust. Three times he'd tried to calculate the load bearing down on the span, and each time he'd come up with a different answer. He pushed aside the drawing board, gazing at his sketch of the new bridge with a jaundiced eye. His heart simply wasn't in it.

Finn had left a set of accounts to be reckoned on his desk, but he'd probably have as much success making those tally as he'd had with calculating loads. There were any number of things to be done for tonight's party, but right at this moment, he couldn't face talking to anyone. All he could think about was Estelle's shocked, pale face, her eyes bright with tears as he turned his back on her.

'You're the one blinded by whatever emotion is eating away at you.'

Obsessed, she'd called him, and she was horribly right, though not in the way she thought. He wasn't driven by shame or by love or by pity or grief. He was driven by guilt.

He groaned, remembering the logical way he'd laid out his proposal back in Florence, his reasoned argument for their marriage, the rationale they'd agreed for managing the risk of failure. It was the perfect recipe for success, yet he was hellbent on sabotaging it, and if he couldn't find a way to stop, history would repeat itself.

He'd wreck this marriage too. He'd ruin Estelle's life too.

His heart twisted, making him groan. He'd hurt her. She didn't understand why he'd lashed out at her. She didn't understand that he couldn't bear it when she tried to make sense of the senseless, to understand what he barely comprehended himself. Estelle, bright, lovely, clever, transparent, impulsive Estelle. He was draining the life out of her. If he wasn't careful, what they'd called their friendship, the foundation for their marriage which they'd taken for granted to be rock solid, would start to crumble, and it would be his doing. With Estelle as his wife, he could have all he ever wanted, yet he was wilfully set on a path that would ensure that he ended up with nothing. Not even his wife.

He didn't want to lose her. He couldn't bear to lose her. The reason he'd dreamt up this practical marriage of theirs in the first place was because he didn't want to lose her, and what he felt for her now was a damned sight more significant after two months of marriage. They could be happy. This morning, they had been happy. Breakfast had given him a glimmer of a future that was rosy, with a lifetime of those breakfasts together, a lifetime of teasing and laughing, and planning their days and then recounting their days, safe in the knowledge that they would have another day and another and another. He wanted to grow old with her, for God's sake, but he was lucky if he'd see another birthday with her, the way he was heading.

He wanted to be a husband to her. A real husband. He wanted to make love to her. Last night had given him hope on that front—but he knew it was false. They would have their family the way they'd discussed, but right now, thinking about children was putting the cart well before the horse. He had to find a way to salvage his marriage before he could even contemplate adding children to the mix.

He could tell her the unvarnished truth. The very idea of that made him feel as if he'd fallen off a cliff edge, but he closed his eyes and forced himself to imagine it all the same. That last debacle. The sick, familiar rhythm of it, what she had said, what he had said, locked in the torment of trying, knowing his efforts would be futile. At what point had he cracked? It didn't matter, he had uttered the fateful words.

'Just do it! Put us both out of our misery.'

Was it bluff-calling or an order? It made no difference. He dropped his head into his hands, his shoulders heaving, though he made no sound. The only certainty that would come from him telling Estelle the truth was that she would leave him, knowing the monster that he was. But the other thing he was certain of was that he didn't want to live without her.

Estelle wore a scarlet gown to the party. Redheads, Mama used to say, should never wear red, which was why all three sisters were irresistibly drawn to the colour. The sleeves were puffed at the top, narrow at the wrist, held in place by a series of little buttons. The stiff cotton was formed into tiny pleats at the back, but the dress front fell straight from the high waist. A wide band of satin ribbon was tied in a bow at the back, and the same ribbon was stitched in three bands on the hem, but aside from the locket Phoebe had given her for her twenty-first birthday, and her wedding ring, she wore no other jewellery.

She had not seen Aidan since he stormed off this morning. She'd emerged from her bout of tears exhausted and depressed. She didn't have the heart to confront him again. Even if there was the time, she needed to conserve her energy to put on a brave front. He too was sub-

dued when they met up at the front door, smiling
stiffly, treating her as if she were made of glass
as they completed the short walk round to the
stable yard where the feast was just coming to
an end.

Fortunately, the atmosphere was already
raucous, with a band playing traditional music,
reels and jigs, a stark contrast to last night's se-
date offering. Aidan's toast was received with
loud cheers, the stream of congratulations they
received seemed both warm and genuine. Under
different circumstances Estelle would have been
more than happy to join in the merriment. This
was much more her sort of party.

'We'll not stay long,' Aidan said in a tone that
brooked no objection, pulling her clear of an
over-zealous dancer. 'I'll check that there's still
plenty to drink to go round and that the leftover
food has been divided up. Will you be all right
on your own for a bit?'

'I'll be happy to be on my own for a bit,' she
said sharply, immediately regretting it when he
flinched. She drew a breath. 'I'll listen to the
music. Go on, go and smoke a pipe with the
men, or something.'

'I've never smoked a pipe in my life. Are you
sure you'll…?'

'I'll be fine, Aidan.'

She was still ridiculously close to tears. Waiting until he disappeared from view, Estelle made her way past the dancers to the furthest corner of the courtyard, where a group of people were gathered in a semi-circle round a lone fiddler. He was playing a lament she recognised, a plaintive song about an immigrant remembering the green mountains of home. A young girl got to her feet and began to sing, the rest of the little group taking up the chorus. Estelle sat down unobtrusively, joining in with the last chorus. The young girl resumed her seat, the fiddle player embarked on another lament, and the next person in the circle stood up to sing. This was followed by a more rousing rebel song, and then two love songs, neither of which had happy endings.

Lost in childhood memories of the days when they had been four siblings and not only three, joining in with every chorus, Estelle immersed herself in the music. Only when all eyes turned expectantly on her as the only one who had not performed a solo, did her inhibitions return. She would have given a great deal for the earth to swallow her up, but it was too late to back out, and she didn't want to set herself apart or have them say that Master Aidan's new wife was a snob. It was a small group, and if she picked something with a chorus, then she'd not be unaccompanied for long. Besides, shy as she was of performing, she knew she could hold a tune. And there was one particular tune that she wanted to sing.

Getting to her feet, she smiled nervously, clasping her hands together to steady herself. '"Mo Ghile Mear"?' she suggested. 'My Gallant Lad' had been one of their governess Bridget's favourites, a love song with two meanings, of a woman mourning her lost love, and a country mourning its lost prince, Bonnie Prince Charlie. It had been the dashing Young Pretender who had appealed to Diarmuid. He'd loved this song.

The fiddle player nodded and began to play the introduction. Estelle closed her eyes to block out her audience and began to sing. She sang in Irish, for the words in translation lost the haunting beauty of the language in which it was written. As the first chorus began, she forgot she had an audience and sang as if she was alone with her little brother, barely aware that her audience had ceased singing along and were listening, rapt, until she finished the song and opened her eyes.

The little circle had become a crowd. There was a moment's silence, before she was treated to rapturous applause. Blushing, shaking her head at any suggestion of an encore, she saw Aidan standing on the periphery, his eyes fixed on her, his expression inscrutable. Excusing herself, she was about to make her way over, when he turned on his heel and for the second time that day walked away from her.

Bewildered and hurt, wanting only to share her bittersweet memories with him, she made to follow him.

'Let him go.' Finn put his hand on her arm, steering her away from the gawping crowd.

'Why did he disapprove so much of my singing? Does he consider it unseemly for his wife to carouse with tenants?' she asked, stung.

'It wasn't your singing, it was the song. It was Aoife's song. She sang it at their wedding ball, accompanying herself on the harp. It was her party piece. And a poor version too, compared to what you treated us to tonight. I've never heard it sung so beautifully.'

'Your blarney is wasted on me tonight, Finn.'

'Ach, sure, it can't be blarney if it's the truth.'

He walked her back, leaving her at the front door of the castle. 'Don't judge him too harshly,

Estelle. He's had to contend with more than any man should have to. I'll bid you goodnight.'

Inside, she hesitated at the foot of the stairs. It wasn't sleep she needed, but the solace of her music. Not the harpsichord, her parlour was too close to the rooms they used in the evenings and she didn't want Aidan to hear her, but the ball-room was at the other end of the castle.

The shutters had been left open from the piano tuner's visit, allowing the moonlight in, enough to let her avoid the various grey lumps of furniture and make her way to the instrument. Estelle opened the top and sat down on the stool flexing her fingers. Closing her eyes, she began to play. She played the old songs. Not only the ones that Bridget had sung to them, but other ballads, English ones and Scots ones, that she had taught herself from a book, a gift from her mother not to her, but to Diarmuid, who had begged for it on her behalf. One song led to another. She didn't sing, but in her head she could hear the words. She played until her tears were spent, until she came back around again to 'Mo Ghile Mear', and then she did sing, softly and in English this time, 'My Gallant Lad', for her long-departed little brother.

Drained, exhausted but calmer she closed the

lid of the piano and opened her eyes to find Aidan standing a few feet away, putting her immediately on the defensive. 'I had no idea that your wife had a soft spot for that particular song, and I certainly wouldn't have sung it if I'd known that she had played it here, at your wedding party.'

'Finn told you?'

'Don't worry, he's not confided any more of your deep dark secrets, he's as loyal as the woman in the song was to Bonnie Prince Charlie.'

'I'm sorry you heard it from Finn. I came looking for you in order to explain.'

'Then why did you walk away from me?'

'To prevent me from making a fool of myself in front of everyone by getting upset. I've never heard that song sung so beautifully. When I heard you sing tonight, I wasn't comparing you, and I wasn't seeing ghosts. I was looking at you and I was thinking, this woman is my wife, and I was thinking of the first time I heard you play in the church in Florence, and how you'd played from the heart. You breathed life into me when I thought I was an empty husk. I don't want to lose you, Estelle. The very thought of it makes me feel ill.'

She sat back down on the piano stool. 'That song was my brother's favourite. That's why I sang it. For Diarmuid. He drowned, you see. He was on his way to school in England. My parents were escorting him. The ship went down and all three of them were lost at sea.'

Aidan sat down beside her looking stricken. 'So what Clodagh told you this morning must have seemed like a horrible coincidence.'

'We decided, Phoebe and I, that Diarmuid wasn't dead, that he'd been washed up on some remote beach, and it was just a case of waiting for him to be found. We knew in our hearts that it was a fantasy, but we kept it going for ages between us, imagining him eating strange fruits and catching fish and getting his skin burnt in the sun. We decided it was a desert island that he was on, you know like the castaway in the story?' She smiled weakly. 'Even though the ship went down in the Irish Sea. I've not played many of those songs since. I'm surprised I remember the half of them.'

'Was your brother musical?'

'Not a bit, but he loved to sit by me at the piano, right from when he was a toddler. I tried to teach him, but he'd no patience and no ear, and when I look back on it, I'd little patience with him. I wanted the piano to myself. I was always scooting him away. It was one of the things I regretted, when we'd finally accepted he wasn't coming back, that I'd not had more time for him.'

'So Clodagh conjured up more than one ghost this morning?'

'I miss my little brother, and I wish I'd made more of the time we had with him, but he doesn't haunt me, Aidan.'

'Aoife doesn't haunt me, not in the way you're imagining.' Aidan gave a ragged smile. 'You see, it seems I can say her name.'

He pushed himself to his feet and prowled over to the window, opening it up to the night and the distant sounds of the dying embers of the party. 'You wanted to know what she looked like? She was beautiful. She had black hair, huge big blue eyes, skin like buttermilk. She barely came up to my shoulder, one of those gossamer, fairy-like women that seemed only just tethered to the ground. One of those women who drew every eye when she walked into the room.'

Another bittersweet coincidence. 'That's what Papa always said of my mother. That the conversation stopped when she entered a room. Not,'

Estelle added hastily, 'that I mean to draw any other comparison. My parents' marriage was…'

'Tempestuous, I think is how you described it.' Aidan closed the window, leaning his shoulders against the frame.

'Did I? They were certainly passionately in love.'

'From the little you've told me it sounds as if they didn't much care for each other.'

'On the contrary. They cared too much for each other and not enough for anyone else. More so my father. He was obsessed with my mother.'

'Obsession isn't love, Estelle. Obsession is wanting someone or something to the exclusion of all else, regardless of the consequences.'

'Wanting something or someone—such as a child, you mean? Are you saying that's what drove Aoife to take her own life?'

'Drove her?' His voice shook. 'Yes, she was driven to it.'

All her instincts were to go to him, but when she moved, he shook his head, shrinking away. She was about to ask him to explain what he meant, when he pushed himself away from the window to rejoin her on the stool, taking her hand. 'I want more than anything for us to put the past behind us.'

What she wanted was for *Aidan* to put the past behind him, but it was the same thing. Aoife had killed herself because they couldn't have a child. Aidan accepted the blame for that, so it was only a short step to him also blaming himself for her death. Estelle pressed her lips to his knuckles. 'It wasn't your fault, none of it was.'

He pulled his hand from hers and got to his feet. 'You don't know what you're talking about.' He took a step towards her, then stopped. 'Everyone thought we were happy, right up to the end. We put on an excellent performance. I don't want our marriage to be a performance, Estelle. I want our happiness to be real.'

Her heart melted. She threw herself at him, wrapping her arms around his neck. 'It will be. We're happy now, aren't we?'

He put his arms around her waist, pulling her closer. 'How could I fail to be happy when you're in my arms, like this.'

'Then any time we are unhappy, all we have to do is this.'

'Kiss and make up?'

Her smile faded as their eyes met. 'No. That's what my parents called it. What we are doing is reuniting.'

'I like that.'

'Good. I do too.'

* * *

Their lips met almost before she had finished speaking, and Aidan forgot everything except this, Estelle in his arms, Estelle murmuring his name. They kissed, melting into each other, and the world righted itself. His eyes drifted shut, and the world narrowed to this moment and this woman and their kisses, healing the rift between them.

Then heating them, for they were no longer kissing for reparation but kissing for the sake of kissing. Kissing to rouse each other, her hands pushing under his coat, his own, seeking the swell of her breast, the moan she uttered making him hard, and her nipple peaking at his touch making him harder. She was saying his name again, but it was urgent now, and he wanted, ached to do what she begged him to do, to be inside her, feel her slick and wet and tight, to feel her clinging to him as she came, and then…

He tore his mouth away, shaking his head, smiling weakly. 'I think that's probably enough reuniting, don't you?'

'You're right,' she agreed, though she looked as he felt, that he was quite wrong. 'I think that's more than enough of everything. It's been a very long day. I think it's time for bed. Onwards and upwards tomorrow?'

'Onwards and upwards,' Aidan agreed, hoping fervently that this time he would be able to deliver on his promises.

She kissed him on the cheek and fled. The doors creaked shut, and Aidan sat back down at the piano, idly tinkling a few of the keys randomly. Had he done enough to reassure her? There had been a moment there, when he'd been poised on the brink of confessing everything. There had been several moments when he'd felt like a liar, even though he'd tried very hard not to utter falsehoods. He longed to tell her the whole truth. It sat so ill with him not to, every passing day making him horribly aware that he was living a lie. But he couldn't tell her the truth because he would lose her if he did.

'It wasn't your fault...none of it was,' she'd said, so fiercely and with such certainty. How many times had he tried to tell himself the same thing? If he managed to convince himself of that, he'd long ago have resigned himself to be content with his life alone here at Cashel Duairc. He wouldn't have gone to Florence to escape his demon, the guilt that consumed him. He wouldn't have met Estelle.

Ought he to have married her, having kept such a terrible secret from her? But he hadn't told her, and they were married and he could not regret that fact. He wanted to remain married. Happily married. He wanted that more than anything.

It was a simple enough equation for a one-time aspiring mathematician. How long ago that seemed! All he had to do was bury his guilt so deeply it would never resurface. If he really did want Estelle more than anything—and he did—then surely he could manage that.

Chapter Ten

Six weeks later

Deciding to change early for dinner and grab a bit of fresh air, Aidan opened the door of the estate office just as Finn was about to enter. 'I'm glad I caught you.'

'Is there a problem?'

'A potential one,' Finn said, looking uncomfortable. 'Something I need to make you aware of regarding Aoife.'

Aidan's heart sank. 'Must you?'

'Look, I'll get straight to the point. You remember Shamus, the footman with the gob on him who used to be in service here? He was here this afternoon visiting his father, who is one of your tenants. He came up to the house to see his old partner in crime, Donal, and the pair of them were reminiscing about old times over a glass or ten. Anyway, Cook, God love her, thought that she'd be doing us all a favour by trying to sober them up by plying them with bread and cheese in the kitchen. It was she who tipped me off.' Finn wandered over to his drawing board. 'Is that the bridge you're thinking of constructing? I thought you'd go for a more elaborate design.'

'It's a work in progress. I'm really not interested in hearing kitchen tittle-tattle, Finn.'

His friend threw himself down on one of the fireside chairs. 'And I'd rather not recount it, but the problem is Niamh, the new maid who waits on Estelle, was there when the pair of them started running off at the mouth. I'm not saying she'll pass on what was said, but there's a chance.'

'Go on then, spit it out. What were they saying?'

'That Aoife fled to the island most nights. That it was a wonder Estelle hadn't done the same, for you've been married long enough to have shown your true colours by now.'

'I beat my wife now, do I?'

'Ah, Aidan, they didn't quite go that far, but they implied you must have mistreated Aoife to make her behave so erratically.'

'I never laid a hand on her.'

'You don't need to tell me that!'

Suddenly extremely weary, Aidan sank down on the chair opposite. 'In actual fact, for over a year, I didn't touch her in any way.'

It took a while for the implication to sink in. 'But she told me—' Finn broke off, colouring deeply. 'She told me in confidence and swore me to secrecy. I think she was so excited by the news that she had to tell someone. Dear God, if it wasn't you, are you telling me that there was someone else?'

Aidan shook his head impatiently. 'No, nothing like that, she would never have—it's complicated. I've already said more than I should.'

Finn got to his feet. 'If the maid reports the kitchen gossip back to Estelle, I've no idea what she'll make of it, though I'd bet my life that she'll defend you to the hilt. Just in case I'm wrong, my advice is to tell her yourself first.'

'Your advice couldn't be more misguided.'

'The poor woman is tiptoeing around you as if you are a volcano about to erupt at any moment, if you don't mind my saying.'

'I do mind, as a matter of fact.'

"Fine! It's none of my business at the end of the day, except for the fact that you deserve to be happy, Aidan, and I believe Estelle is the perfect woman to help you achieve just that.' Finn threw open the door. 'Don't muck it up. Right, I've said my piece, I'll make myself scarce.'

'Finn.'

'What?'

'Thank you. That can't have been easy.'

After he left, Aidan stared blankly once again at his bridge. Finn was right, it was an eye-wateringly boring piece of architecture. Should he talk to Estelle? There was a chance that Finn was being over-cautious, and he'd give almost anything not to bring the subject up. But he was loath to have her hear it from anyone but him, given his past record in that regard.

The urge to tell her the whole truth behind the gossip was like a physical longing. He was finding it harder and harder to resist, ironically, the more and more he was coming to care for her. He could come clean on both accounts. That would be a hell of a confession to make, and to hear!

Aidan groaned. Like it or not, Finn *was* right. He'd no option but to present Estelle with another piece of the puzzle for her to slot into place.

* * *

It was pouring with rain outside, and above all, the thing Estelle loathed most was getting soaked to the skin. She had a pile of letters to answer and a stack of invitations to consider, but neither task appealed, so she had made her way once again to the attics of the west wing. She'd taken to spending a good deal of time up here in the last month, attempting to impose some order on the chaotic archives. Today, she had uncovered a bundle of plans, including the drawings Aidan's mother had made for the planting of the walled garden, but not even this treasure trove could hold her attention.

She was starting to wonder if her marriage had been a mistake. As each day passed, it should be getting easier for them to relax in each other's company, when in fact it was the opposite. Aidan was in an almost permanent state of alert, waiting for something to jump out and remind him of the past, preparing himself not to allow it to overset him. And she was just as tense, watching him, walking on eggshells around him lest she inadvertently say the wrong thing.

Far from cooling their ardour, the weeks of not kissing and not touching had turned desire into a tangible presence in the room every time they were together, a simmering, quivering creature only barely chained. She was getting to the point where it seemed the only thing that would clear the air between them was to do the very thing she had insisted they must not.

It had been three years since Aoife died. Estelle couldn't imagine the depths of despair a person must be in to throw themselves into a lake, but she couldn't rid herself of the notion that in some ways it was a selfish act. Despite his best efforts to hide it from her, Aidan was still struggling with some element of guilt. He'd never said so, but a man who assumed complete responsibility for his wife's inability to conceive would be bound to assume culpability for her taking her own life.

It's not your fault, she wanted to shout at him, but simply saying the words would be enough to set him off. Aoife was a deeply troubled woman, who wanted something so passionately that she didn't care or couldn't see what it was costing her marriage and her husband. Aidan had suffered. He was still suffering, and still blaming himself for failing. She'd seen the tension in him when he heard Hera bark, the way he held himself quite still, his fists clenched tightly by his side. She'd seen the wretched look on his face when he'd spotted Aoife's signature in an old book of household accounts on Estelle's desk. And worst of all, she'd seen the look of abject despair when he looked at her, thinking her unaware of him. That look made her blood run cold. She couldn't think of any other reason for it, save regret.

Sometimes it seemed to her that Aidan was wilfully keeping the past in the present, deliberately allowing it to destroy their chance of happiness. She didn't want her marriage to fail because of a ghost. She didn't want her marriage to fail, full stop. Aidan cared for her. She suspected he might care a great deal for her. Almost as much as she cared for him.

Shocked, she let the plans roll to the floor. She liked him, but she wasn't in love with him. Was she?

When she was younger, she'd taken her parents' claim to be wildly in love with each other at face value. She'd seen and heard enough evidence of their passion, and she'd assumed that the fights, the screaming matches, were just another side of the same coin. Later, much later, when she was old enough to make sense of the things she'd overheard as a child, she'd been shocked to the core by the realisation that her mother had conducted numerous *affaires*, had a string of lovers, but she'd never doubted her father's enduring and singular love for his wife. Aidan had said it was obsession not love. It was true that sometimes, when Papa had shouted very convincingly that he wished he'd never met Mama, that she tormented him mercilessly, and it had sounded closer to hate than love.

If that wasn't love, then what was? She loved her sisters, and Aunt Kate, she'd loved poor Diarmuid, but that was a different kind of love. It meant wanting to protect someone, even if it meant putting yourself second. It meant putting someone's happiness before yours. That wasn't the same as the love between a man and a woman, was it? It couldn't be, because that would mean what she felt for Aidan was dangerously close to love.

Estelle dropped her head on to her arms. She was twenty-five years old, why had it taken her so long to ask herself these questions? And why was she asking them now! She was married to a man so racked with guilt about his first wife's death that he was in danger of destroying their marriage. Why did he feel so guilty when he'd done everything he could to make Aoife happy, even to the extent of making himself miserable? It didn't make sense, but she daren't raise the subject again for fear it would break his already fragile mental state.

'I've been looking for you everywhere.' Aidan pushed the door into the attics open to find Estelle perched on a metal box, a number of maps spread out on the floorboards. 'What have you got there?'

She eyed him warily, clearly assessing his mood. 'I think it's the original plans for the rebuilding of the castle.'

'May I see?'

He pulled up another metal chest and squatted down on it beside her, studying the map. 'The east wing is missing.'

'I know, and see here, where the foundations of the old castle are, it looks as if the intention was to rebuild them, incorporate them into the new castle.'

'So it does. I wonder why they didn't.'

'There's no explanation here, but I hope to find something in the other papers from the time. There are whole boxes full of stuff, accounts books, bills, even a diary.'

'Enough to write a history?'

'It's a huge project to embark on. It would take years.'

Did they have years? It made his heart contract, seeing the unasked question in her eyes, knowing that the seeds of her uncertainty had been sown by him. Warning her that there was ill-founded speculation that Aoife's midnight wanderings were a result of his mistreatment of her seemed an inadequate response. He needed to repair the shattered trust between them. Dammit, he claimed he wanted to build things! A solid foundation for his marriage was much more important than any bridge or canal.

As ever, he longed to pull her into his arms and hold her, tell her everything would be fine, but she deserved more than that. In any case, he didn't want her to misconstrue his desire to break down the barriers between them. 'Estelle.' He reached for her hand, rubbing it against his cheek. 'We have years and years ahead of us, more than enough time for you to write an archive and reconstruct the gardens. Ample opportunity for me to build a bridge and a canal and add another wing to the castle if you want. Time to establish the most important thing of all.'

'A family?'

He kissed her knuckles. 'It's not that I've forgotten why we married, I promise you.'

'Oh, Aidan, do you think I can't see that? I just wish you'd tell me what you're finding so difficult. You blame yourself in some way, I know, but I can't understand why.'

He jumped to his feet, pulling her with him, needing to act before his confession spilled out. 'Come with me. I'll show you something that might explain better than words ever could.'

'Where are we going?'

'The east attics.'

His heart was pounding, his mouth was dry as he led the way down the stairs along the corridor to the east wing.

Estelle watched with astonishment and some trepidation as Aidan searched through his chain for the key. 'Mrs Aherne told me the key to the east attics was long lost. She said that the door hadn't been opened in years, that the attics held nothing of interest. Broken furniture, old hangings. I take it she was lying?'

'Not lying, protecting someone.' Aidan turned the lock. 'Before I show you what's behind this door, I need you to know I haven't kept it from you because I too was protecting someone.'

Icy fingers clutched at her heart. 'Aidan, you're starting to frighten me.' Was this where all the relics of Aoife had been stored? Was she about to see some sort of macabre shrine?

'It's not frightening, it's simply tragic,' he said, holding the door open. 'I won't say any more. There's no need, this place tells its own story.'

Heart pounding, Estelle stepped through the door. She was standing in front of a set of thickly carpeted stairs leading to a landing with a door off it, before the stairs continued up. The walls were not merely whitewashed, as they were in the west attics, but painted a pretty primrose yellow.

The landing door opened into a furnished room. Picking her way carefully to the shuttered windows across a carpet thick with dust, fingers shaking, she opened the catch and threw them wide to reveal what was unmistakably a day nursery, lavishly furnished. The furnishings had not been covered. Save for the dust, the room had been left as if the owner had simply stepped outside, and would return at any moment. A nursing chair sat ready at the empty grate, a patchwork blanket folded neatly over the back of it. Beside it was a wooden cradle made up with linen which the moths had made a meal of. A baby carriage had been similarly made up with linen. An ivory teething rattle replete with silver bells sat exactly in the centre of the pillow. A beautiful carved wooden rocking horse occupied one corner. There was a child's wooden high chair beside the table in the centre of the room, and a set of child's china set out on the table itself. It was perfect and pathetic. A thwarted dream frozen in time, a fossil set in amber.

Aidan was standing in the doorway, his own deep sadness at this tragic tableau writ large on his face. His own lost dream was reflected here too. For the first time Estelle felt she was truly beginning to comprehend what he had endured, the enormity of what he had lost, and why he found it so difficult to forget. In the face of this shrine, she felt naïve and selfish.

Chastened, she made her way to the top of the stairs to the night nursery, leaving Aidan to his own thoughts. A day bed was made up beside the child's cot. There were stacks of linen in the closet, all moth-eaten. Tiny nightgowns, exquisitely embroidered in white but now mottled with mildew, were folded beside a heap of hats and mittens. Tears streamed down her cheeks as she imagined the hope and tender love that had gone into making this layette.

She closed over the shutters and returned to the day nursery. Aidan had gone back down the stairs. Looking around with fresh eyes, it struck her as extremely odd that Aoife had chosen the attic as a nursery, when there were any number of rooms which would have served the purpose much better, rooms which she had already marked out for her own nursery that could accommodate a nanny's bedchamber and sitting room. It wasn't usual for a nanny to sleep in the night nursery alongside her charge, was it? Why choose such a cramped place? And such a remote one. If she had been Aoife, expecting her first child, and such a desperately longed-for child too, she wouldn't have wanted to let it out of her sight, let alone have it sleep a ten-minute walk away from the master bedchamber, in an attic. But there was no doubting the love that had gone into furnishing this little suite. It was heartbreaking to think it had never been used, and now never would be.

But Aidan had said there had never been a child. She set the rocking horse going. It was not unusual for a mother to furnish the nursery in eager anticipation of their child's imminent arrival. What sort of person furnished a nursery for a child that had never existed?

Aidan locked the attic door carefully behind them. 'We'll talk in the library.'

Rain teemed down, battering the leaded panes of the normally cosy room. It was unseasonably cold. Seeing her shiver, he stooped to put a light to the kindling in the grate. Estelle sat on one of the wingback chairs by the fireside, clasping her hands together to stop them from trembling. He stood at the window, leaning his cheek against the panes.

'Obsession,' he said, breaking the tense silence. 'Do you remember, I told you that I understood it.'

'Wanting something to the exclusion of all else, regardless of the consequences.'

'Do you understand now, Estelle?'

She nodded, holding her hand out to him. 'After what I've just seen, I'm beginning to. What made you decide to show me that place now, Aidan?'

He crossed the room to join her, pressing her hand before taking the seat opposite. 'When I first met you, one of the things that drew me to you was that I could read you like a book.'

'So much for my carefully cultivated air of mystery.'

He shook his head impatiently. 'Don't, not now.'

'I'm so sorry, I'm...'

'Nervous. I know.' He smiled at her wanly. 'But there are too many occasions now when I've no idea what you're thinking. It's my fault, I know that. You feel I've shut you out and made it difficult for you to ask.'

'It sounds to me as if you can still read me perfectly.'

'I've had a lot of practice at reading between the lines. Unfortunately, I've also become expert at keeping my thoughts to myself.'

There was a world of suffering contained in those two understated sentences. She yearned to comfort him, but his hands were gripped so tightly on the arms of the chair that his knuckles gleamed white. She daren't risk oversetting him, so she remained silently in her seat.

'I should have shown you that place earlier, but I couldn't bring myself to face it. It's like a mausoleum. The last resting place of dead hopes and dreams.'

'It must have been very difficult for you to

open the door at all. They were your hopes and dreams too.'

'No.' Aidan uncurled his fingers, stretching his legs out in front of him. 'That place was not of my making. I didn't show you it before, out of loyalty to my—to Aoife. It's too private. It meant so much to her, what people thought of her, but anyone can see, looking at that place, that it's the work of a deeply troubled mind.'

'It's certainly not a place for a child,' Estelle said carefully. 'Not a real child.'

'I knew you'd see that. You're right. There was never a child to occupy that nursery, not even the possibility of one. I knew it. She knew it, but she wouldn't accept it. I found out today that she told Finn she was expecting, a few weeks before she died. I can only assume she also told Mrs Aherne too. I really have wronged that woman.'

'You made it up to her by providing her with a glowing reference and a very generous pension when she left.'

'And for releasing her from her bondage by marrying you, which I'm pretty certain is how she came to view her time here, after—after. Perhaps even before. This wasn't a happy home for a long time, Estelle. When Aoife and I married we were both set on having a big family. After a while, with no sign of a baby, she resorted to prayer, then quack remedies, any number of well-meaning natural healers and a good few charlatans who prey on desperate souls like her. I didn't interfere, for on the whole it gave her comfort and did her no harm—save that it did, for it offered her false hope.'

'What about seeking help from a doctor or a midwife?'

'Oh, we had both come along and ask all sorts of intimate questions.' His cheeks stained with colour. 'The only practical advice they gave us was to keep trying and not to give up hope.'

'And she didn't,' Estelle said softly. 'The evidence is there, in the attics.'

'That was later, not more than a year before she died, when we couldn't keep up the pretence between us any more.' Aidan gazed into the fire. 'Sometimes, she gave in to her frustration. She'd shout, or throw things at the wall. I could deal with that, she always calmed down quickly enough, but I couldn't stand it when she cried. That was the worst. She didn't sob, she never made a sound, but suddenly, right in the middle of dinner or a conversation, the tears would start, and she couldn't stop them. I'd have done anything then, if I could have.' He shuddered. 'The worst thing was that she'd say she was sorry afterwards. She knew she was making me unhappy, but she couldn't see a solution beyond the one thing we couldn't have. In the last months, her moods became more and more erratic, and it frightened her, I think. She made me keep the likes of Clodagh and some of her closer friends away. If you'd seen her then, you'd have thought she was ill.'

'Couldn't you persuade her to see a doctor?'

'There was nothing a doctor could do, save dose her up with laudanum, and that was no solution. There was only one solution, and it was the one we couldn't have. It was a vicious circle.'

'Oh, Aidan.'

'Don't pity me. I can't bear it and I don't deserve it. She was my wife, it was up to me to take care of her.'

'You did.' Stoically enduring what sounded to Estelle exactly how he had described it, a living hell. 'You did all you could and more.'

But once again, he shook his head. 'Latterly, she took to fleeing to the island at night.'

'The island?'

'She called it her sanctuary.'

Estelle's hand flew to her mouth. 'She drowned trying to reach it?'

'That's the story we put about. We tried to pass it off as an accident, but there were too many things that didn't add up. It was a perfectly calm night, and the boat was still upright when it was found.'

'She could have fallen. Reaching for an oar perhaps.'

'The oars were in the boat. We found stones in her pocket.'

Estelle shivered. 'Oh, God Aidan, please don't tell me it was you that found her?'

'No, Hera her faithful hound did, at daybreak. Her barking attracted a few people before I was summoned. Some of them must have talked. There were whispers. No one could understand why would someone so young and so happy, with everything to live for, would take her own life.'

'But you knew why.'

'Oh, I know exactly why.'

Aidan was clutching at the arms of the chair again, his head bowed, taking deep breaths. She couldn't decide whether this confession was cathartic or destructive. He didn't want her to comfort him. All she could do was wait. *It wasn't your fault*. She daren't utter the words. Poor Aoife. And poor, poor Aidan. He'd tried so hard to do what his wife wanted, to bear the burden of their problems himself. A terrible pity welled up inside her for the desperate woman, but it was tinged with anger. Aoife had not given up hope, and so Aidan could not be allowed to. 'I take it that the question of adopting never arose between you?'

Aidan looked up, rolling his shoulders. 'To be honest, it never even occurred to me. It's not exactly common practice, but I'm pretty sure it would have been a pointless suggestion. Adopting someone else's child would have been admitting defeat for her. She wanted her own baby, her own flesh and blood.'

'But if it was clear she couldn't have what she wanted…'

'You mustn't blame her, Estelle. She wasn't being rational, it was more like a kind of primitive urge. The nursery, that was an offering. She thought that if she—oh, I don't know, if she demonstrated that she was ready, then fortune would smile on her.'

'But it didn't?'

'By that time, it would have required more than dame fortune's intervention,' he said heavily. 'When I first discovered what she was doing in the attics—not that she made any attempt to hide it from me—I knew in my heart it was wrong, but I couldn't bring myself to do anything about it. Perhaps I should have.'

'You're being very hard on yourself, Aidan. She was a grown woman, and capable of fooling almost everyone into thinking that she was perfectly happy. You can't take responsibility for her every decision and action.'

'I knew she was overwrought, not thinking straight.'

'Under the circumstances, I don't think you can have been expected to be clear-headed either. I take it you didn't unburden yourself to anyone? Finn?'

'I couldn't. It would have felt like a betrayal. She was so ashamed of being childless. She couldn't bring herself to admit it to anyone.'

'Which is why she blamed you?'

He flinched, jumping to his feet and making for the window again. 'She had just cause.'

She didn't, Estelle wanted to shout. Why did he persist in the belief that it was his fault?

'It's time that travesty of a nursery was dismantled. You're my wife now and this is your home. We can't have a shrine to my previous marriage locked away in the attics. It's time for it to be consigned to the past along with everything it represents. I want you to be happy, Estelle, I want us to be happy.'

She joined him at the window. 'I'm not altogether unhappy.'

'You're not yourself. I don't want you looking at me as if I'm a pot about to boil over. I don't want you having to think about what you are about to say before you say it.'

'How do you know I do that?'

'You catch the corner of your bottom lip between your teeth, like you're biting back your words, when you're debating a tricky issue. At breakfast time, you turn your cup around and around in its saucer when you're trying *not* to say something.'

'I had no idea I was so transparent.'

'There's no sides to you, my father would have said. He'd have liked you.' He slipped his arm around her waist, edging her closer. 'I know we can't live in our little glass dome for ever, but these last few weeks, it's felt like one of us has been trapped inside it while the other has been stuck outside. I've missed you.'

'I've missed you too.' She turned in his arms, leaning her head against his shoulder. 'And I've missed this.'

'You have no idea how much I've missed this.'

She closed her eyes, burrowing closer. 'When we're like this, nothing can come between us.'

'It was because you didn't want intimacy to come between us that we agreed we'd banish it.'

'I know.' She lifted her head to meet his eyes, smoothing his tousled hair back from his brow. 'But I'm pretty certain I was wrong. I thought that making love would turn us into my parents, tearing each other's clothes off one minute, then tearing each other's eyes out the next. No, don't laugh, you know exactly what I mean.'

'I do. What has made you think differently?'

'You.' Wrapped in his arms, smiling into his eyes, the world felt as if it had been righted. She *knew* that they were meant to be together. She knew now what it was she was feeling. 'You made me look at my parents in a very different light, for a start. They couldn't possibly have loved each other. Loving someone means being kind and gentle. They were never kind. And they never *cared* about hurting each other. While you and I, we can't bear to hurt each other.'

'I have hurt you, though.'

'Mainly due to an understandable but misguided desire to protect me. You've taken a huge step today, in trying to put that right. I know how difficult that was for you, it was painful enough to listen to. Thank you, Aidan.'

'I want to make *us* right.'

She laughed. 'Not only does that sound like something I'd say, it's almost exactly what I was thinking.'

'I mean it.'

'I know you do.' She was almost giddy with the emotional turmoil of the last hour. Aidan had finally managed to put their marriage first. There was an *us*. It seemed imperative to her that they prove it. Right now. 'Has it occurred to you that the reason we can't resist one another is because we're not meant to?'

'That's a very interesting way of looking at it.'

'I'm serious, Aidan. I think the time has come to stop resisting and try submitting.'

He smiled, the slow, sensuous smile that made her insides melt, a smile she hadn't seen in weeks. 'You've no idea the image that has conjured up.'

She smiled back, the wicked smile she knew had the same effect on him. 'I don't, but I'd like to find out.'

Aidan gazed at his wife in awe, teetering on the brink of something that felt extraordinarily like it might be happiness. 'You are irresistible.'

She laughed, the breathy laugh that made his stomach clench. 'You've been doing a remarkable job of resisting so far.'

'Ah, but for how much longer?' He slid his hands down to cup her bottom, pulling her up against him. He was already hard.

She blushed, but then she wriggled, and when he groaned she wriggled again.

'Temptress,' he whispered into her ear, nipping her lobe.

She slid her hands under the skirts of his coat, mirroring his hold on her, curling her fingers into his behind. 'I warn you, I'm at the limit of my knowledge. You're going to have to tell me what to do next.'

'I don't think you need any instructions,' he said, and he was right, for she was already lifting her face to accept his kiss. Their kiss. She kissed him back just as fervently, just as passionately, just as deeply, as he kissed her. Her tongue darted into his mouth and his shaft throbbed.

If they hadn't left it so long, he thought hazily, if they hadn't denied themselves, they wouldn't be so inflamed. But all that simmering anticipation, all that frustration, had led to an inferno. He should stop. But when she sucked his bottom lip like that, he couldn't stop. He really should stop, but she was making that little panting sound that meant she wanted him to touch her nipples, and he absolutely had to touch her nipples.

They were in the library. Someone could come in. No one would come in. He had lost his coat. Her hair had come undone. He'd unfastened her gown, just enough to be able to kiss the tops of her delicious, delightful breasts, but not enough. He kissed her, she kissed him, and they sank on to the hearth rug. The hearth rug! But it meant he could unfasten her gown, and she was wriggling free of it, and her corset was easy enough to unfasten and dear heavens, how could he resist taking her nipple into his mouth when she was almost begging him to, and how could he resist sliding his fingers inside her when it made her gasp like that, when she tightened around him like that, and she was so hot and so wet and when she pulled his face down, her tongue pushing into his mouth as he touched her, and she came with such abandon, with such overt delight, he could die of pleasure himself, just watching her. Though he wanted to do more than observe her abandon. Now really was the time to stop.

'What now, Aidan?'

Estelle, her hair falling over her breasts, her gown twisted half off and half on, rolled towards him, flattening her hand over his chest. He didn't even remember losing his shirt.

'Are you not satisfied, you wanton woman?' he teased.

She laughed. She kissed him. 'I am, but you're not.'

'Estelle…'

'I want to, Aidan. It's not fair.'

He laughed. 'It's not about fair.'

'Tell me what to do. I want to do to you what you just did to me.'

He tried, he really tried, to resist her entreaties, but somehow he had placed her hand over his erection. He still had his trousers on. So technically…

'You still have your trousers on.'

'Estelle, you're pushing me to the brink.'

'You have made me tumble over the brink. Three times now, to be precise. You're not breaking your promise, Aidan, I've already released you from that. Don't you want to?'

'I think it's very clear that I do want to.' He had unbuttoned his trousers. She slid her hand inside. He groaned. 'Estelle, that is so…'

'What should I do now?'

'Nothing.' He covered her hand, curling her fingers around him. He must not come. Not yet.

'Aidan?' He opened his eyes to find her gazing at him, that smile on her lips, her eyes glowing. 'You look nothing like the statues in Florence, in fact you put them utterly in the shade.'

He laughed, a low growl. Her fingers tightened around him and he groaned. Then she kissed him, and he rolled her on to her back, covering her, and she parted her legs so that he was between them, and he was aching to be inside her, pressing against the hot, soft flesh of her inner thigh. He summoned the last of his resolve. 'Not this. We can't.'

'Yes, we can. Would it be so wrong?' She wriggled under him. 'We're married, Aidan.'

'We're married, Aidan. This is why we married. What is wrong with you?'

The memory Estelle had unintentionally evoked had an instantaneous effect. He felt himself falter, physically diminish, emotionally shrivel. He rolled off her, mortified.

'Did I do something wrong?' Estelle was still smiling. 'I did warn you you'd have to coach me.'

He pulled on his clothes quickly, but not

quickly enough to cover the evidence of his shame. Estelle's smile faded. 'Aidan, what's the matter?'

'Do you know why I could be so certain she wasn't pregnant? Because I hadn't been near her in months. And do you know why I stopped trying? Because I couldn't perform my duty as a husband. Because each time I tried, this was the outcome. So I think it would be best if we resumed our policy of resisting, don't you? That way neither of us will be disappointed.'

He knew he was being unfair. He knew he was being cruel. None of this was her fault. But at this precise moment, all he wanted was to get out of the room and as far away from Estelle, and the source of his shame, as possible.

Chapter Eleven

Estelle stared in disbelief at the closed door of the library which Aidan had just stormed through, trying to make sense of what had just happened. One minute they had been kissing passionately, he had been fully aroused, they had been about to make love, and then the next minute—what had changed?

Shivering, she tried to wriggle back into her dress only to realise when she had that it was back to front. Tears splashed on to her hot cheeks as she stood up to try to right it and caught sight of her corsets wrapped around the leg of the table. Where were her shoes? Her hair had come undone. Where were the pins? What the hell would she say if one of the servants came in and caught her in this state? The challenge of putting her corsets back on defeated her.

She managed to put her dress back on the right way, but the effort drained her of energy. She slumped on to one of the fireside chairs, staring at the spot on the hearth rug where she and Aidan had almost made love.

What had gone wrong? What had she done? Or not done? Had she hurt him?

I hadn't been near her in months.

I stopped trying.

I couldn't perform my duty as a husband.

Each time I tried, this was the outcome.

Whatever had happened, had happened before, so it couldn't be her fault. If only it had been. Aidan's face had been a mask of abject shame and horror.

Aidan couldn't make love. Why couldn't he make love? It seemed to her, until the very last moment, that he had been very ready to make love, but what did she know of such matters? Until she met Aidan she hadn't even been interested in making love. She'd thought she would never want to make love. She'd resigned herself to the fact that it was necessary in order to have a baby, but she'd never imagined it would be a pleasure. Then she met Aidan, and from the first kiss they'd shared, all those months ago in the *piazza* in Florence, making love with him is what she had wanted to do, even though she hadn't actually admitted as much to herself. And the reason she wanted to make love with him now, which she might as well own up to, was because she had fallen in love with him.

Her hand went to her heart. She was in love with her husband! It shouldn't be such a shock. From the moment they'd met she had been drawn to him in a way she'd never been drawn to any man. She liked him. They were friends. The more she came to know him, the more she cared, and the more remote and unhappy he became, the more she ached to make him better. She loved him, it had simply taken her a very, very long time to put what she felt into words. She was in love with her husband. And her husband was…

Her mind skidded to a halt. She didn't have a word for what Aidan was suffering from, and even if there was a word, she didn't want to apply it to Aidan.

Each time I tried, this was the outcome.

Aidan hadn't been able to make love to his first wife. Slowly, her dazed and shocked mind began to sift through the implications of this, and her blood ran cold. From the very first, he had insisted that the childless state of his first

marriage was his fault. He had failed, she dis-
tinctly recalled him saying that, because she'd
been quite indignant about it. It took two to
make a child, she'd thought. But Aoife blamed
Aidan. And Aidan blamed himself.

She tried to recall exactly what he'd said.
They hadn't been blessed at first, she was sure
he'd said that, and the medical people had told
them to keep trying, which meant they had been
able to try. No, she didn't want to think about
that. She didn't want to think of Aidan making
love with anyone save herself.

Or not making love.

She covered her ears, for it truly felt as if
the jumble of emotions might explode from her
head. She was far too overwrought to make any
sense of it at the moment. She loved Aidan. That
was what mattered, and that was what she must
cling to. She loved Aidan, and Aidan had fled
from her, mortified, unnerved and unmanned.
She half got to her feet, then sank back down
again. Best to leave him alone to recover. She'd
see him at dinner. After today, and those tragic
revelations he'd made of his own accord, there
was no longer an invisible barrier between them.
He wouldn't retreat from her again, she was sure
of it.

He had run away just now, admittedly, but that was different.

I want to make us right.

And she so wanted there to be an *us*. She loved him so much, and she was almost certain he loved her too. Surely that was all that mattered. If they had each other, they could overcome anything.

Two weeks later

Aidan sat on the grass verge on the edge of the lake, his hand cradling the rusty iron mooring ring. Three years ago today he had made his last journey out to the island, on a day not unlike today, with sullen skies and a gusty breeze. Aoife's family hadn't wanted her remains returned to them. They hadn't sent a single representative to the funeral, for fear that the shame would contaminate them by association. The local vicar had been deeply embarrassed, but word had come down from well above him in the hierarchy. Given the circumstances, the church wouldn't accept her being interred in hallowed ground. He was immensely touched when the poor man defied his superiors to preside over the ceremony.

When Aidan had first suggested the island

as her final resting place, Finn had been horrified, not at the idea but by the difficulties it presented in terms of practicalities. Desperate for any form of distraction, he had thrown himself into the task of designing a barge to transport her on her final journey. There had been far fewer mourners than she deserved. Finn had ferried them across in three trips on the little yacht his father had used to teach him and Clodagh to sail. He had followed the barge across in *her* little rowing boat. They could hear Hera howling plaintively from the shoreline all the way through the service. He'd had the barge broken up for firewood afterwards.

'Just do it! Put us both out of our misery.'

The heavens opened, soaking him through in an instant, but Aidan didn't move. She'd been dead three years. He had to work hard to remember her face, yet he could recall every single word of that fraught last conversation, could pinpoint every single stage of it where he might have said something different or said nothing at all. He hoped that her suffering was at an end. He hoped that all the words the vicar had said that day about her finding peace were true, but unless she'd been handed a babe in arms in the afterlife, he doubted it.

Her death had given him no solace, no sense of peace, merely catapulting him into a different corner of hell. How many times since he'd met Estelle had he tried to escape that wretched state of mind? How often had he fooled himself into believing it was possible? But each fresh start had been destroyed almost before it started. His guilt was a living, growing entity, forcing him to look back and back and back over his shoulder. He didn't give a damn that it was destroying him, but he couldn't bear to see what he was doing to Estelle as a consequence.

What would have become of them, he and Aoife, if things had been different? If she had accepted they couldn't have a child, would they have been able to fashion an alternative life together here at Cashel Duairc? Would they have drifted apart and eventually separated? Would his inability to be a proper husband have merited an annulment? The very thought of what they'd have had to endure in order to prove that made his face burn, but if she'd thought that it would give her the freedom to find another husband, a potent husband, he didn't doubt that Aoife would have put them through it.

With an exclamation of disgust, Aidan got to his feet. Rain streamed down his face, but there was no point in going back for a greatcoat now, he was already soaked through. Digging his hands into his pockets, hunching his shoulders, he set off in the direction of the river, with the vague intent of trying to revive his interest in the new bridge which was intended to span it.

He stared at the plan for hours on end every day, but he made no progress with it. Some days, the time went by in the blink of an eye, and he'd find he'd done nothing *but* stare at the drawings or at the account books. On those days it was all he could do to sit opposite Estelle at dinner, to pretend to eat something, then to fall on to his pillow exhausted, falling into an abyss of unconsciousness that wasn't sleep, waking just as exhausted the next morning. Other days, it seemed to take a year to get from morning until night, and then another year to get from nightfall to the next morning. Today was one of those. All he wanted was for it to be over.

Three years. Could today finally be the day he drew a lasting line under it all, and would tomorrow finally be the fresh start he craved? The first day of the rest of his life with Estelle. Why was it so damned difficult to make something happen when it was what he wanted more than anything in the world!

He loved her. It had crept up on him, the love he felt for his wife, growing with every passing day, so imperceptibly that he'd scarcely noticed until the day he decided to show her the contents of the east attics. They were all gone now, and the hope that had flared that day, that he and Estelle would find happiness, was gone too after his spectacular failure, though his love, contrarily, still continued to grow. Estelle was a part of him, bedded deep inside of him, entwined around his heart. He'd do anything to keep her there. Anything to be able to tell her, and to hear the words repeated back, for he knew that she loved him, just as much as he loved her. But the words remained unsaid, and he was beginning to wonder if they ever would be spoken aloud. Love was supposed to conquer all. It was no match for deep-seated guilt.

Looking back on those golden days in Florence, Aidan couldn't believe he'd been so naïve. His desire for Estelle had been so utterly different from anything he'd ever felt for his first wife, it hadn't occurred to him that his body would fail him. It hadn't failed him, not once, when he was intent only on her pleasure, on satisfying himself by satisfying her. But when they had been on the brink of making love he had failed dismally. Even now, weeks later, the memory was excruciating, all the more so because this time, he'd failed even though he wanted, desperately wanted to succeed.

Since then Estelle, his lovely, brave Estelle, had tried to talk to him about it numerous times, had begged him to explain, then had begged him to forget it and to try again. And each time, he'd simply refused. Refused to discuss. Refused to act. They had agreed to a platonic marriage for her sake. He wished to hell that they'd kept to it for his.

Which left him where? At a crossroads. The end of the road, or a new direction? Could he try again? He was terrified of failing, but if he didn't try, what would be left of their marriage? Living without Estelle was an even more terrifying prospect. Tomorrow, he'd think of a way of making a real fresh start.

It wasn't until a tear splashed on to the keyboard of the harpsichord that Estelle realised she was crying. She closed the lid, wiping her eyes with the back of her hand. Everything she played sounded like a dirge, for the spark had gone from her music as well as her spirit. Phoebe's latest letter lay on the desk. Eloise was making a rare trip to London in December. Phoebe thought it would be a wonderful surprise if Estelle and Aidan joined them. She longed to see her sisters, but at the same time, she dreaded the very idea, for they would take one look at her and know she was unhappy.

Besides, Aidan wouldn't go. He could barely bring himself to dine with their closest neighbours, and had cancelled most of the other invitations they had received and originally accepted. She had no idea what excuse he'd given, but the spate of callers following their wedding party had died to a trickle. He was becoming a recluse, and perforce so was she.

She picked up her pen and dipped it in the inkwell, but after writing *My Dearest Phoebe* she was at a loss. Even if her twin was sitting opposite her in this room right now, she couldn't begin to imagine confiding in her. What would she say? *I'm in love with my husband, I think my husband might be in love with me, but he can't make love to me?* She didn't really care about whether or not Aidan could make love—well, only a little bit—but Aidan cared. If only she hadn't begged him to, then they wouldn't be in this mess. It was her own fault. If they had stuck to the original agreement to keep their marriage platonic, then everything would be fine. At this very moment, they might be discussing how and when to make a start on establishing their family.

She knew that wasn't true. The real issue wasn't that Aidan had been unmanned, the question was why? He believed he had deprived Aoife of what she wanted most in the world. It was a short step from there to believing that he was responsible for her death. The sinking feeling in the pit of her stomach told Estelle that she was edging closer to the truth. Such an extreme step as Aoife had taken could only have been contemplated in the depths of despair. When all hope was lost, as it must have been, if Aidan could not...

She was crying again. Her heart was wrenched with pity, and a desperate desire to find some way to make him see that he was wrong, that the final act had been Aoife's decision alone. *It wasn't his fault.* He had done everything he could to give Aoife what she wanted, but what she wanted was impossible. Why hadn't he been able to see that? Why couldn't Aidan understand that you simply couldn't make the impossible possible, no matter how much you wanted to.

She understood that. Though their parents

had been washed up and were buried together, Diarmuid's body had never been found. That had been one of the most difficult things any of them had had to come to terms with. There had been times, in the first months with Aunt Kate, when she and Phoebe had returned to their fantasy that he was living on a desert island somewhere. They convinced themselves that though they might never see him again, he was alive. Other times, they played the *if only* game. *If only* Papa had chosen a school in Ireland. *If only* Diarmuid had been ill and unable to travel. *If only* the ship had sailed later or earlier. *If only* their brother had learnt to swim. *If only* they had made more of their goodbyes.

If only Aidan would accept that it was Aoife and Aoife alone who took her own life. *If only* Estelle could make him see how happy they could be together without ever making love.

The ink had dried on her pen. She set it down. The only person she wanted to discuss her troubles with was the only person who could help resolve them.

'May I come in?'
'Yes, of course.'
Estelle, seated at her desk, turned away from

him, and Aidan saw her surreptitiously wiping her eyes. She'd been crying again. He pretended not to notice because that was clearly what she wanted him to do, hovering in the doorway until she turned round sporting that rigid smile he had come to dread. 'What was it you wanted?'

'I thought we might take lunch together, for a change.'

It was a simple request, or should have been, but nothing between them was simple these days and he deserved that guarded look she was giving him, as if his request for lunch masked a darker purpose. 'I thought you preferred to get something sent over from the kitchens to the estate office.'

'I thought it would be nice to eat together, like we used to.'

'And talk?'

'Of course we'll talk,' Aidan said, as if they always talked, as if dinner hadn't become an ordeal, akin to a meal taken under the auspices of a silent order of monks. 'We can talk about old times, meals we've shared.'

Estelle's expression had lightened, but it darkened again at this. 'I no longer have the healthy appetite I used to have for lunch.'

Or dinner, Aidan thought heavily. She was

very good at rearranging the food on her plate to look as if she'd eaten, but he was sadly vastly experienced in spotting such a tactic. He was squeezing the life out of her, quite literally. They couldn't go on like this. 'Please, come and have lunch with me. I've taken the liberty of organising it.' He held out his hand. 'I want us to sit down together and try to be ourselves again. Do you think we could try to do that?'

'Oh, Aidan.' She hurried over to him. 'We shouldn't have to try, should we?'

He ushered her out of the room, deciding not to reply to this because the honest answer was too depressing. In the hallway, he picked up her cloak from the chair where he had placed it, and her brows lifted in surprise.

'I know the castle can be draughty but I'm not at the stage of needing a cloak indoors.'

'We're not eating indoors.'

Where are we going?'

'Wait and see.'

Outside, the rain had stopped, leaving the sky a pearly grey. Estelle took his arm as he led the way past the kitchen gardens, and though she was still holding her smile in place, he was aware of her studying him from under her lashes, aware of her trying to understand his mood, and to align her own. It sickened him that she had to do this, that this was what they had come to, so polite and careful when they should be carefree, both of them afraid to speak their thoughts.

Tell her, tell her, tell her, was the rhythmic chant that accompanied him everywhere these days. It was never silent. All he could to was drown it out by speaking over it, but when the words threatened to spill out, when Estelle looked at him with that particular mixture of hurt and yearning, he had no option but to rush from the room.

Tell her.

It was there now, an insistent demand to be heard. He had tried to pacify the voice in his head by revealing some of the truth, then with more of the truth and then the bulk of it. It still wasn't enough, and his body had punished him for not recognising that fact.

He couldn't tell her. Not yet. He had one last throw of the dice left and this was it. Recapture what they had. Bring those memories to the forefront of his mind, let them displace the other ones. Estelle was all he wanted. Estelle, for herself alone, not as the mother to their adopted family, but as his wife. She was everything to him. He had to cling on to that, and somehow make things right between them.

Opening the main door of the succession houses, he led her through to the fern house, where the air was sweet with the smell of warmed peat, and the earthy, slightly sickly scent of the ferns themselves. The wrought-iron table had been set up in the warmest corner as he'd specified, the matching chairs padded with cushions, the table set without a cloth, using the plainest crockery and silverware. Two glasses sat next to a jug of wine. Their food was set out on a separate table with heated dishes.

He was nervous. Desperately nervous. 'Well, what do you think?'

'Our own private *osteria*,' Estelle said softly.

'Under glass, as I'm sure you have noted. I'm sorry I didn't have time to have it redesigned into a dome.'

Tears sparkled on her lashes. 'This is lovely, Aidan.'

'It wasn't meant to make you cry.'

'I'm not.'

'Of course you're not.' He wiped her tears away gently with his fingertips. Her breath caught when he touched her. He wanted to kiss her. He could see in her eyes that she wanted him to kiss her. But he hesitated, and the moment was gone, so instead he pulled out her chair with a flourish. 'Would the *signora* care to be seated?'

'She would. *Grazie.* And how are you today?'

Delighted to see her enter into the spirit of his homage, Aidan adopted a suitably lugubrious expression. 'God has spared me for another day, but you have brought the sunshine into our impromptu dining room this afternoon,' he said, flicking a cloth over the table, before pouring the wine.

If Estelle's laugh was forced, it was still a laugh. 'Signor Giordano! I remember him.'

"I'm sure he remembers you to this day too. I'm afraid that Cook struggled to source some of the ingredients, but I am hoping that she's been able to bring a little taste of Tuscany to County Kildare.'

'Pinzimonio,' Estelle said, when he set down a plate of raw vegetables. 'Irish style, I see. And with an anchovy dressing, if I'm not mistaken.' She lifted her glass, chinking it with his. *'Saluti.'*

She didn't tuck in with her usual gusto, but then she had not done so for weeks. She did eat though, and he forced himself to do the same, knowing her eyes were on him. They talked of that first lunch in Florence, and by the time he brought Cook's version of *affettati misti* to the table, they had both begun to relax a little.'

'Blood sausage, ham and piccalilli,' Estelle said, with a nod of approval. 'Cook has been extremely inventive. Do you remember...?'

Day by day, they conjured up the hours they had spent together under the benign Florentine skies. What was the best lunch? Which café served the best coffee, the best ice? What was their favourite walk, their favourite church?

'I sincerely hope it's not tripe,' Estelle said as he removed the cover from the heated dish. 'No, that smells far too good.'

'Pappardelle sulla lepre,' Aidan said, 'though it's rabbit and not hare. You gave Cook the recipe along with several others some time back.'

'I'd forgotten. This pasta is delicious.'

They continued to talk, though there were moments of silence now, when they gazed at each other and when they smiled, and the tense, awkward silences that had become commonplace between them were banished. When the rabbit was finished and he'd put the plates on the side table, she leaned her chin on one hand,

and he covered her other hand with his, just as they used to do.

'Thank you, Aidan,' she said. 'That was wonderful.'

'I'm afraid there's no ice to finish, but we could take a turn around the fernery and pretend it's the Parco delle Cascine—or a scale model of it.'

She let him help her to her feet, and she tucked her arm in his. 'The fernery was your grandfather's idea, did you know that? I found a notebook of his in the attics full of all sorts of complicated architectural drawings for heating and irrigation pipes. It looks as if your engineering bent extends at least a generation further back than your father.'

'It seems to have deserted me of late. I can't even come up with a decent design for a modest bridge.'

'Build a new Ponte Vecchio. Or forget all about the bridge, and build us a dome.'

'I wish we'd never left Florence.'

Estelle came to an abrupt halt, her smile faltering. 'Don't say that. We left Florence to build a future for ourselves here, together. We'll always have our memories of our time in Florence, and this has been a lovely reminder of how happy we can be, but wallowing in our shared past isn't going to make everything right between us in the here and now.'

'I'll never forget Florence.'

'You say that as if it's all we have, Aidan.'

'I didn't mean it that way.'

But he'd sounded horribly as if he had meant it exactly that way, as if there was no hope for them. She wouldn't accept that. 'It's not about forgetting Florence, it's about forgetting what happened to make you run there,' Estelle said, 'and why you're still not able to consign it to the past, after all this time. I know you feel guilty, I know you think that it was all your fault.'

'Please!' He pulled her into his arms. 'Can't you see, I don't want to talk about it.'

'Then why did you bring me here?'

'I don't want to lose you.'

'Aidan!' She put her arms around his neck. 'Don't say that. It's surely not come to that.'

'I don't want it to. You do know that, don't you?'

He sounded so desperate. She tried not to panic. 'I'm not going anywhere,' she said, smoothing her hand over his cheek, pressing closer against him.

'I can't bear to contemplate it.'

'Then don't.'

The anguish in his voice terrified her, but the need in him made her desperate to reassure him, and herself too. She pulled him towards her and their lips met, clinging without moving for an agonising moment, as if they were afraid to move, and then they did, and she forgot her fear because the taste of him and the touch of him and the way he groaned when their tongues touched had the same effect on her as it always had. She lost herself in kissing him, and he kissed her back wildly, urgently. Her hands smoothed and stroked, clutching at his shoulders and his back and his behind, and his hands were on her too, smoothing and stroking and cupping, and it felt so right and she had missed him so desperately.

Aidan wrenched himself free, his chest heaving. 'This isn't working.'

Estelle stared at him in confusion, for she'd felt the physical evidence that everything was working perfectly well pressing against her.

'It solves nothing, I can finally see that,' Aidan said, confusing her further.

'What solves nothing?'

He was staring at her as if she was a stranger. 'I'm so sorry.'

The tone of his voice made her blood freeze, for it was gentle, the kind of voice that a person used when they knew that what they were about to say was going to be hurtful. 'Please don't, Aidan. Whatever it is you're going to say...'

He covered her hands with his, but the gesture, far from reassuring her, sent a shiver down her spine, as if someone was walking over her grave. She snatched her hands away, steeling herself. 'What are you sorry for?'

'I brought you here thinking that if we could forget for a while, and remember what it was like in Florence then it might change things.' He covered his face with his hands. 'But it's impossible. I can't be the husband you deserve, Estelle. I am so very sorry.'

He dropped his hands. His eyes were bleak, so bleak that she wanted to look away.

'When I married you, I never expected we would make love. In fact I married you on condition that we wouldn't.'

'It's not about making love or not making love.'

'Then what *is* it about? Please, Aidan, don't

say you can't be my husband, you *are* my husband.'

'Estelle, I'd agree to almost anything when you look at me like that, but I know in my gut it would be wrong. I'm sorry, I simply can't do it. I'm not going to make the same mistake twice.'

'What on earth do you mean by that?' She took a stumbling step away from him. 'I'm not Aoife.'

'I don't mean you might kill yourself, I'm worried that I'm destroying you.'

'Aidan...'

But he shook his head violently. 'I thought I could put it all behind me, but I can't.'

'Aidan, I don't understand.'

He eyed her sadly. 'No, but you will. It doesn't matter how deep you bury the past, it's still there and always will be. The only solution is to confront it head-on. I love you too much to live a lie with you.'

Despite everything her heart leapt. 'Oh, Aidan, I love you too. I love you so much.' Aidan loved her. She loved him. Surely that was all that mattered. But one look at his face told her that she was wrong. This wasn't a beginning. It was an ending.

'Estelle, I love you as if you're part of me, but

ultimately it makes no difference. I shouldn't have married you.'

'Don't say that!'

Aidan paled, but his mouth remained set. 'We need to visit the island.'

'The island?'

'The past is buried there and so is the truth about what happened.'

No sooner were his words out than a crack of thunder sounded overhead, and rains started pounding down on the glass of the fernery. Cursing, Aidan pushed open one of the windows used for ventilation to reveal a sky iron grey with black clouds, the wind so strong that the window was nearly wrenched from his hand. By the time he'd wrestled it shut he was drenched, and the fernery was enveloped in gloom. 'There's no way we can go out in that. It's going to be a struggle to get back to the house. We can talk here.'

'No!' Whatever he had to say, she needed to prepare herself to hear. 'In the morning, when the storm has passed, we'll go to the island then.'

'Estelle, I won't change my mind. Putting it off until the morning will only prolong the agony for both of us.'

She knew that, she could see it in his face,

but she wasn't ready. It was too big a leap, from their Florentine lunch to this. 'In the morning,' she said stubbornly. 'Please, Aidan, let's wait until then.'

A flurry of rain rattled the windowpane, and a gust of wind found a gap in the casement, making the curtains billow. Shivering, Estelle curled up under the sheets, knowing that sleep would never come. How could it, when in a few short hours she'd finally discover the true reason for her husband's tortured and self-destructive behaviour.

Another strong gust of wind blew the window open. Jumping out of bed, she wrestled to close it over. A storm was brewing in more ways than one. A shaft of moonlight pierced the thick cloud casting a shadow on the lake, illuminating the ruined tower on the island. It looked stark, brooding, ominous, as befitting a place harbouring dark secrets.

Secrets which had already blighted their marriage. They had lived—no, barely existed—in the shadow of those secrets for far too long. Was it too late to salvage something from the wreckage?

She lay awake waiting for morning, staring

wide-eyed into the darkness. She wasted little effort speculating about what it was he was going to reveal to her. All she could think about were the consequences of him doing so.

I love you as if you're part of me, but ultimately it makes no difference.

I shouldn't have married you.

Aidan clearly believed their marriage was over. Every time she tried to imagine what that meant, her mind became a complete blank and her heart began to race. She loved Aidan. Aidan loved her. A proper kind of love, a caring kind of love, and a passionate kind too, which didn't rely on making love to express it. She loved him with all her heart and soul. Losing him would be like losing an essential part of herself. She couldn't lose him. But no matter how many times she said so over and over in her head, she couldn't convince herself.

She'd begged for tonight to prepare herself, but she would never be prepared to say goodbye. If he truly felt that he couldn't live with her, would she have the courage to leave? In just a few hours, she thought despairingly as the storm died down and the first fingers of grey dawn poked through the curtains, she would find out.

Chapter Twelve

Estelle glanced up at the heavens. There was barely a trace of last night's storm. It was one of those days where the weather was hedging its bets, yet to make up its mind whether to be fair or foul. White and grey clouds bled into one another making the sky look like a huge swathe of crumpled silk with rents torn in it where blue peeked through, though there was no trace of any sunshine. It was mild, and though last night's rain sparkled on the grass, the air had the crispness of autumn.

'Ready?' Aidan asked.

She nodded, though it was a lie, but though she'd happily never hear whatever was to come, she could see that Aidan wouldn't rest until he'd spoken. He led the way, taking the path that followed the lake to the far side, pulling aside a swathe of brambles to reveal a gate which she hadn't noticed before, standing aside to let her precede him. The boathouse sat low on the ground, projecting out on to the lake. It was a simple wooden building, the roof moss-covered from the overhanging trees.

Taking a large key from his pocket, Aidan set it in the lock. 'You haven't asked me why we're going to the island.'

'Aoife's buried there, isn't she?' Estelle answered, for that was one of the few things she guessed. 'Her sanctuary, you called it, and I assumed that the church wouldn't permit...'

'No, they wouldn't.' Aidan visibly braced himself as he turned the key and opened the lock. 'I've not been out there since the funeral, but Finn keeps the boats in order in the hope that one day I'll take a notion to sail again.'

Inside, there were two boats tied up, a small yacht and a rowing boat, both bobbing on the waters which lapped against the narrow platform which ran around the walls. Aidan made his way to the end of it, heaving the sliding door to one side, letting the daylight in, before jumping into the rowing boat with practised ease.

'Just step down carefully, I'll not let you fall,'

he said, holding out his hand. 'Don't worry, this isn't *her* boat. We scuttled that one.'

He really had done everything in his power to eliminate all trace of Aoife. What she'd taken previously for an extreme form of grief, Estelle now saw was something decidedly odder, not the actions of a man trying to forget, but of a man with something to hide. Her cloak got tangled around her ankles as she stepped into the boat, making it rock alarmingly, but Aidan was as good as his word, catching her around the waist, holding her until she and the boat were steady, then for just a fraction longer than necessary before letting her go.

She sat in the stern, her heart leaden, and Aidan took up the oars. There was scarcely a breeze. The waters of the lake lapped gently against the hull. Above them, the clouds parted to allow a weak sun to shine. He rowed steadily and efficiently and as far as she could tell, instinctively, for he made a direct line for the island without the need to check over his shoulder.

'There's an iron ring over on the little shore by the house,' Estelle said.

'We always tended to moor the little boat— this one, or its predecessors—there.'

Until Aoife drowned, he meant, after which

they were hidden away in the boathouse. Out of sight but not necessarily out of mind. 'The tower isn't actually unsafe then, I take it?'

'It was built to resemble a ruin.'

'So there was never any chance of my being injured by falling masonry.'

'It was the easiest way to stop you going anywhere near the place. I'm sorry for lying to you but at the time I thought I had no choice.'

'In the same way that you now think you have no choice but to tell me the truth now?'

His acknowledging smile was bittersweet. 'It is a perfect spot for a picnic, you were right about that—or at least it was once. My father used to take Clodagh and me out there in the summer months. We used to swim from the small beach where I'll land the boat in a minute.'

A lump rose in her throat, for this was exactly the sort of family outing she'd imagined them having. A family which would now never exist? Panicked, Estelle pushed this thought to one side. She had to save her marriage first, before she could even begin to think of introducing children to it. She had to save her marriage, not for the family they might have, but for the husband and wife they could become. If only. How she loathed those two words. So deceptively simple to say and yet so difficult to achieve.

As they approached the island she could see that the tower was indeed an artfully constructed ruin, the deliberately ramshackle wall neatly pointed, no trace of the wooden rafters that would have been needed to support a roof, if one had ever existed. The island itself was smaller than she'd imagined, oval-shaped and almost completely flat, with the tower on an ellipse nearest the castle. Aidan beached the boat on the little shore, pulling the oars in before helping her out.

'Are you sure you want to do this?' she asked, desperate for one last chance to avoid her fate.

'I have to,' he said. 'You were right all along. I can't pretend she never existed.'

The grave was in the lee of the tower, in a small dip in the ground, on the side of the lake facing the boathouse.

Aoife Isolde Malahide, née Kilpatrick
May she finally find peace here

Estelle studied the grave. She read the stone. Then she pressed his hand, and murmured that she'd leave him to his thoughts, and headed back down to the boat.

* * *

Alone, Aidan was grateful for her absence, though he'd needed her presence to give him the courage to make those last few steps. He stared at the gravestone he'd never seen, the inscription he'd agonised over but had never read, for he'd left it to Finn to make these final arrangements. The last time he'd been here, the grave was freshly dug, the earth had been heaped to one side, slowly turning to mud in the steady rain. If it weren't for the marker, it would be hard to spot her last resting place.

Had she finally found peace? Crouching down, he took the baby's teething toy from his pocket and set it down carefully beside the headstone. It was the one thing he'd kept when he'd had the sham nursery cleared. Made of ivory with silver bells, he'd found it on the pillow in the baby carriage, and kept it on impulse. He closed his eyes, and said a rare and fervent prayer for her, and for himself too. He didn't ask for forgiveness, it was too late for that, and it would make no difference anyway. Aoife was dead, and nothing could change that.

Aidan got to his feet. He couldn't change the past, but he could stop history repeating itself. He couldn't save himself, but he could save Estelle. She hurried towards him when she saw him approach, catching his hand, pressing it against her cheek, kissing his knuckles. She didn't tell him she loved him but he could see it in her eyes, and he had to fight with himself to refrain from pulling her into his arms one last time.

'We'll go round the other side of the tower,' he said. 'It's sheltered, and there's a stone bench built into the ruined bit of the wall.'

'Your grandfather thought of everything.' Estelle sat down. 'I feel horribly like a condemned prisoner exiled to an island prison.' She tried and failed to smile. 'Sorry, that was a terrible thing to say.'

'But accurate. I feel pretty much the same.' Aidan leaned against the wall, closing his eyes, struggling for calm. Over and over last night, he'd reviewed the logic of what he was about to do and reached the same conclusion. He no longer questioned the telling of his sorry tale, but he dreaded the consequences. Opening his eyes, he forced himself to meet Estelle's gaze. 'Nothing I've told you about my first marriage has been a lie, but I've not told you the whole truth.'

'I know you think you're responsible for Aoife's death, Aidan, but...'

'Estelle, I *am* responsible. I didn't push her over the side of the boat, but I may as well have. I killed her.'

She stared at him in utter disbelief. 'You don't mean that.'

His heart had been racing, but it began to slow now, and though he still dreaded what he must say, his dread was tempered with relief. This was the right thing to do. 'I've told you that my marriage had become a living hell. I still don't think I've managed to get across what it was like, to be locked in that particular purgatory together. It was all-consuming. The only escape would have been for us to have a child, and that was the one thing that there was no prospect of. And in the end, the very last thing I wanted.'

'But I thought you said that you married because you wanted a family.'

'Oh, I did. I was every bit as eager as she was to have children, and every bit as confident as she was that we would. We were both healthy, we were young, our married life was what it should be, the odds were on our side. But as time passed, nature stubbornly refused to comply. I did try, as I told you, to find out what we could do to improve our chances of success. There was little to be done save keep trying. And so we did.'

The recollection of those nights made him cringe inwardly. There had been some nights when his performance had relied on his imagination taking him far away from his wife and the marriage bed. It had become an act. But a successful act.

'Time passed,' he continued. 'She grew more frantic. I began to lose hope, and that made her furious. Having a child was the most natural thing in the world, which meant that not having one was unnatural, to her way of thinking. Since there was no reason why we couldn't have a baby, then we simply needed to persist. It was my duty to persist, I'd be failing her as a husband if I didn't.'

'Oh, Aidan!'

He shook his head to cut short Estelle's indignant protest. 'You couldn't fault her logic. She didn't want a husband, she wanted a father for her children, and to be brutally honest, that's why I married her, to be a mother to my children. I was failing her.'

'You don't know that.'

Aidan flinched. 'I didn't know it, not at first. Part of the problem was that there seemed to be no explanation. How can you admit defeat when you aren't sure you're beaten?' He sighed wearily. 'In truth though, I began to lose hope and I began to lose the will to persist.'

He stopped to swallow, taking a deep breath before he continued, unable to look Estelle in the eye. 'I no longer wanted a child, not with her. I no longer believed that a child would make her happy and I worried that there was every possibility we'd make any child miserable, for we were so miserable ourselves. But how the hell could I tell her that? I couldn't tell her what I felt, but nature intervened and took the decision out of my hands.'

Estelle got to her feet. He made a half-hearted attempt to fend her off, but when she persisted, putting her arms around his waist, burrowing her head into his shoulder, he allowed himself to take succour and strength from her embrace before gently disengaging and waving her back down on to the bench.

'You're still thinking I've no reason to feel so guilty, I can tell. Bear with me, for I've never even allowed myself to recount this last chapter. Just bear with me.' He closed his eyes, leaning his head back against the wall, and forced himself to remember.

* * *

'What are you frowning about?'

'This.' Aidan held out the bill. 'Take a look.'

Aoife remained where she was at the drawing-room door, eying him warily. 'We should go through for dinner.'

'A rocking horse, Aoife? This has to stop.'

She sidled into the room. 'Every child loves a rocking horse, Aidan.'

'We don't have a child.'

'Not yet, but soon.'

'Aoife, you're not pregnant.'

She covered her ears with her hands. 'Don't say that! I'm not listening.'

'You're not pregnant!' Aidan swore. 'You know perfectly well that you're not pregnant.'

'And I know perfectly well whose fault that is!'

She glared at him for a moment, then she smiled, and his heart sank for he had come to loathe that smile.

'Please, Aidan, won't you come to me tonight?'

'There's no point,' he said flatly.

'How do you know, if you won't try?'

'We have tried repeatedly, and I'm sick of failing.' He held out the bill. 'This has to stop, Aoife. It's one thing to fit out a nursery before a *child is born, quite another to do so when there is no child, nor any prospect of one. We'll give the stuff in the attic away. It won't go to waste.'*

'Give it away? That's our child's nursery.'

'There is no child!'

'Don't say that.' Her eyes flashed. 'I won't listen.' She began to back towards the door. 'I mean it, Aidan, if you say that again I won't be responsible for my actions. You'll live to regret it.'

'You say that every time we have this discussion. You don't mean it.'

'I do mean it. This time I really mean it, Aidan. If you won't give me a child I don't want to live.'

'I don't know how many times I'd heard her say those words, or something similar. I don't know how many times I'd backed down, or said something—anything—to pacify her. I don't even know what it was about that damned bill for the rocking horse that felt like the final straw, but it was. So when she opened the door and announced she was going to throw herself in the lake, I told her to go ahead. "Just do it," I said. "Put us both out of our misery." And she did.'

Aidan stopped speaking and drew a shaky

breath, looking confused when he realised he was sitting on the bench beside her. His knee was shaking uncontrollably. Estelle's heart went out to him as tears streamed down her cheeks. 'It wasn't your fault,' she said. 'You had no reason to believe she'd act this time, when she'd cried wolf so often. How were you to know?'

He took her hands, for the first time since he'd begun his heart-wrenching confession, looking straight into her eyes. 'I knew her mind was unstable, but I did nothing to stop her. Worse, I dared her, virtually ordered her to do it.'

'You didn't force her to jump from the boat, Aidan, she chose to.'

'I didn't call her back. I didn't go after her. I didn't stop her taking the boat out. If I'd done any one of those things, then she wouldn't have killed herself. She was at the end of her tether because I had destroyed the last vestige of hope she had left.'

What if. A game Aidan had played even more than she had. 'Aoife couldn't have hoped,' Estelle said, 'not when you could not...'

He coloured, but didn't drop his gaze. 'Even if I could have, I wouldn't have, and I finally told her so that night. That's what I mean about taking away any residual hope she might have had. That was the final straw that pushed her over the edge, and it was my doing. I killed her.'

'You didn't kill her.'

'Then why can't I live with myself? For three years I've been trying to get over this, but it's not going away. I shouldn't have married you. It was very wrong of me, but I'm going to put it right.'

'I don't see how you can.' She sounded desperate. She felt desperate. The more she protested, the more implacable Aidan was becoming. 'We're married. You can't mean we'll get a divorce?'

'Or an annulment. You'd be entitled to one.'

She was icy cold. This couldn't be happening. She wouldn't let it happen. Carefully, she disengaged her hands and shifted away from him on the bench. 'Aidan, you love me, and I love you.'

'I do love you, with all my heart, but I can't live with you, Estelle. It would be wrong. I can't make you happy, and I refuse to be responsible for making you unhappy.'

'But you will. I'll be miserable without you.'

'Believe me, not as miserable as you'd become living here with me.'

'But now I understand why you are so unhappy…'

'I told you so that you'd understand why we

can't be together. You can't help me, Estelle. I'm beyond help, can you not see that? I have to live with what I've done, but I won't—I can't drag you down with me while I do. The man you married in Florence wasn't me. This is me. I'm not fit to be a husband and I'm certainly not fit to be a father.

'My love, think how we've been these last weeks. I've made you so unhappy that you barely eat. You can't even bear to play your harpsichord any more, and it will only get worse.'

'I'm not your love. If I was your love, you'd want me to stay here with you no matter what.'

'I wish I could, but it's because I love you more than anything that I can't. I don't deserve to be happy but you do. Don't you understand?'

There was such anguish in his voice it tore her heartstrings. She did understand, though she thought his logic was inherently flawed. He truly believed he was responsible for Aoife's death, and being the man he was, now he'd admitted it, he wouldn't be capable of forgiving himself. Giving up his own chance of happiness was his way of atoning. She knew it was pointless, but she had to try one more time to make him see.

'I think you're wrong to blame yourself,

Aidan. I understand why *you* think it was your fault. I know what I say won't make any difference. I know you would never have forced yourself to tell me what has so clearly been eating you up for three years if you felt there was the slightest chance of our marriage succeeding. And I promise you I've no intentions of forcing myself on you if you don't want me to stay.'

'It's not a question of what I want.'

'But it is.' She sounded cold, but that was better than hysterical, and if he took it for hurt then he was right. He had hurt her, he was in the process of breaking her heart, but she wouldn't add that to his already overflowing burden of guilt. 'You did everything in your power to make Aoife happy. The fact is that you were doomed to fail because she wanted something that between you was impossible. That's tragic, Aidan, but it's not a crime.

'She couldn't face the truth. Because you knew it would hurt her, you went along with her, though it cost you dear. One time, and only once, you tried to confront her with reality. Once, Aidan, you tried to make her see the situation from your point of view. She couldn't face it. She took her own life rather than face it. That was her choice. Whether you could have saved her that night, you'll never know, but I'm fairly certain if you had there would have been another occasion and another, and the outcome would eventually have been the same.'

She reached for his hand again, unable to stop herself from rubbing it against her cheek. 'She was sick, Aidan, and you were at the end of your tether. You're not a murderer, you're an honourable man who made some flawed decisions for the best and most loyal of reasons. I wish you believed you deserved to be happy, but you don't believe that, do you?'

'I'm sorry.'

'So am I. For myself and for the little ones we're depriving of a happy home.'

He flinched at this jibe, as she'd known he would, for it was a cruel one, but he didn't throw himself at her feet and beg for another chance. Estelle got up. Her legs were trembling but they held her upright. 'I'll make arrangements to leave as soon as possible. A few days should be enough.'

'A few days!'

'I don't think either of us wishes to prolong the agony now.'

'What will you do?'

She had absolutely no idea. At this moment

in time, the only thing that appealed was to shut herself away in a darkened room as far away from Cashel Duairc as possible. 'I rather think you have abdicated any right to ask me that.' She shivered violently. 'Now, can we get off this godforsaken island?'

In the next few days, Estelle did her best to maintain rigid control over her emotions as she made arrangements for the journey to Dublin then on to London. She didn't always succeed. She allowed herself to cry alone in the attic which housed the newly ordered archive which she would never now turn into a history. She wandered alone in the pouring rain in the walled garden she wouldn't be here to restore either, her tears falling unchecked. Playing music, which had always been such a comfort in the past, was unimaginable now. She couldn't bear to look at her harpsichord, and took to working in the library in order to avoid her parlour.

She didn't beg Aidan to change his mind, but the meals they took together were strained. She could not bear his attempts to make polite conversation, or to pretend that the situation was in any way normal. At breakfast, she recited the list of tasks she had set herself for the day, and at dinner, she updated him on her progress.

She might as well have set a clock on the table between them to count down the hours until her departure, but Aidan, though each recitation pained him, endured it and did not beg her to delay her leaving, or to cancel it altogether.

She didn't beg him to change his mind, but it was a daily battle not to. They hadn't even been married six months, not nearly long enough to have failed conclusively. Could she put her case more forcefully? She could, and she could repeat it endlessly, and Aidan would listen, but he wouldn't hear. She'd only make him even more miserable. He believed his way was the only way, the best and only solution. Which was the cruellest of ironies given that once upon a time they had considered themselves the best and only solution to each other's problems.

There was nothing she could do or say to counter his conviction of his culpability and guilt. The only thing to be done was to mitigate the damage by removing herself. Unlike Aidan, Estelle believed she did deserve to be happy. And in time, she was determined that she would be.

Her last day at Cashel Duairc was spent supervising her packing and saying her goodbyes. With Cook and Niamh, the story she and Aidan had agreed made it less painful, for they believed she was merely paying a visit to her sisters. She had no words for Finn, and he had none for her, save to tell her, as he enveloped her in a hug, that she would be sorely missed, and that he would pray every night for her return. She wore her blue gown for dinner, Aidan's favourite, though it was no longer too tight. They ate next to nothing. They said next to nothing. She gazed at him across the table, thinking this is the last time, this is the last time, willing him to speak, willing him to beg for even one more day. Silence fell between them.

She pushed back her chair. 'I think I'll go to bed. I've an early start in the morning. Goodnight, Aidan.'

She was out the door before he could reply, but then she waited, on the other side of it, her heart thumping. She heard his chair scrape back, heard him cross the room and hesitate, but the door wasn't flung open. Furious at herself, she went to bed, forcing herself to lie still and close her eyes, though she had never felt less like sleeping. A while later, she heard his boots on the floorboards, and waited for his bedroom door to open, but instead the footsteps stopped outside her door and her heart leapt. Foolish,

foolish heart. After an agonising wait, the footsteps retreated and she heard Aidan's bedroom door close.

Was this how their marriage was to end, with the pair of them lying in separate rooms yards apart, counting down the hours to dawn when they'd say a tense, chilly farewell for fear they would break down and let each other see that their hearts were breaking? This last week, she had been punishing him for forcing her to leave, but he wasn't forcing her. She was choosing to leave because she loved him too much to hurt him by staying. It was her choice, a painful choice, but it was still hers, not Aidan's.

This was the wrong ending. Without giving herself time to consider, Estelle acted on instinct, jumping out of bed, tapping on his door, opening it before he had time to answer.

'Estelle.' He was in his nightshirt, standing at the window. 'Is there something wrong?'

'Yes.' She crossed to him, throwing her arms around him. 'We deserve a better goodbye. It shouldn't end like this.'

He wrapped his arms tightly around her, burying his face in her hair. 'I've been standing here looking up at the stars and thinking the same thing, and kicking myself for letting you go like that, after dinner.'

'I'm here now, Aidan.'

He laughed softly, pulling her closer. 'I'm very, very much aware of that.' He kissed the top of her head, then loosened his hold. 'Thank you.'

'I thought you would come after me when I left. Then I thought you might come to my bedchamber to say goodnight, even though you never have before.'

'I wanted to, I almost did, but how could I? I've already asked so much of you, and you've been so...' His voice broke. 'I couldn't have done this without you. I know, that's a completely irrational thing to say, but it's the truth. You gave me the courage to confront the past because I couldn't bear to lie to you. And God love you, your courage in facing up to the consequences since I told you has made it almost bearable. You're an amazing woman, Estelle. I should never have married you, but I will never regret having met you.'

'I don't want to go. No,' she added hurriedly, 'I don't mean tomorrow. Let me stay here tonight, Aidan.'

'There's nothing more to say.'

'I don't want to talk. They say actions speak

louder than words.' She hadn't intended this when she leapt out of bed, but once again, she surrendered to her instincts. 'Love me, Aidan,' she said. 'Just love me.'

Without giving him time to consider, she kissed him, and the instant their lips met, she knew she'd been right. This was what they needed, this was how they should say goodbye, this was how they should remember each other.

She curled her fingers into his hair, pushed herself hard against him, opened her mouth to deepen their kiss, wanting to eliminate every little bit of space between them. He matched her every move, murmuring her name between kisses, his hands on her back, on her bottom, pulling her closer and still closer. She could feel his arousal pressing through the flimsy fabric of their nightwear, could feel the heat of his skin as she let her hands roam across his shoulders, down his back, to the slope of his buttocks, wanting to learn every contour, wanting to remember.

Their kisses were wild, their hands frenzied. She was burning up inside and out. He kissed her throat, undoing the buttons at the front of her nightgown to kiss the valley between her breasts, and then her breasts and then her nipples. Her heart began to hammer, and the sweet, aching tension inside her began to build. He eased her backwards on to the bed, undoing the last of the buttons. She could see his chest heaving as he looked at her, could see the effect she was having on him, the jut of his arousal beneath his nightshirt, though she dare not touch him.

He kissed her again, easing her legs apart, stilling her hands when she reached for him, telling her to wait, to be patient, and before she could ask him what he meant, he kissed her again, so that she forgot all about the question. He was kissing her mouth and her breasts and then her belly and then lower. The creases at the tops of her thighs. And then between her thighs, kissing and licking, rousing her to new heights so delightful that she wanted to cling there for ever, and as if he sensed it, he held her there, taking her to the edge then stopping, until she thought she would die of the waiting, and she heard herself begging, please, and before the word was out, she was tumbling over, pulsing and arching up under him, calling his name, clutching at his shoulders, mindless with wanting.

'Aidan.' Pushing herself upright, she wrapped her legs around him, tugging at his nightshirt. He yanked it over his head, and for the first time she saw him naked, refusing to allow herself to think that it would be the only time. She pressed her mouth to his chest, kissing him, rubbing her cheek against the rough hair, licking his nipples, relishing the way he moaned at her touch, the way his heart was hammering, all the time conscious of the hard ridge of his arousal pressing between her legs, against her tummy. 'Love me.'

'Estelle, I...'

'Just love me.'

Estelle lay back on her elbows, gazing up at him boldly, the look of a woman who knew she was desired, and who was relishing it. One long tress of her hair lay over her breast. He leaned over to suck the nipple that was peeking through and she shuddered. He kissed her mouth again, slowly, and he began to enter her, slowly. She was hot and wet and it took all his powers of self-control not to thrust deep and hard, but he held back, and she opened up to him, so he pushed higher, until he was inside her.

He pushed a fraction higher, and she moaned. He began to pulse and she tightened around him. He slid his hands under her bottom to pull her closer, and thrust. She moaned. He didn't think he'd ever been so hard. He thrust again and this time she met him, holding him then tilting towards him, and he lost himself, forgot himself, thrusting harder, higher, faster, until she cried out, and her climax sent him spinning out of control into a gut-wrenching climax of his own that left him utterly spent. Chest heaving, he fell on to the bed beside her, wrapping his arms around her, kissing her, desperate clinging kisses, telling her he loved her with his hands and his mouth, not wanting to let go of her, not ever.

It was Estelle who finally moved, gently disentangling herself. 'Don't get up,' she said. 'And please don't see me off in the morning. I want to remember you like this.' She picked up her nightgown and pulled it on. She leaned over him, her hair trailing on his chest, for one last gentle kiss. 'Goodbye, Aidan.'

All the same, he forced himself to watch her leave the next morning, from one of the upstairs windows, and for the first time since his confession on the island, he doubted the wisdom of his decision. If she had looked up, he'd have gone to her. All she had to do was look up. But she didn't look up.

Chapter Thirteen

December 1832—Fearnoch House, London

'Has she finally gone to sleep?' Phoebe asked. 'You've been up in the nursery for ages.'

'She dozed off a good half an hour ago, after only the third retelling of her favourite story,' Estelle answered, 'but I couldn't tear myself away. I can't believe how big she is. Or how adorable.'

'I know, I do believe Matilda is my absolute favourite niece.'

'Tilly is our only niece, Phoebe.'

'So far. Alexander and Eloise are such besotted parents I don't expect it will be long before we gain another little niece or perhaps a nephew. We are very privileged you know, Twinnie, to have been entrusted with the care of their little poppet. I reckon if Alexander had his way, he'd have taken her with him to the Admiralty party.'

'She might be a little poppet now, but she's Eloise's daughter. I've no doubt she'll grow up every bit as strong and independent as her mama.'

'I have to admit, Eloise has astonished me. For someone who was so absolutely adamant that she never wanted children, she's taken to motherhood like a—well, I'm not sure a duck to water is the right phrase, but you know what I mean. The other day, I overheard her arguing with Alexander over whether their daughter's first word was Mama or Papa. Would you like a sherry before dinner? It's not as good as the one we have at home, but it's very palatable.'

'Talking of which, where is Owen tonight?'

'Oh, he's having dinner at his friend Jasper's.'

'Is he the one who married Owen's former fiancée?'

'Olivia. She is expecting now, so I'll be another sort of aunt.' Phoebe handed Estelle a glass of sherry and dropped on to the sofa beside her. 'So, how are you really? Since Eloise and Alexander came to town, you chose to abandon my humble abode for their enormous mansion, I've barely seen you.'

'Phoebe, I've only been here ten days. I was more than a month living under your roof.'

'You were there in body, but I'm not sure you were there in spirit.' Phoebe clinked her glass and took a sip of sherry. 'Palatable, as I said. Have you talked to Eloise?'

'What about?'

'The thing you've not mentioned at all to me. The small matter of what on earth is going on with your marriage, Estelle, and where your husband is?'

'He's in Ireland, as you very well know.'

Phoebe rolled her eyes. 'Eloise said I should wait until you're ready to talk, but...'

'You've discussed me with Eloise?'

'For goodness sake, Estelle, of course we've discussed you! We're worried sick about you. You're a shadow of your former self. In all the time you've been staying with me, you've never once had a letter from Ireland and even more worryingly, you didn't go near the piano.'

'How can you possibly know that, since you spend most of your time at one or other of your restaurants.'

'I would have happily taken leave of absence if you'd shown the slightest sign of wanting my company. Well, apart from Friday and Saturday, which are the busiest days.' Phoebe took another sip of sherry, wrinkling her nose. 'And as for the piano, I know you haven't played it because when I first noticed you hadn't been near it I sprinkled some talcum powder on the keys and it was still there the last time I checked. What's more, Eloise tells me you've not even opened the door of the music room here, and I remember when we first visited, when she was just married, you thought you'd died and gone to heaven.'

'How does she know that, has she sprinkled talcum powder on the door handle on your advice?'

'Eloise knows everything, she has eyes in the back of her head, you can't have forgotten that! But never mind Eloise. Please, I need to know, because there's only so much *not* interfering a twin can bear.' Phoebe paused to draw breath. 'What is going on?'

Estelle shook her head. 'Nothing.'

'I know that's nonsense.' Phoebe set her sherry down and took her hand. 'Can't you tell me?'

'No, I mean there's nothing going on. There's nothing to tell.' But the weeks of keeping her feelings battened down, wandering the streets of London under the guise of sightseeing, in an effort to avoid the perennial question of what Aidan was doing right at this moment, were suddenly too much for Estelle. 'I love him so much, and he loves me, and yet it makes no difference whatsoever.'

Phoebe, to her astonishment, laughed. Then she burst into tears. 'I'm so sorry, you can have no idea. Oh, Estelle, come here.' Without waiting for her to move, Phoebe threw her arms around her. 'I don't know why I'm crying, save that I've known something was wrong and I've not wanted to ask because there are some things that you can't talk about, even with a twin. I know that better than anyone, believe me.'

'What do you mean?'

Phoebe sat up, dabbing at her eyes with her sleeve. 'I'll tell you, though I've never talked about it before, not even to Eloise. But I'll tell you because I hate seeing you so miserable, and because it might help.'

'Tell me what?'

'About Owen and me.'

'So you see, even though I loved him desperately by then, and he loved me, it would have been wrong to beg him to stay."

'How could I not have known any of this?'

'I made very sure you didn't. I wasn't at all sure how you'd react to me telling you I'd fallen passionately in love for a second time. Not that I was in love the first time, but I thought I was because I imagined myself and Pascal like Mama and Papa.'

'While you and Owen are nothing like.'

'No, though we are *very* happily married in every sense, if you understand my meaning. Ah,' Phoebe added with a knowing smile, 'I can see from your blush that you understand me perfectly. That is not the issue, then?'

'No, it's certainly not. I can't believe I'm having this conversation with my little sister.'

'Ha! Imagine having it with your big sister.'

'No!' Estelle giggled. 'Though I have to tell you, I suspect that Eloise and Alexander are also *very* happily married. The other day, I caught them kissing at the breakfast table, and exchanging a look.'

'Like this?' Phoebe fluttered here lashes, rolled her eyes and flopped theatrically forward with her lips pouted.

'Exactly like that.'

'So, do you want to tell me about this Irishman you've married?'

'I don't know that I can.'

'I find that sherry is ideal for soliciting confidences. I'll pour us another.'

When Estelle had finished a very much abbreviated form of her tale, Phoebe was silent for a long time, chewing on the corner of her mouth. 'How strange, I had no idea you felt that way about children.'

'I had no idea you had fallen in love with your husband.'

'Unfortunately, as you now know, the simple act of falling in love doesn't guarantee happiness. If you really want a family Estelle, you're going to have to find a way to fall out of love with Aidan. If he's right when he says your marriage can be annulled, then you'd be free to marry someone else, and...'

'I don't want to marry anyone else. I'm married to Aidan. I want to remain married to Aidan.'

'Aha! So it's not really about wanting a family after all?'

'It is. It was. Stop looking at me like that, as if you can see inside my head.'

Phoebe held up her hands. 'I'm saying nothing more.'

'We married because we wanted a family, or that's what we told ourselves, though we both admitted afterwards—ages afterwards—that neither of us could bear to say goodbye. We weren't in love, but we were—' Estelle broke off, sighing. 'Don't laugh, but right from the start, from the moment I set eyes on him, I was drawn to him, as if we were meant to be together.'

'I don't think that's silly at all. Did he feel the same?'

'I think so,' Estelle said. 'No, I know he did.'

'But even though you both feel you're meant to be together, you've decided to live apart. Why did you leave, Estelle? I mean, I understand all you've said about not being able to have a family together because his behaviour is so—well, frankly, he sounds troubled in much the way that Owen was, and so I do perfectly understand the destructive effect that has on a household, but is that really why you left?'

'I left because Aidan didn't want me to stay.' Estelle twirled her empty sherry glass between her fingers. 'I would love to have children, but if I had to choose between a family and Aidan, there's no question of what I'd choose—whom I'd choose. What's more, I don't want children at all unless Aidan is the father.' She set her glass down on the floor. 'When did you get to be so wise, Phoebe?'

'Has Phoebe been dishing up advice? I thought I had exclusive rights to that role, as big sister.'

'Eloise! What are you doing home so early? Couldn't you bear to be parted from your first born for more than a couple of hours?'

'I've already checked on her, and she's sound asleep. The truth is, I couldn't bear to miss out on a rare opportunity to have both my sisters' company, or to be the subject of your gossip in my absence, though it sounds as if I had no cause to fear on that account.' Eloise pulled a chair over to the sofa and sat down. 'So tell me, what have I missed?'

'Estelle is in love with her husband, and her husband is in love with her, but he sent her away because he said he couldn't make her happy, and she left because she thought it would make him even more unhappy if she stayed, but now she's not so sure.' Phoebe slanted Estelle a glance. 'I think that's it in a nutshell, isn't it?'

'Estelle is in love!' Eloise exclaimed. 'Good heavens, who would have thought it.'

'Well you clearly did, for one. You're using

your classic "I'm pretending very hard to be surprised but I've known all along" voice,' Phoebe said drily.

'It wasn't difficult to guess. I've never seen anyone try so hard to be cheerful, or so determined to change the subject whenever it veered even close to Ireland or her husband. Besides, she's been here ten days and she's not once ventured into the music room.'

Phoebe threw Estelle a triumphant glance. 'I told you.'

'In any case,' Eloise said, reaching over to pat Estelle's hand. 'I recognised the signs, for I was the same myself, when I first fell in love with Alexander, and though he loved me, he would have none of me.'

'What!'

'Eloise!'

'Tell us!'

'I'll explain after dinner.'

'It can wait,' Phoebe said. 'That's how important this is!'

The three sisters talked long into the night, but Estelle was still wide awake when Phoebe left and Eloise retired. The music room of Fearnoch House was too far away from any of the bedchambers for her to worry about disturbing anyone. She lit a candelabra and set it down on the open lid of the harpsichord, but made no attempt to play.

Loving someone, according to Phoebe and Eloise, meant letting them go if that's what they wanted. It's what both her sisters had done. It was what Estelle had done. Her sisters were convinced they'd done the right thing, for they were both now reunited with their husbands and extremely happily married. Would absence make Aidan realise that he didn't want to live without Estelle? But it wasn't a question of what he wanted, it was a question of what he thought he deserved.

What about what she wanted? Closing her eyes, Estelle began to play, and for the first time in months, the music flowed. Bach's *French Suite*. The fifth movement, which she had played in the church in Florence back in May. She had known then that she and Aidan were meant for each other. She had known that from the moment she set eyes on him. It had taken her a long time to put her feelings into words, to realise what she felt was love, but that's what it had been, right from the start. For both of them.

She stopped playing abruptly. She hadn't let

Aidan go at all, she'd simply walked away because he'd asked her to. She'd persuaded herself that it was the right thing to do, because that's what he wanted her to believe. But she didn't believe it, as Phoebe, her clever little sister, had pointed out. She loved Aidan. The idea that she'd find happiness with someone else was preposterous, children or no. She would never marry someone else, because she was in love with Aidan. She could fashion a life of sorts for herself, she could found her music school or do any number of things independently, and she could reconcile herself to that life, perhaps even find contentment. But contentment was not happiness.

Aidan didn't believe he deserved to be happy. He had proved very adept at making himself miserable and she couldn't deny that she had been unhappy living in Cashel Duairc, but it was a very different kind of unhappiness to what she felt now. She couldn't force herself on him, she wouldn't want to, but if she waited patiently, as both Eloise and Phoebe had, she wasn't at all convinced he would ever change his mind. He'd endure, and while he was enduring, she was trapped in limbo, and wasting her life.

She had to try again, one last time. He might

refuse point-blank to see her. She might return to Cashel Duairc only to discover that he had been right, and that they simply couldn't be together. But at least then she'd know for sure. She *had* to try again. The idea terrified her, but for the first time since she'd arrived in London, she felt a flicker of hope. She owed it to herself to try. She owed it to them both to try.

Gently closing the harpsichord over, she blew out the candles. Outside, the dawn had broken. Checking the clock on the mantel, she saw that it was almost breakfast time. Eloise and Alexander were both early risers. The Earl of Fearnoch's name and reputation had greased the wheels of her Continental journey. Getting her to Ireland with all possible haste should be a piece of cake in comparison.

Cashel Duairc

Aidan beached the boat and almost before it had stopped moving, Hera leapt out, her tail wagging. Leaving the hound to enjoy her long overdue rediscovery of the island, he made his way around to the stone bench on the castle-facing side to consider his own plans. The sun shone brightly in the cold December sky, melting the morning's frost. The air was cold and crisp, stinging the lungs when you inhaled, making a little cloud when you exhaled, making you aware, with each breath, that you were alive. The perfect day for making a fresh start, but he needed to be absolutely certain, this time, it would be a lasting one.

Here on this very spot he had effectively put an end to his marriage. When Estelle left, all those weeks ago, he'd known she was taking his heart with him, but he'd been unprepared for the sense that she'd taken the essence of him as well. He'd waited for the anticipated sense of relief that he'd surely earned for having given her up, but as the days passed, what he had felt was a growing belief that he'd made a terrible mistake.

Her leaving had successfully banished Aoife's ghost, but now he was haunted by different memories. Estelle playing the piano and the harpsichord. Estelle, with her chin on her hand, across the table from him at breakfast and at dinner. Estelle poring over plans and rearranging furniture. Estelle laughing. Estelle kissing him. Estelle telling him that she loved him. And here, on this spot, Estelle agreeing to walk away from that love, because he asked her to. It was the last thing she'd wanted to do, but she hadn't begged him to change his mind. She had made their goodbye as perfect as any goodbye could be, and then she'd gone, as he had asked her to do, and she hadn't looked back.

He'd heard nothing from her since. He assumed she was with one of her sisters, but for all he knew she could have headed off on her travels again. Not knowing was one of the many things he was finding almost impossible to bear. As to wishing she would forget him, find someone else, have a family with another man—he couldn't wish any of those things. Not for the want of trying, but he found it impossible.

She was meant to be with him. He was meant to be with her. Now that she was gone, he couldn't understand why he'd not understood that incontrovertible truth. That was why their eyes had met across the crowded *piazza* in Florence. That was why they'd extended that first encounter from coffee to lunch to a walk and another coffee and another walk. That was why they'd met each other every day in Florence, and why they'd not been able to say goodbye. That was why they'd constructed the notion of a practical marriage between them. Not because they so desperately wanted to be parents, but because they so desperately wanted to be man and wife.

When Aoife died, the ghosts that had haunted

him had all been sad, pathetic creatures. When Estelle left, he was not tormented by recollections of how unhappy he had been. He could hardly conjure up the tense silences, the determined distance he'd put between them. He was haunted, not by the past, but by the future he'd given up. What had seemed so clear to him, standing on this very spot all those weeks ago, had begun to seem misguided, from the moment Estelle gave him what he'd asked for.

He loved Estelle. She loved him. It was a simple equation that should guarantee happiness, were it not for the guilt he bore for Aoife's death. Guilt he had been so certain would eventually destroy him. Guilt he had been sure he'd have to endure for the rest of his life. Guilt which meant he and Estelle could never be happy. Guilt which had gradually, in the weeks since she left, begun to shrivel and to change shape into something he now believed he could live with.

Aoife wanted what she could not have. She refused to accept that it was impossible. She took her own life because she couldn't accept that her deepest, most fundamental desire would never be realised. Had that been his fault? In the last year of their marriage, he'd been unable to try to father a child, but for four years he had tried, and for most of that time, he'd wanted a child just as much as she had. His desire had faded with their hopes, but he'd subverted his wishes to hers, had put her wishes over his own, because otherwise, their marriage had no purpose. They weren't enough for each other, they never had been. If he was guilty of anything, it was marrying her in the first place, and that decision was Aoife's as much as his.

They shouldn't have married, but they had, for the same reason that countless other couples had married in the past and would in the future. Their marriage had failed, and that failure had driven Aoife to the grave. His fault, but only partly. Her childlessness had made her ill. Her illness had made him impotent. But it had been her illness, not his impotence, that had sent her to her grave. Could he have saved her life that night if he'd not been at the end of his tether? He'd never know, but he did know now that he wasn't a murderer. He was, as Estelle said, simply a man who had made some flawed decisions for the best and most loyal of reasons. He couldn't undo some of them. Aoife was dead. But there was one, vital decision, which he had got wrong, and which he was now determined to reverse.

But first he had to say goodbye. He was not surprised to find Hera sitting sentinel at the grave, but he was taken aback at the joyful bark she gave when she saw him, jumping up, her tail wagging madly. 'In a moment,' he said, scratching her head affectionately. 'Go and wait by the boat, there's a good girl.'

The rattle he'd left on the grave when he'd last visited the island with Estelle was tarnished and weather-beaten. He dug a hole for it and covered it over, before kneeling down on the damp ground to whisper a prayer.

His breeches were soaked at the knees when he got up. 'I hope you have found peace, Aoife, for there's nothing more I can do.' He waited, but there was no familiar pang of guilt or regret. Finally, he believed the truth of his words.

In a week's time the year would be over, but he wasn't waiting another week to try to claim his chance of happiness. Whistling to Hera to jump into the boat, Aidan pushed it away from the shore and leapt in beside her. He rowed quickly, making for the shore beside the castle. He'd have to replace the rusty mooring ring, or maybe he should think about building a little jetty. And on the island, where the stone bench was, he should think about some sort of covering, so they could still enjoy their picnics even in the rain. It might be an idea to build something similar in the walled garden too, once he'd had the walls rebuilt. And then there was the bridge. Finally, he could picture the bridge. As he beached the boat and Hera leapt out before him, Aidan's head was full of plans.

First things first, though. Before he could put any of them into practice he had a journey to make and a wife to reclaim. If she'd have him, after all he'd put her through.

Chapter Fourteen

Dublin Bay—one week later

Standing on the upper deck as the ship sailed into the wide expanse of Dublin Bay, Estelle was already suffering from a severe attack of butterflies. At this rate, by the time she had completed the one remaining leg of her journey, she'd be too sick to get out of the carriage. Which would suit Aidan very well, if he didn't want to speak to her. In retrospect, sending a letter warning him of her arrival might have been a mistake. Perhaps she should have surprised him, left him no time to prepare. If she simply turned up unexpectedly, perhaps he'd be so delighted to see her that he'd forget that he had decided never to see her again, by which time it would be too late. No, if anything, she liked that scenario the least. It had been the right thing to do, to warn him. Though there was a chance she could arrive at Cashel Duairc to find he wasn't there at all. Then what would she do?

What she had to do was get herself off the boat and get in the carriage and get there in the first place, without making herself even more nervous. Retiring to her cabin to assemble her luggage, she could hear the cries of the stevedores and feel the ship sway and settle as the sails were lowered and they docked. Assuming that the knock at the door was one of the crew come to take her trunks, she bid them enter and picked up her hat.

Except it wasn't one of the crew. Her hat fell to the cabin floor. 'Aidan!' She took an instinctive step towards him, then stopped and her heart, which had leapt at the sight of him, plummeted. 'You don't want me anywhere near the castle.'

'Estelle!' He stepped into the cabin, closing the door behind him. 'I'm here because I was too impatient to wait for you to arrive at the castle. I got your letter on the very day I decided I was going to come looking for you.'

'You were coming to look for me?'

'And I'd have combed the world if I'd had to.

But I didn't have to. I was so wrong to send you away. I don't want you to be happy with someone else, I want you to be happy with me.'

'Aidan! I was coming here to tell you exactly that, but I wasn't even sure that you'd hear me out.'

'I should have listened to you months ago. I had it all wrong, upside down in my head. How could my making us both unhappy make anything right? I thought I was miserable before, but when you left, I felt as if I'd lost a limb or two as well as my heart.'

'That's exactly how I felt.'

'I know there are some things that I can't undo. I will always feel partly responsible for what happened to Aoife, but it would be wrong of me to destroy my life and yours too, in some misguided attempt to atone.'

'Do you really believe that?'

'I truly do. This time, I am absolutely certain that our marriage can work. Some good has to come of this tragedy. It's not just our lives that I'd ruin either, is it? There's the little ones we could give a home to, as you pointed out. I'd like to think that Aoife would approve of that too. I'm sorry for what I put you through, Estelle, I'm sorry I had not your clear sight, but I'm seeing clearly now. It took your leaving to make me see what existed between us right from the start. We were meant for each other.'

Tears were streaming down her face. She had never seen him so adamant, had never seen him look at her with such unconflicted love. 'We were,' she whispered. We were meant for each other.'

She held out her hand. Aidan took it, he kissed it, and then still holding it, he dropped to his knees. 'I love you with all my heart and my soul, Estelle. I want you to be my wife, not for any practical reason or for any other reason at all, save to share our lives together, and to make a future together, whatever that may be, and to love each other, always. Will you marry me, be my wife in spirit, this time, and not in name only?'

'As many times as you like.' She dropped to her knees beside him. 'And I promise that I'll love you more every day we're together.'

Finally, he wrapped his arms around her, hugging her tightly to him, and then kissed her gently. 'I have missed you so much.'

'I've missed you too. So much.'

He kissed her again, and this kiss was deeper. 'I never want us to be any further apart than this,' Aidan said when it ended. 'Not ever.'

She laughed softly. 'That's going to make for an interesting journey back to County Kildare.'

He smiled, a smile she thought she'd never see again, a smile that sent her pulses racing in a way that she thought they never would again. 'We're not going back to County Kildare,' he said, getting to his feet and locking the cabin door before pulling her upright beside him. 'Not yet.'

'Aidan! We can't possibly, not here.'

'Why not? You are my wife, after all.'

His lips found hers again, and one kiss merged into another, and she forgot everything save the driving need to make love to the man she loved. The man she would love always, more deeply every day, for the rest of their lives. It was the only thing that mattered. The only thing that would ever matter.

* * * * *

Historical Note

Brian Dolan's excellent book, *Ladies of the Grand Tour*, was my main source for Estelle's Continental trip. Lucky Estelle to have a very influential brother-in-law to deal with the logistics of handling multiple currencies, vermin-ridden beds, agonising and prolonged passport controls, and to allow her—and you, I hope—to enjoy the scenery.

Thanks to Alison L., once again, for the gift of Dolan's book, as well as *Great Houses of Ireland*, which I made extensive use of in creating Cashel Duairc.

Huge thanks to my sister-in-law, Eabhnat ni Laighin, who helped me name Cashel Duairc, and who suggested 'Mo Ghile Mear' as the song which forged a bond between Aoife and Estelle. There are many haunting versions of this song on YouTube, but the one which inspired me was by Folky Macfolkface, which I was privileged to hear before it was released, thanks to Eabhnat, who sang it, and my brother, who played in the band and produced the recording.

Regular readers will know that I like to give real historical figures walk-on parts in my stories. Sir George Hamilton Seymour, who plays a minor role in the Florence part of this story, was Minister Resident to the Grand Duke of Tuscany, of which Florence was the capital, before Italy was united. He married Gertrude in 1831, a year before I sent her off to Siena with Estelle, and they eventually had seven children.

A great big thank-you to my Facebook friend Margaret Murray-Evans for naming the Irish wolfhound Hera. I hope I've done her justice.

Finally, I think it must be very obvious that this story is a homage to Daphne du Maurier's *Rebecca*. I first read the book when I was fifteen and still have my original copy, which I bought with a book token from a school geography prize.

A recent re-read made me wonder what would happen if the second Mrs de Winter hadn't been so shy, if she'd spoken up a bit more, or even challenged Max a bit on his studied silences?

And, come to think of it, what about giving Max a makeover?

The result is this book, one of the most challenging I've written to date, and one I'd probably have given up on if it had not been for the support and encouragement and enthusiasm of my fabulous editor, Flo Nicoll.

Is it a fitting tribute? I leave it up to you to decide.

MILLS & BOON

Coming next month

CONTRACTED AS HIS COUNTESS
Louise Allen

He was dangerous, reports said, but they were hazy about who he was a danger to, other than the aforementioned blackmailers, presumably. The judgement was that he was ruthless, but honest. Stubborn, difficult and self-contained.

No one had reported on Jack Ransome's looks, on that straight nose, on that firm, rather pointed, jaw that gave him a slightly feline look. Certainly there had been no mention of a mouth that held the only hint of sensuous indulgence in that entire severe countenance. Other than those faint laughter lines…

So far, so…acceptable.

'You show no curiosity about why I have engaged your services, Lord… Mr Ransome.'

'No doubt you will inform me in your own good time. Whether you decide to employ me or not, I will present your man of business with my fee for today and for the time I will spend travelling to and from Newmarket and for my expenses incurred en route. If you wish to expend that money on chit-chat, that is your prerogative, Miss Aylmer.'

Very cool. Very professional, I suppose.

She stood, glad of the table edge to steady herself, and he rose, too, a good head taller than she, despite her height. 'Please. Sit.' The lid of the coffer creaked open until it was stopped by a retaining chain, standing as a screen between Mr Ransome and its contents. Madelyn lifted out the rolls and bundles of paper and parchment that it contained and placed them on the table in a pile at her left hand, except for one which she partly opened out. She kept her right hand on that as she sat again.

'What I require, Mr Ransome, is a husband.' She had rehearsed this and now her voice hardly shook at all. In some strange way this situation went beyond shocking and frightening into a nightmare and nightmares were not real. Father had left careful and exact instructions and she had always obeyed him, as she did now. Even so, she kept her gaze on the parchment that crackled under her palm.

'Then I fear you have approached the wrong man. I do not act as a marriage broker.' When she looked up Mr Ransome shifted on the carved wooden chair as though to stand again.

'You do not understand, of course. I have not made myself plain. I do not require you to find me a husband. I wish you to marry me. Yourself,' she added, just in case that was not clear enough.

Continue reading
CONTRACTED AS HIS COUNTESS
Louise Allen

Available next month
www.millsandboon.co.uk

COMING SOON!

We really hope you enjoyed reading this book. If you're looking for more romance, be sure to head to the shops when new books are available on

Thursday 28th November

To see which titles are coming soon, please visit

millsandboon.co.uk/nextmonth